Mixed Blessings

RICK HAMLIN

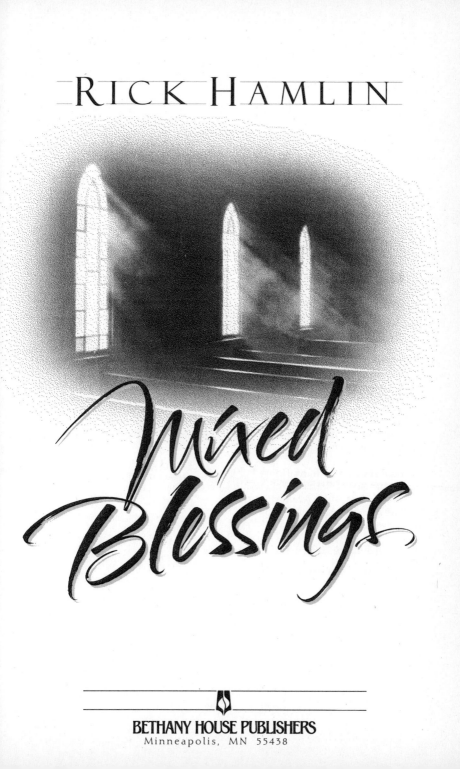

Mixed Blessings

BETHANY HOUSE PUBLISHERS
Minneapolis, MN 55438

Cover design by Lookout Design Group, Inc.
Cover Photo: © 1999 Will & Deni McIntyre/Tony Stone Images
Inset Photo: © 1999 R. B. Studios/The Stock Market

Unless otherwise identified, Scripture quotations are from the King James Version of the Bible.

Published by Bethany House Publishers
A Ministry of Bethany Fellowship International
11400 Hampshire Avenue South
Minneapolis, Minnesota 55438
www.bethanyhouse.com

Printed in the United States of America

ISBN 0 - 7394 - 0779 - 1

For Sweetie, as always

RICK HAMLIN is the managing editor of *Guideposts* magazine and the author of *Finding God on the A Train*, a Book-of-the-Month Club alternate selection. A graduate of Princeton University, Rick worked as a professional actor and singer before beginning his writing career. He makes his home in New York City with his wife and two sons.

CHAPTER 1

LURLENE LOOKED UP from her computer screen and gazed over at the potted philodendron cascading haphazardly down the file cabinet. She wrinkled her nose in disapproval at its condition, its partially exposed roots as shriveled and brown as the roots on a bleached blonde. Peering over the top of her glasses, she noticed the biblical concordance left by her boss on the windowsill. No doubt he was already wondering where it was. She slipped the tip of a coral-hued fingernail into her auburn hair and rubbed a patch of scalp above her ear as she looked into the courtyard.

The garden was a source of comfort to her. The azaleas were blooming in feathery tufts of tissue-paper colors. Survivors of past Easter services, they had decorated the altar before being transplanted into the garden. Each was given in remembrance of a parishioner or a relative who had passed on. Every year Lurlene typed up the names and had them printed on a green leaflet that was inserted into the Easter program, the spelling rigorously checked: *Flowers given in memory of . . .* She had never made a mistake in twenty-two years. A potted azalea was thirty dollars, an Easter lily forty. The way Lurlene saw it, those who spent thirty got a better deal because the azaleas could last for decades in the flagstone border, while the more popular Forest Lawn lilies died in a month or two. What would a dead parent rather have? Something that looked cool, white, and waxy for a day or a plant that splashed color around for years?

Gazing at the azaleas, Lurlene could remember each memorialized person by the plants that had survived. Helen Bradford's mother in the burnished pink, Doris Matthew's father in the white with red flecks, Althea Bruington in the bush that was as bare as a monk's head on top and ratty around the rim. Too bad, for Lurlene had always liked Mrs. Bruington. Sad to see her go through a second demise. A little plant food might have helped, but it probably wouldn't bring lasting revival. She would make a mental note to check with the gardener. She was not one to forget her mental notes.

That was how Lurlene had helped Pastor Bob over the years. "Mrs. Scott," he would call to her over the intercom in the mellifluous tones that had once made him hope Hollywood would beckon, "do you have my schedule for Thursday? Who is my twelve o'clock? Can I make it to the hospital by one?" "Mrs. Scott, have you typed up last week's sermon yet? Someone asked me for a copy." "Mrs. Scott, what hymns are we singing on Sunday? Have you put them down in the bulletin?" "Mrs. Scott, I've got what's-his-name on the line. He's asking if I can perform the marriage ceremony for his daughter in June. Do you remember what her name is?''

Of course Lurlene remembered their names, and she knew exactly which Saturday in June he was free. Referring to her records, she would discover a slot between a 10:00 A.M. wedding and one at 6:00 P.M. If the Fletchers wanted a 2:00 P.M. June wedding officiated by Pastor Bob, that was their only choice. Otherwise, one of the other ministers on staff would have to do it.

Pastor Bob didn't expect her to dispatch his dirty work for him. When a church member had a complaint, he met the person directly. ''If you're talking about me behind my back,'' he said frequently enough, ''speak directly to me. Let me know what's wrong.'' He fielded gripes about the choir or the choice of hymns. He listened to comments about his sermons—some people found them too long, while others felt they were too short. He was ready to settle the dispute that arose when one member of the decorating committee wanted flocked trees at Christmas and another argued for fresh green ones. And he was on hand when two trustees marched into his office, lowered the blinds, asked Mrs. Scott to hold all calls, and claimed that the treasurer, an upstanding citizen, had embezzled half the mission fund—Lurlene heard it on her intercom. As it turned out, to everyone's relief, the fellow was in the early stages of Alzheimer's and had simply botched his records.

Unlike some bosses, he never expected his secretary to lie. Not even a white lie. If he was taking an afternoon nap she wasn't expected to say ''He's in a meeting,'' or ''He's in a conference.'' She was supposed to say ''He's napping,'' as hard as that was to do. In fact, she couldn't do it. It sounded so unprofessional. "He's away from his desk" was the best she could manage.

That meant he was on the black Naugahyde sofa that sat beneath his bay window, a box of tissues on the table nearby for church members who burst into tears as they bared their souls. Once two boys from the playground nearby peeked in through the leaded glass just as the reverend rose from his perch, appearing right in front of their eyes as though resurrected. They ran from the window in terror.

The Reverend Robert F. Dudley Jr. was a big man, standing six foot four in his stockinged feet, his head round and heavy. As he approached middle age, it had become as craggy as Mount Everest. His broad brow that had looked regal in youth now cantilevered out over his eyes in a remotely simian fashion. Laugh lines cut a swath through his cheeks deeper than a crevasse in a glacier. His round nose was rounder, his chin more pronounced, and his ears—never small—drooped like a tent about to collapse. When speaking he could marshal all these features into a handsome, distinguished face. But when he woke up from a nap, they were as disjointed and scattered as the plastic parts on a Mr. Potato Head.

"Mrs. Scott," he called just now over the intercom, "where's my concordance?"

She resisted the impulse to say "Right where you left it." After all these years they were like a couple in a marriage that had survived the long haul. He knew her habits, and she knew his. He could complain, she could complain, and neither of them held out any hope of changing the other. Lurlene found it easier to sigh, roll her eyes, and think *"Right where you left it*'' as she congratulated herself on her great restraint.

''I think it's here, Bob,'' she said out loud. Point made. ''Yes, it's on the windowsill. Shall I bring it to you right away?'' A magnanimous offer of assistance.

''Thank you, Mrs. Scott,'' he said. ''I'll be there in a sec.''

The green light went off on the intercom. She could hear him standing up at his desk, the squeaky chair rolling back as he shuffled to the door. The door opened. She didn't move. Neither did he. He still had the ability to pause in a threshold and capture the attention of an entire room. It was as though he were waiting for the applause to die down before he went about his act of business.

''There it is,'' he said, smiling. ''I can't understand why things just walk away from me.''

''I can't either,'' she said, maintaining their comfortable fiction.

He walked to the windowsill and took the book down. ''I was looking for the passage about the widow's mite. Both Mark and Luke have it. Sometimes those familiar parables are worth reading again just to see if new meanings have cropped up. I never know what I'll find. I've been reading the Gospels from front to back again and again, year after year, different translations, different printings, different commentaries, and still I see new meanings in them.''

He turned to his Bible and began thumbing through it.

Years ago he would have talked through his sermon with her, enumerating his major points, maybe testing out an anecdote or two, but that time had passed. It wasn't that he didn't trust her judgment. He knew she could be depended upon to straighten out grammar when she transcribed the sermon from his tape. She would edit out the parenthetical pauses and little stumbles that served to remind his congregation and radio audience of his humility. But for now, for him, a sermon only existed in the time and space in which it was delivered. It expanded or contracted according to the whims of the moment and the yawn of a front-pew parishioner. It rose and fell with the nodding of heads and the blinking of eyes, as significant to him as the crescendo of "amens" that greets a black Baptist preacher. As much as he outlined his sermons, mentally listing his points, he felt preaching was an improvisatory art like jazz. Too much practice prevented him from being open to the inspiration of the moment.

"You're not going to change the title?" she asked from her desk. His whims could make her nervous. The Sunday bulletin went to the printer on Thursday, and she liked to have it finished by Wednesday. And here it was already Tuesday afternoon.

"No, I think not," he said. "How does it read now?"

" 'Money and Power.' "

"Catchy. Do you think it'll draw them in?"

"It can't help but do so."

"But nobody will really want to hear what I have to say."

He looked crestfallen for a minute, reminding her of a little boy needing encouragement. Though his confidence was immense and his personality large, he could be easily crushed by self-doubts. It was her job to diffuse them as quickly as possible. To clear the air.

"Nonsense. That's what people are searching for today. Answers. Not just a lot of talk."

"If they only knew how paradoxical the answers can be."

"I'm sure you'll make that clear."

The funny thing was, she *was* sure. It confounded her that he would hem and haw, proclaim his weaknesses and failures, explain how he'd really bitten off more than he could chew—yet on Sunday morning he would deliver sparkling examples of such clarity that they stunned her as she listened to them on her Dictaphone the next morning. One thing she'd never doubted in her twenty-two years under his employ—he was a great preacher. He was one of the very best speakers she'd ever heard. "You'll do just fine," she said.

"Thank you, Mrs. Scott. I know you mean that."

With the concordance, he returned to his paneled lair, lost to the world. He would be reading and scribbling on a yellow legal-sized note pad for the next hour. He would take down more books and leave them open in a stack on his desk. He would refer to theology but never quote it, then he'd consult several commentaries, shaking his head at their opposing views. Finally he'd open his newspaper clipping file of heartwarming stories to find a touching human-interest anecdote to support his message. He had never let her touch this file, no matter how many times she suggested that she could reorganize it in a neat thematic way. "I know what's here," he'd say. "If you move things around, I won't have any idea where to find what I'm looking for."

Once, just as a test, she rearranged two clippings. Sure enough, he came barging through the door. "Lurlene, you must never touch this folder. It is my personal property. Do you understand?"

"Yes, Pastor Bob," she had said. He had called her by her Christian name, a sure sign of his agitation.

"Never again," he said.

"I understand," she had said. Forever afterward she left the folder alone.

She had pouted a bit that day. His anger was a formidable thing, and just a small glimpse of it made her wary of its depths. Well acquainted with the pastor's wife, she was certain that they had stormy arguments at home. Once or twice she had heard his raised voice coming through the office wall when he was talking to his wife on the phone—Lurlene never eavesdropped on family conversations. She understood his anger and was relieved that the full force of it had never been directed at her.

She returned to her computer screen and retyped an address for one of the weekly birthday letters. She was not a church member, but she knew the policy. Every church member was sent a letter on the week of his or her birthday. Another one of Pastor Bob's innovations. "A church is a family, and we should show we care for one another." By now that meant nearly fifty letters a week. Thank God for computers—it made the caring a little easier.

She had to admit that she viewed such efforts with cynicism. She wondered if he used such techniques because they had been suggested by some church marketing expert to increase the offerings in the plate.

Her cynicism wasn't an attractive thing, and most of the time she kept it under wraps, but for twenty-two years it had never left her. What she didn't discuss with Pastor Bob, what she hated to admit, what she would never have told one of the parishioners who gave her preserves at Christmas and asked about her son or sent her flowers on National Secretaries Day was that she found the whole faith-God-religion thing utterly incomprehensible. She worked for a church, but she didn't believe in what it did. She didn't believe one word of it. Not one word.

CHAPTER 2

THEY JOKINGLY REFERRED TO themselves as "the women upstairs." They were not, in fact, all women. Sometimes men joined them, though not very many and mostly retirees. An occasional male teacher with an irregular schedule or an earnest young man searching for his vocation—once an engineer who worked a night shift. Generally, though, they were women, and they did their work upstairs.

The room was in an attic above the chancel, so they could hear the organ pipes below. When George, the organist, played a pedal point in the low bass range, it made the walls of their upper room reverberate so that some feared another earthquake was on the way like the one that had required extensive restoration of the bell tower and the removal of two cast-concrete gargoyles. The women upstairs had first gathered during World War II. That was when journalists and pundits had begun to say, by way of encouragement, that more battles were won through prayers at home than through warfare in the field. It might not have been a comfort to the poor soldiers dodging bullets at Monte Cassino, but it sure made their mothers, sisters, and wives slaving in front of ironing boards and hot stoves feel better.

Back then, at the time of Guadalcanal, one such group had come to white-haired Dr. Sandifur and asked where they could gather for prayer. Because it was California, many of the women had relatives in the Pacific theater, and their fears for the men's safety were well grounded.

"What you need is a prayer closet," Dr. Sandifur had said. A former army man who had served as a chaplain in the last world war, he was sympathetic to their plight. "You need a place that will remind you to pray whenever you go there. A place that calls you to that vocation." The very walls and floor would be a holy reminder, the smell of the plaster like incense to a High Church Anglican. He also had a practical concern. He wanted it to be somewhere in the church complex where people could come and go without having to pass through other rooms or offices, a place where some privacy could be preserved. Where the door could be left unlocked without leaving the rest of the building vulnerable.

When he came upon the upper room, it seemed perfect with its separate entrance and narrow set of stairs in the back of the church so that no one would have to traipse through the sanctuary. Until then the space had been used to store stacks of old hymnals and yellowing sets of music scores. More storage was found elsewhere, the room was painted and carpeted, and bulletin boards hung from the walls. One woman donated her dining room table and chairs. The group had their prayer closet.

At first they gathered several mornings a week. Maps of the Pacific were hung from the wall with little colored pins marking bases of loved ones. The men's destinations were not marked. In fact, the women didn't know the half of it. After all, loose lips sank ships. They talked a bit as they knit and crocheted, sharing their concerns. Then they prayed. For half an hour on weekday mornings the place was dead silent. A dozen ladies gathered around a table with bowed heads. "Prayer warriors," they called themselves, to distinguish their mission from that of the men overseas.

Their efforts did not go without success—if the word success can be applied to prayer. Several young men in the heat of battle described a strange calm even in the foxhole. Helen Bradford's fiancé wrote, "Although I could barely pray myself, I felt as though many were praying for me." Doris Matthews' husband said he actually heard his wife's words of prayer when his submarine was dodging depth charges in the Pacific.

In the group more than one prayer warrior recalled a moment when she felt an urgent need to petition God. Later she would discover through a carefully censored missive that yes, indeed, her son, boyfriend, brother, or husband had been facing grave danger at that very moment. When a relative was wounded or killed, a member of the prayer circle could feel sustained in her worry or grief by the intercession of friends.

Soon an article appeared in the local paper in the religion section, and when it did, others sent in their concerns. "Would you pray for my son in the Pacific?" "Would you remember my grandson in the submarine corps?" "My boyfriend is a medic in constant danger—would you pray for him?" Even after the war the prayer requests continued to come in. There were other dangers, other challenges, some much closer to home. The women who had started the group kept coming back, and others joined them. Not everyone went to the room upstairs every day, but they'd drop in one or two mornings a week to bow their heads.

Prayer requests were left on the table in a breadbasket. Ongoing concerns were posted on the bulletin board. Every once in a while some member would make an effort to organize the requests with military precision by putting illnesses in one corner, financial concerns in another, and death on a special shelf. From time to time notes on the walls appeared. "After you've prayed for a request, please put a red *X* next to the name." "Absolutely no food or beverage in this room." "Did anyone find a gold bracelet here last week?" All told, Dr. Sandifur's original goal was remarkably well served. The people who came to the room prayed. There were better venues for church gossip—the upper room above the chancel was strictly reserved for a holy purpose.

By the time Pastor Bob was brought on staff at First Church, there were few women left from the original group. One of the stalwarts had had a slight stroke and couldn't make it up the three steep flights of stairs. Petitions were made, phone calls flew across town, a design team explored the possibility of installing a small elevator. The woman herself had to put an end to the debates. "I can pray here at home," she said. "Don't change the center of our operations on account of me. When people go to the prayer room they get serious. They can't overhear any meetings or classes. Their only distraction is the organ playing, and that's not a distraction at all. We shouldn't move to another space."

Back then Pastor Bob's dynamic preaching brought new crowds to the congregation. People who had heard him on the radio came to see him live. They thrilled at the sight of his large body leaning over the pulpit, a proud man humbled before God. They delighted in his casual asides. They were charmed by the smiles that punctuated jokes or appeared on his face when he was overcome by the ineffable goodness of the Lord, a look that said, "Words can't express." This was stuff you couldn't get from the radio. They came in droves, lining up for the 9:45 A.M. sermon at 8:00 A.M. Then the lines drew the curious and the unchurched like long queues outside a movie theater. "If those folks are willing to get up early on a Sunday morning, get dressed, and wait outside," people told themselves, "there must be something there. . . ."

"We need a new and bigger church," the Reverend Robert F. Dudley had announced to his board of trustees. "We can't fit under one roof. We can barely house our homeless shelter in the basement." In principle, the board agreed. With an eye on the bottom line, they were grateful for the heaping offering plates brought in by Pastor Bob's sermons. The debts that had accumulated in Dr. Sandifur's waning years—when his dyspeptic comments about the sins of living off a blue-chip portfolio had alienated some big donors—were erased in two short years. If Pastor Bob wanted more space to house the congregation, he deserved it. It was just that . . . well, people were rather fond of the old building.

They loved the milky green stained-glass baptismal window that depicted a white dove descending through an opalescent haze. It was the very image of the Holy Spirit on a smoggy Southern California day. They had grown accustomed to the old oak pews that curved in banks like seats in a Roman theater, rising up beneath a half-moon balcony. They had a sentimental attachment to the mosaic floor in the vestibule in back. They felt keen serenity under the bronze Byzantine chandeliers with their incandescent lights glowing brightly at the processional and dimming respectfully for the long pastoral prayer.

The congregation had been shown architectural plans for a white concrete, earthquake-safe building that would incorporate some of the old elements into a larger building on the same busy corner, but as much as they admired the practicality of such a solution, they gazed at the options with a sense of loss. They knew what they liked, and they liked what they already had.

Unable to change the trustees' minds, Pastor Bob backed down. In the meantime, he agreed to preach twice on Sunday mornings, at 9:45 and 11:15, and the fellowship hall was enlarged so that the people who didn't get in the sanctuary could watch him with other worshipers on a closed-circuit TV. After a time, he, too, became attached to all the incongruous elements of the building.

In a few years the church had become infused with memories for him. He decided it would be heresy to bring the place down. Not that a church isn't more than a building or that art has any greater sanctity than the people viewing it. But this place had become holy ground to him. It put him in the right mood on Sunday mornings. When God seemed far away, it reminded him of times when the Lord had felt close, and it reminded him of people whose lives had been changed by God. They had sat in the second pew to the left or had wept silently in the very back pew, observed by him as he looked up from his text. Sometimes they had mourned tragic deaths or devastating losses, clinging to faith by a thread. He needed his congregation more than they needed him. When he stood in front of them and preached from the pulpit, he felt their belief, and it took him out of himself. No, he couldn't touch the old First Church building. It would remain safe from the wrecker's ball for as long as he was here. The prayer room behind the organ and above the chancel would be preserved for another generation.

"Helen, would you pass me that stack of letters?" Doris Matthews said to her companion that afternoon in the prayer room. Small and birdlike with white hair, she exhibited the beginnings of a dowager's hump, stooping over the long table as she shuffled through a pile of opened correspondence.

"These were prayed for this morning," Helen Bradford replied. Tall, lanky, with a golfer's body, she had dyed-brown hair and spoke in a smoky contralto voice. As she gazed at the stack of letters, licking her index finger, a row of silver bracelets clanked against her tanned wrist.

"All of them?" Doris asked.

"I think so," Helen said.

"Have they been stamped?"

This was procedure. Requests that had been prayed for received a red stamp of the praying hands. Helen thumbed through the pile she was holding, the envelopes stapled to the letters. A neat red outline of Durer's praying hands emblazoned the upper corners. The stationery ranged from thick creamy rag bond to lined foolscap. Some people had typed their requests on office letterheads, others had scribbled them on note cards.

"All of them," Helen affirmed.

"Then they're ready to label."

The two women were here to label the letters. It was a system that had evolved over recent years. The prayer warriors prayed in the morning. Others sorted and labeled the requests in the afternoon according to a huge list of categories.

"Do you have an extra list?" Helen asked Doris.

"Yes, right here." She pulled one out of the table drawer and scanned the entries, following the categories with the tip of a ball-point pen. Each entry had a number that followed it. Presumably this was to help the pastor's secretary, Lurlene Scott, who would have to type the form letter that went as a response to each prayer request.

Helen returned to her letters and studied them. "We've had a lot of 'Cancer' this week," she observed.

"I've had one or two 'Heart Problems,' " Doris said.

"So many people seem to be having heart surgery these days. It makes such a difference. I've known people who couldn't walk up a flight of stairs, and now they're playing two sets of tennis. . . ."

"How about prisoners' letters?" Doris asked.

"You can see them coming miles away. All those pages of bad spelling and messy handwriting, with all those prison numbers in the return address."

"Poor dears, they do go on."

"Not much else to do with their time, I suppose."

The two women talked for several minutes as they went about their tasks. Efficiency experts would point out that valuable time would have been saved if the morning prayer people also labeled the letters after they read them and prayed for the requests. But the old-timers saw wisdom in the division of the tasks. A prayer was a prayer. The labeling was a more cerebral activity. It was a question of devotion. The morning was devoted to prayer, the afternoon to talk.

"Listen to this," Helen said, holding out one letter. " 'I don't generally play the lottery, but recently I've taken to buying a ticket. I figured if God wants me to win, the least I can do is help Him. I can't ask you to pray for me to come up with the right numbers—that doesn't seem right. Can I ask, though, for maybe a couple hundred dollars in two weeks? Or earlier if He wants. Thanking you in advance . . .' "

"I'd file that under 'Financial.' "

"You don't think she has a gambling problem?"

"Not yet."

There was the silence of careful reading for a few more minutes, then Doris interrupted. "Here's a sweet one. 'I am twelve years old. My brother is ten. In two years he'll be twelve and I'll be fourteen. I hope he'll be nicer to me when he's twelve than he is now at ten. My mother says he is young, but I realize that he will always be younger than me. She says that when we're older we'll feel like the same age. I hope I can last that long.' "

"That is sweet, but what's her request?" Helen asked.

"To get along with her brother."

"I'd file that under 'Relationships,' " Helen said.

"That might be too serious for a girl her age. I'll suggest something geared to kids."

"Don't we have a couple of form letters just for children?"

"We should."

The form letters were generated by Lurlene. They had been written and updated over the years by Pastor Bob. Filled with helpful advice, they quoted appropriate Bible verses, but the most important message they seemed to contain was simply "We prayed for you." That was all people asked. That was all they wanted to hear.

"I'll mark it 'Youth.' "

"Good idea."

A warm February breeze came in through the dormer window at the top of the room while downstairs George was running through a Bach partita on the organ, rehearsing for Sunday's worship service. Once a month the congregation was treated to a Bach postlude. Usually by that time people were so busy greeting each other in the aisles that they paid no more attention to it than to background music in a department store, but George valiantly played on.

In the middle of a florid musical phrase, Doris clicked her tongue. "More drug problems," she said at the prayer table. "I just don't know where they buy the stuff."

"Do you see the return address?" Helen asked.

"A nice neighborhood." She looked at the back of the envelope as though she would find out who the writer was. It didn't really matter. Letters were held in the strictest confidence. People had come to trust the ladies upstairs. In over five decades there had been no leaks of confidential information. Pastor Bob said it was God's grace.

But at just that moment Helen held up a long typed letter with a neat feminine signature, and as it turned out, the contents of this letter would break a perfect record. Had the subject been a little different, had the writer expressed herself less succinctly, had her request not touched one of the readers, that record might have gone unbroken. Maybe it was, as the Chinese would say, the flaw on the vase that made it perfect. Or perhaps it was as the Latin phrase goes *felix culpa*, a happy mistake.

"A dating service letter," Helen said in her smoky voice.

"Another request for the perfect husband?" Doris asked in her high, birdlike soprano.

"We get so many of them."

"Anything different about this one?"

"The description of what she'd like is pretty good. 'Six foot two, dark hair, a love of laughter, great sensitivity, mid-twenties to early thirties, nice singing voice, stable in career, willing to travel. I'm sorry to burden you with a list of qualities, but I've heard that it helps to be specific in prayer. At this point I'd probably settle for half of what I've put down, but my best friend said to aim high. I'm aiming high. Pray that I don't become bitter and small-minded. Pray that I don't become desperate either, like some women I know. And pray that I'll recognize this Prince Charming when I meet him.' "

"True Love. The Perfect Mate. 'Marriage' is probably the easiest category to use," Doris said.

"If prayer can help anything, it should help here."

"Does she say anything about herself?"

"No. Not really. Just what kind of man she wants. But God knows who she is."

"And knows what she needs."

"I have no problem praying for that."

"Amen," Doris said as she looked down her list.

CHAPTER 3

AT 5:30 P.M. ON THE DOT, Lurlene turned off her computer and spread the beige cover over her still warm monitor, tucking in the sides like a Jaguar owner covering his car with parachute cloth. She closed one of the casement windows and locked it—even in a church, one could never be too careful about the possibility of a burglary. Her white purse sat next to her desk, and her sweater hung loosely from the back of her chair. When it got cool in the office, she sometimes draped it over her shoulders. Now at the end of her work day, Pastor Bob helped her into it, one arm at a time, and then she picked up her handbag.

"Shall I lock the door?" she asked him.

"No. No need to. I'll be right behind you."

"Well, then, good night."

"Good night, Mrs. Scott, good night! Get safely home."

For exercise, Lurlene Scott walked to work every other day, and today was one of those days. She was an attractive woman—well preserved, some might say—with looks that were a combination of good genes and fate. Walking was her way of helping nature's generosity.

The light was disappearing from the cloudless sky and the blue gave off a phosphorescent glow, as though the atmosphere had held the day's sunshine in reserve. Lurlene swung her hands purposefully as she walked, her handbag hanging from her shoulder. She crossed San Anselmo, with its broad cedars set back from the street, and turned onto a quiet oak-lined block. It was an older neighborhood of modest pretensions, California bungalow style giving way to Spanish revival. In the fading light she could still see the stucco and clapboard fronts of her neighbors' homes, the windows illuminated like stage sets. A girl practiced the piano behind the curved plate glass of a living room window. A boy slouched over something at the kitchen table, his homework no doubt. An elderly couple stared at a TV that glared back at them in shades of blue.

She liked gazing inside homes. One or two people she knew. Most she didn't. At one time she had supposed their lives weren't as difficult as hers or didn't hold the same heartaches. But after twenty-two years at First Church, she had heard enough hard-luck stories not to be fooled by appearances. Quiet desperation came in many shapes and sizes. Financial setbacks, death, depression, failed marriages. At least she had known love, she told herself, no matter how badly her marriage had ended up. No matter how much pain that failure had given her.

When her son was nearly two, her husband had left her for good. That's why she clung so tenaciously to the job at the church. It was a point of pride with her. She didn't want to be dependent on any man for her livelihood, especially her mate. It was just as well, because after those early days of marriage she never was. Feckless, irresponsible, and charming to a fault, her husband was her biggest mistake.

When she first set eyes on him, she thought he was the most handsome man she had ever met—tall, dark haired, gracious, dandyish. He looked at her across a tray of canapés, insisting she take the last Vienna sausage. They were at the wedding of her best friend, and he was a classmate of the groom. He had grabbed her hand when she was still eating and swept her off her feet, dancing with her until she was breathless and her side ached. Before the bride and groom had come back from their honeymoon, she had fallen hopelessly in love with Jonathan Walter Scott. He courted her with orchid corsages and heart-shaped boxes of chocolates and witty letters that made her laugh out loud. Generally she had been the roommate who stayed at home on Saturday nights, filling the evening with macrame projects and needlepoint. Now she went out eagerly two, three, four times a week.

At the bowling alley he had proposed, just like that. "Let's get married," he had said, taking a platinum and diamond engagement ring out of his madras jacket. She cried that night, cried for the thrill of it all.

"He could sell ice cubes to Eskimos" was the most complimentary thing her best friend's husband could say about Jonathan Walter Scott. "He could sell anything." Maybe what the man was trying to say was that Jonathan had sold Lurlene a bill of goods. He'd sold insurance for a while—or so he said—and pinball machines to bars, and bowling equipment, which is why he knew everyone at the alley. She had wondered why they never took him up on the offer to pay for a round of drinks for everyone until she figured out that they knew they'd never get their money. He liked to drink, but then, a lot of other men did too. He could down tall glasses of beer while shooting the breeze, and it never seemed to affect him.

What she loved best about him was that he was a dreamer. They could sit up half the night outside among the camellias that grew beneath Lurlene's apartment. There he spun tales of the things he'd like to do someday. He hoped to own and run his own restaurant. Then they'd have a chain of them, just the two of them. He wanted to travel. Maybe they'd have a travel agency. They'd live in a big colonial house with white pillars and black shutters and enough rooms to house the underprivileged children they would adopt someday. For Lurlene's wedding present he actually gave her a miniversion of his dream house—a one-story with red brick, black shutters, and no pillars. How he ever put the cold hard cash together she never knew. After he was gone she sometimes thought he'd robbed a bank to pay for it. He never had any money otherwise. The house was the only thing he left her. That and their son.

A springlike breeze blew a whirlwind of leaves across the gutter as she crossed an intersection. The smell of orange blossoms was in the air. She was grateful for this leafy neighborhood. Her son had ridden his bicycle along these safe streets, had played with the children who grew up in these houses, had climbed these trees. When the boy was old enough to get around by himself, he would drop by the church on his way home from school to check in with her.

Business was what took her husband away at first. That had been his excuse. The trips took longer and longer as he traveled farther and farther afield. "I can't tell you where I'll be," he'd say, "but I'll call you."

From motel rooms, where the sound of passing cars and muffled shouts could be heard in the background, he called. From bars, where the noise of the TV and hearty laughter rang out, he dialed collect. He was selling pinball machines or jukeboxes or electric-powered lawn mowers, and he had a potential customer that was really big. Really big, he promised. When he came home he'd bring her a new sweater, a gold charm for her bracelet, an autographed baseball for their son. Maybe the pressure to bring back bigger and better presents after each trip kept him away longer. Or maybe it was the anxiety of having to produce a bigger and better lie. By the time Jonathan Jr. was a toddler, Lurlene realized she had to get a job just for her own peace of mind—she was already handling the checkbook. The church was nearby, her secretarial skills were good, and the place was starting a day-care nursery. "Something to keep you busy when I'm not around," her husband had said, as though she didn't have enough to keep her going already.

On her first day of work, Lurlene put Mr. Scott's picture on the shelf and another one next to it of her toddler son in an engineer's hat and overalls, a present from her vagabond husband. Over the years the pictures of Jonathan Jr. had changed from grinning school shots—head cocked to one side—to Little League photos of the would-be slugger holding his bat. There was a wistful, serious high school graduation portrait of a young man in cap and gown and an equally serious college shot with coat and tie and a brief flirtation with a mustache. The most recent picture came from the parish directory when a traveling salesman photographer—reminiscent of her former spouse—took pictures of the congregation before a backdrop of quaking aspens, the like of which had never been seen near First Church. Jonathan and his mother, just the two of them. The photos of her husband had long since been put away. That chapter in her life was closed.

Lurlene whistled as she walked through the neighborhood. She'd learned over the years that the little things she could do to keep her spirits up were worthy investments. Hum, whistle, maintain a positive attitude, smile. When she was younger, people had often commented on her upbeat outlook. One could still hear the perkiness in her voice when she answered the phone at work. "Pastor Bob's office" or "Pastor Bob's line" or even "Lurlene Scott. Can I help you?" There was a little bit of the cheerleader in her demeanor, but beneath it resided well-masked bitterness and anger. Sometimes it came out in a sharp remark that Pastor Bob noticed. Otherwise she kept her disappointment under wraps.

She passed through the opening in the white picket fence where a gate had once stood. A vivid memory came to her of seeing her husband slam it closed with his foot as he carried a plaid suitcase to his car. He had hugged his son, who was holding a red ball against his hip, kissed his wife good-bye, and was gone. Maybe the way his eye had refused to hold hers for very long should have given an indication of his intention. The heartiness of his laughter had begun to sound forced, and his conversation often dissolved into silence. At any rate, this was the last time she saw him. The memory of it was still painful.

"Jonathan!" she called as she walked up the brick steps, her heels clicking against the ground. She knew he was home, for the kitchen light shone through the louvered windows and his beige Toyota was dripping a small patch of oil in the driveway. She already had her key in her right hand when he pulled the door open to let her in.

"Hi, Mom," he said.

He was tall enough so that he consciously stooped through thresholds, although he wasn't so tall that he would graze his head. He seemed to do it out of a desire not to appear overwhelming. Sometimes he looked like a camel drooping its neck, a camel with heavy dark eyelashes. He led with his head when he walked. "Stand up straight," Lurlene had told him many a time, but to no avail. He'd bend forward, kindly, winningly, as if to say, "I'm not all this towering presence. I'm right at your level. Don't worry. Don't be afraid." And since his level was mostly kids, he must have hunched even lower.

"How was work, dear?" Lurlene asked.

"Same thing."

"A big group?"

"Not much bigger than usual."

She put her keys in the dish by the front door and took off her sweater. "Which school were you at today?"

"Dawson Elementary."

On weekday afternoons he led puppetry workshops in after-school programs for children whose parents didn't pick them up until five o'clock. He was good at what he did and very much in demand. She was so proud of his accomplishments.

Setting up his own curricula, he taught the youngsters how to build puppets and how to develop their own original plays. Bringing in cartloads of beads, tinsel, buttons, fringe, pipe cleaners, yarn, string, glitter, ribbons, and paint, he helped them decorate their paper-mache creations as elaborately as possible. Even now his bedroom and basement workshop were a treasure trove of seedpods that fell from carob trees and dried stalks of yucca he found in the foothills. He gathered peacock feathers from a peafowl farm and pigeon feathers from beneath a guano-encrusted statue. He recycled LEGOs, Happy Meal prizes, hairnets, and steel wool, which was great for eyebrows and beards. From the time he was a little boy he had used his mother's discarded nylon stockings, empty Clorox bottles, egg cartons, and toilet paper rolls.

"A nice couple from church have their boys at Dawson."

"I don't have many boys in my class."

"Maybe they're not into puppetry."

"There are a lot of choices available for them. Most of the boys seem to go for basketball or soccer."

Jonathan had gone out for sports when he was a boy, probably, Lurlene reflected, because he knew it was something that would make her happy. He was good in volleyball and basketball and could have made one of the varsity teams in high school, but by then she recognized his heart wasn't in it. She kept telling herself it was because he didn't have a dad out on the sidewalk tossing the ball to him or dribbling layups in the driveway. The basketball hoop, rusty and basketless, still hung above the garage door, a memorial to her efforts. That Jonathan never took it down said something about his own sensitivities: He hated to acknowledge his failure to make it as a jock.

"I thawed out some ground round in the refrigerator," she said. "I thought I'd make some patties for dinner."

"That sounds good, Mom," he said.

"Let me change my clothes first," she said. "We'll eat at seven o'clock, if that's okay."

"Fine by me."

She took her purse to her bedroom and changed from her work clothes into a comfortable knit outfit. Jonathan went back down to his workshop to cut some Styrofoam for a puppet. He would work until dinner was ready.

Lurlene knew it would be better for him to find his own place and move out. A twenty-three-year-old man could live on his own, but Jonathan would never be able to afford much on his scattershot income, and she honestly enjoyed his company. In fact, each of them would say that this arrangement of theirs was something one did for the other, but both derived equal pleasure from it.

By candlelight they ate hamburger patties with sautéed mushrooms, green peas with butter on top, and strawberry ice cream for dessert. Jonathan talked about the students in his Tuesday after-school class. They were creating a version of Peter Pan where Captain Hook was a frustrated rock star, Peter was a superhero with magical powers, and the Lost Boys were a football team. He allowed them great license with their plots. They were especially fond of their set with its vinegar and soda volcano and glass-mirrored lake.

"And how was your day?" Jonathan asked his mom.

Lurlene described the bulletin she needed to get out and Pastor Bob's usual delay over choosing hymns and deciding the best title for his sermon. "He can never make up his mind until the last moment," she said.

Jonathan smiled at the familiar complaint before turning to wash the dishes while Lurlene watched a rerun of her favorite TV show.

The window was slightly ajar, and the sound of the laugh track wandered outside, rising up to the heavens and traveling into infinite space. During a commercial break Lurlene stood up and walked to the open window, breathing in the air and the faint scent of a blooming pear tree and a camellia bush. As she looked at the sky, she wondered, *If there are Martians out there or some form of life in another solar system, what would they think of these blue TV rays or the sound of taped laughter rising from metal boxes? What if one person out of all those millions of homes sent out a cry of distress? Who would hear him? Who would listen? Who would care?*

Gazing at the heavens, she thought of the nights when she had looked at the stars with her former husband and listened to his dreams. Back then she had accepted as a given that her husband had dreams and the wherewithal to follow them. Staring skyward, she had felt his longing for a better life and believed fate would bring it. He almost made her believe that dreaming was enough. She would have thought it presumptuous to ask God, had she believed in God.

In the end, fate hadn't complied. None of her husband's dreams had panned out. She told herself that it was just as well she didn't believe in God because that meant she didn't have a God to complain to. She could only be angry with herself.

From down in the basement, she could hear Jonathan running a block of Styrofoam through his jigsaw. He was so talented and hardworking. He would go somewhere with his art, do something important with it. She was sure of that. Only one crucial thing was missing in his life right now.

My Jonathan needs a wife, she said to herself. It came from a deeper part of herself than the usual inner monologue. She could have said it out loud. Jonathan couldn't hear her. The sound of the jigsaw and the TV would cover any sound she made. And he usually kept the basement door closed to keep out the sweet, toxic odors of paint, turpentine, and glue.

Lurlene remembered girls he had dated in college and high school. Sweet girls, the kind who volunteered for babysitting, filled in at the church nursery, and made jam. She suspected that he was madly in love with one of them, but not much came of it, and she didn't want to intrude. It was not her place. Recently he hadn't gone out with many girls, retreating instead to his studio in the evenings. He would get calls from girls, but they were just friends.

Lurlene had heard of women in the church who put their sons' and daughters' photos in their Bibles and prayed every day for the perfect spouses for them. She'd typed up a few anecdotes like that over the years in Pastor Bob's sermons. Some mothers went so far as to visualize and actually describe the features of this perfect spouse to God. Short with auburn hair, hardworking, patient, sexy, devoted, loving, and tolerant of in-laws. She laughed at the idea. When it came to the perfect mate for Jonathan, Lurlene could think of nothing she wanted more than a woman who would love her son as much as she loved him. Was that asking too much?

She shrugged her shoulders and put the idea out of her head. She was being silly. Yet there it was again, that deep, deep wish she couldn't quell, couldn't silence. Eminently practical, she found its concerns had nothing to do with practicality. Or happiness. Or even her selfish desire to see him settled. She looked at the stars one more time.

When Jonathan was a boy, they'd looked at stars together many times, and she'd taught him the old rhyme, "Starlight, starbright, first star I see tonight. I wish I may, I wish I might, have the wish I wish tonight." He would make a wish then. She would too. She had told him about wishing for things when he blew out the candles on his birthday cake, and she gave him a few pennies from her red change purse to throw in the fountain when they went to the zoo. She didn't deny him Santa Claus, the Easter Bunny, the Tooth Fairy, or Sunday school. So why not pray?

If I ever said a prayer–if I believed–I would pray for the perfect wife to come into my son's life. That was all she said to herself or to the air or to God–if she had believed in God. It was a wish, a longing that she was half-embarrassed to admit. But there, now it was done. She'd made it to the empty air. Enough.

The commercial was over. The laugh track had resumed. She returned to her TV show.

CHAPTER 4

"I'M WORRIED ABOUT LURLENE," Pastor Bob said the next morning as he sat on his brick patio next to the pool. He was eating half of a pink grapefruit at a glass-topped table.

"Hmm," his wife, Mary Lou, said, barely looking up from the newspaper. An attractive, no-nonsense type, she provided ballast for her husband's creative flights. If he was worried, she was optimistic. If he fretted, she made practical suggestions. When he went out on a limb, she stood on the ground, assuring all that he was quite sane. At the present moment she had finished her grapefruit half and was sitting across from him in a heavy wrought-iron chair—a tax-deductible gift from a congregation member who owned a gardening store.

"She seems distracted. Not really with it. I wouldn't notice it in someone else, but she's usually so sharp. Yesterday I misplaced my concordance, and she didn't interrupt me and bring it into my office as she usually does. I had to ask her for it."

"Maybe she's cutting you some slack. Isn't that

what you've wanted all these years?" Mary Lou balanced one of her bedroom slippers on the tip of her toe. She breakfasted in her bathrobe, while her husband never went outside without being fully dressed. The patio and pool area was fenced in. No one could see them without deliberately spying over the redwood fence, but Pastor Bob never ate breakfast without getting dressed first.

"It's not like Lurlene to be so aloof."

"You've complained in the past that she was too much of a busybody."

"I'm afraid she's going to forget something important."

"Has she done that yet?"

"Do you think she's getting tired of her job?" he asked, ignoring her question.

Mary Lou folded her newspaper and looked over the top of her glasses. Her husband needed her attention. "That's possible. She's been with you a long time."

"Almost as long as we've been here." He always referred to his pastorate in the first-person plural, the way young husbands talk of their wives' pregnancies, saying things like, "We're expecting sometime in January."

"It's no wonder she's tired." Mary Lou put her glasses down on the table. "The woman needs a break."

"She already gets four weeks of vacation," Pastor Bob said sheepishly.

"Has she ever used it? Does she ever go anyplace on her vacation?"

"A week at the beach. Yosemite one year . . ."

"But has she ever taken four weeks off at once?"

"Not that I can remember. She says she prefers to stay in town. Even when we go away in the summer, she stays in town. She says it's restful to go to the office when I'm not there. No interruptions. She catches up on her correspondence."

"And she knows that you'll be calling her from wherever we are, requesting this or that book or a copy of some sermon you delivered five years back. You always want her to fax something to us immediately or send it Federal Express."

"Summers are when I do my best work. It's the one chance I have to plan out my sermons for the entire year."

"What about when we were on sabbatical?"

"She worked in the office. The staff was short one girl, and they depended on her for a lot of regular stuff. You know, the prayer letters, birthday greetings, new member welcome packets . . ."

"The point is, she hasn't taken a full vacation in twenty-two years."

"No, I guess she hasn't."

"No wonder she's tired." Mary Lou picked up her glasses and returned to the paper. When she had a point to make she didn't linger over it. She found a little silence could work wonders. Besides, ever since their children had grown and left the nest, she relished the morning quiet. Her husband had been trained to cut the grapefruit and pour the coffee. Some days he made a plateful of eggs. And she got to read most of sections A and B of the newspaper before going off to work.

The silence only lasted a moment, then Bob asked, "How can you make someone take a vacation if they don't take time off?"

"Talk them into it."

"How would that work for Lurlene?"

"Leave her a few travel brochures."

"She'll never read them."

"Give her some specific suggestions."

"I can't see that they'll convince her to take a trip."

Mary Lou looked up from the article she was reading about a group of chimpanzees that were led by the female of the species. With the patience of a woman who had raised four children, she spoke to the man who appeared to be her fifth. "Make it a gift, Robert."

"A gift?"

"A present. Something special. No one can afford to say no to a gift, dear."

"You mean she'll have to accept it."

"Surprise her. She'll never say no." Smiling, she got up from her chair and kissed Bob on the top of his head as though that would help her idea sink in. Then she carried her plate back inside.

Alone, Bob picked up his grapefruit half and swiveled in his chair so that he could face the mountains. The sun crested over the highest peak in the distance, shining on the melting snow. The nearer hills, soft and green from the winter rains, picked up the long slanting light and warmed in its glow. Faulted by nature in a series of violent earthquakes, the mountains looked comforting and protective, shielding this valley from the harsh desert winds. Bob tipped back his head and squeezed the grapefruit juice into his mouth, savoring every last drop of the sweet bitterness. Another reason he liked to eat breakfast outside. His wife would never allow him to squeeze a grapefruit half into his mouth at the dining room table.

He picked up his Bible sitting on the glass-topped table and turned to the Psalms. Three psalms a day. That was his quota. Sometimes he read them at his desk. When his children were younger and he had to take them to school, he read his three psalms first thing in the morning, leaning into his Bible while sitting on the edge of his bed. But this location, where he could stare at the hills, was the best of all. *I will lift up mine eyes unto the hills, from whence cometh my help. My help cometh from the Lord. . . .*

The Psalms had been his friends over the years so that he'd learned to pin all his hopes, desires, frustrations, and needs on those ancient verses. Even when they spoke of warlike anger, royal devotion, or shepherding in long-gone times, they also sparked the language of Bob's inner dialogue with God. When the psalmist asked God to wreak some terrible violence against his opponents, Bob could look at the enemies he faced—sometimes a trustee or an assistant minister, but more often his own cowardice, timidity, or rage. When the Psalms spoke of a glorious Jerusalem, protected and loved by the Lord, he substituted his own modern benighted city. " 'As the hart panteth after the water brooks . . .' " Well, it wasn't hard to feel such desire on a summer day in this arid place watered by aqueducts and wells with its citizens regularly hydrating—the term they used—from large bottles of labeled water. He had understood that language of longing. " 'By the rivers of Babylon, there we sat down, yea we wept. . . .' " Hadn't he known moments of loneliness like that in his own backyard, in his own home?

He'd grown so accustomed to those words that he said them softly out loud to himself. Like a first grader, he moved his lips as he read, and his usual stentorian baritone rumbled at a low pitch like the small earthquake that wakes a person up in the middle of the night and is dismissed as the vibration of a passing truck. The sound drove his wife crazy, so she never lingered when he prayed.

Bob didn't think of the words as he read them. He knew countless verses, but he had never tried to memorize them. This was not the time for textual analysis or comparing translations. It was the only point of his day when he absolutely depended on the King James Version of the Bible. Other translations might have been more accurate or more sensitive to gender issues or more plainly put, but none of them had the texture of that Shakespearean tongue. This moment of his day was sacred, like the pitcher warming up in the bullpen, the singer going through his scales, the golfer taking a few practice swings. If he didn't have his psalms, he was lost. He wasn't speaking to impress someone else, he wasn't praying for a whole congregation to hear. There was no hidden agenda in this moment. He was warming up with the words of one speaking to God.

He thought of all the times in a week that he promised "I will pray for you" or "We'll be praying for you" or "You're on our prayer list." At times he worried that those phrases sounded terribly empty, like two acquaintances vaguely promising to do lunch. He was aware of his countless failings, but he hoped hypocrisy could not be leveled against him here. *I will pray for you*. True to his promises, he kept a list in his Bible of the people who asked for his intercession. *This is my job*, he told himself. As an obligation it used to be down near the bottom of his list, after preaching, visiting the sick, burying the dead, raising money, going to meetings. Now he put it at the top. He would pray for his congregation. He was reminded of Jesus' words to Simon Peter: "*. . . lovest thou me? Feed my sheep. Lovest thou me? Feed my sheep . . . feed my sheep . . . feed my sheep.*"

A car skidded around the corner on the other side of the fence. He could hear the radio playing full blast and a volley of high-pitched laughter. High school kids on the way to class, no doubt. Driving too fast and living foolishly the way his own boys had when they were in high school. Thanks be to God, his sons had arrived at early adulthood all in one piece. *Thank God.*

Often he became tired of people. It pained him to see them do the same stupid things year after year. He remembered a short story he had read somewhere—or was it a play?—about a man who lived to be six hundred years old without ever aging. Life became torture for the man because he had to see the same mistakes repeated again and again, so he finally begged to be put to death. A dark Methuselah. In his darker moments Pastor Bob could imagine feeling the same way. Sometimes his joviality, his laughter, his earnest care barely covered up his impatience, his irritation, his sinking into a dull misanthropy. He learned to depend on an innate curiosity about people's motivation to pull him out of his uncharitable thoughts. If he could learn enough details about a person and construct a conceivable story, he could find their human errors comprehensible. Perhaps that's what Will Rogers must have meant when he said, "I never met a man I couldn't like." *Couldn't* not *didn't*.

And he used prayer. It astonished him sometimes—his willingness to separate himself from people and their sorrow. To explain it away and dismiss it. Even the inexplicable disasters he could shield himself from. This was the secret he hoped his congregation would never discover. That such a warm-hearted man could harbor such cynicism. Once when he heard of a miserly parishioner's impending death, he was shocked to realize that his first thought was whether the man had mentioned the church in his will. *Lead me not into temptation*, he prayed silently. It's no wonder that Christ's biggest enemies were Pharisees. Pastor Bob could be one. Were it not for prayer.

He looked down at today's list of parishioners who'd asked for his prayers. He glanced at the names of people and their problems. Lurlene herself had typed them out. Cancer, divorce, expectant mother, financial troubles, looking for a new job, struggling through college, bypass surgery. He mumbled the names and the needs to God. Intercessory prayer was always a mystery to Bob, but he depended on it. He had called on it himself. He could feel it happening many a Sunday while he preached, knowing his congregation was praying for him. Maybe they thought he was good and kind and saintly. He himself knew he could be mean, small, and selfish. But if he prayed for others, as he was now doing, God would work on his own heart. Break it open. Heal it. "And Lurlene, too, Lord," he murmured. "Be with Lurlene."

What was that his wife had said about Lurlene? Leave her a brochure? Give her a present?

Over the years he had disciplined himself not to use his prayer time as a think session. He didn't look for sermon illustrations or phrases for a stewardship letter during this time. He didn't plan agendas for meetings or rehearse speeches for his office staff. The ideas came to him, of course, but he tried to let them go.

Mary Lou is right. We should do something special for Lur-

lene. Shame her into taking a vacation. He continued reading the list. *We could have a party. A celebration of her years of service.* Then he began to consider possible days to have it and people to organize it. *What day could we do it? What sort of present should we give her? How can we ever raise the money without her knowing?*

"Enough of this, Lord. I'll take care of it later." He wrote a note to himself and then put the thoughts behind him. Closing his eyes, he searched for the numinous peace that came to him sometimes. If he gave these fifteen or twenty minutes to God, God would be with him the rest of the day. That was their arrangement. He would pray, then give the petitions up to God. God would have to do the rest.

The air stilled. Hardly a breeze marred the surface of the swimming pool. He could hear more cars pass on the street outside. Parents taking their children to school, adults driving off to another day of staring at computer screens or looking at marketing reports. How little he knew about the work lives of his congregation, yet how much he knew about their home lives—their affairs, their chemical dependencies, their disastrous marriages, and their disappointing children. His flock usually came to him in times of crisis, and he listened to them. He was a good listener, and he'd learned that a sympathetic ear was usually all that was expected of him. That and a few words of prayer.

The birds chirped loudly this morning. They darted between the camellias and swooped up to the branches of the pear tree. They called out from the eaves of the neo-Tudor house that served as First Church's manse. One waddled on the brick wall beside the pool. "Give Lurlene happiness," Bob prayed. "Grant her deepest wish, whatever that may be."

As always, he ended with the Lord's Prayer. What a blessing there was in the mere familiarity of it. " 'For thine is the kingdom, and the power, and the glory, for ever. Amen.' Amen!" he repeated loudly, then stood up from the table and looked out at the hills. It was going to be a good day. " 'This is the day which the Lord hath made; we will rejoice and be glad in it,' " he declared in a firm voice.

Ready for work, he balanced his plate on his Bible and headed inside.

CHAPTER 5

LURLENE WAS HAVING a terrible day. Wednesdays were always busy. There was the program for the Sunday worship service to finalize and send out to the printer and advertisements to proof for the local newspaper, not to mention typing the first draft of Pastor Bob's sermon and changing the title on the message board in front of First Church. In addition, there was the usual stack of prayer letters waiting to be answered. "Hump Day," she used to call it. If she got through a Wednesday, she got through the hump of the week. Then she could coast for a few days before starting all over again on Monday. She usually was able to work at a high level of energy and efficiency on Wednesdays to get everything done. But lately she kept getting behind and slipping up. She found herself falling off the back side of the hump.

First thing in the morning the ladies from the prayer room upstairs had come down with a big stack of letters to be answered. Fortunately they had done the sorting, which let her know exactly what form letter she should use in response. Still, she always read the letters carefully to make certain the designations were correct. Sometimes the ladies put down categories that were a little whimsical—one couldn't expect people who spent a valuable portion of their days in prayer to always understand the practicalities of a person's situation. Sometimes they were downright wrong. She had never forgotten the time they labeled a letter "Forgiveness" when it was clear that the woman's trouble with her boss had to do with her lack of qualifications for the job. Lurlene changed the label and sent the correspondent a form letter on the subject of "Career/ Calling."

Then there was Pastor Bob. She couldn't understand what had gotten into him. He had been unusually solicitous all morning. He greeted her especially warmly when he came in, then pulled up a chair next to her desk to chat for a few moments—right when she had a stack of work to do. He asked her about Jonathan, how his puppetry workshops were going, and if he was getting enough work. He asked if there was anything he, Pastor Bob, could do. Then he said he'd always liked Jonathan and thought him very talented.

Lurlene was utterly bewildered. The one thing worse than being taken for granted was to suddenly not be taken for granted. What was on her boss's mind? Did he have some terrible news for her that he was trying to soften? Was he going to let her go? Perhaps he wanted to ship her off to the business office or the drudgery of bookkeeping, and he just couldn't tell her.

After quizzing her for fifteen minutes about her son, he suddenly said, "I think the two of you should go on a vacation."

"But we just took a vacation ten days ago," she said.

"Where did you go?"

"Didn't I tell you?"

"Yes, you did, but remind me once again."

"We went up to Solvang during the President's Day weekend. Had a wonderful time. We ate Danish pastries and visited the Santa Inez mission. . . ."

"I just want you to know how much we appreciate you here, Mrs. Scott. You are a deeply valued employee," Pastor Bob said, then he rose from the chair he had been straddling and went into his office whistling "Rock of Ages."

As if that weren't enough, around ten-thirty she received a telephone call from a newspaper reporter who was doing a feature story on prayer. The woman wanted to talk to the minister at First Church because she understood that the church had a special program of praying for people and their problems.

"He's not available right now," Lurlene said in her coolest, most polite voice. "I'll tell him you called." She took down the message on a pink slip of paper and hoped Pastor Bob simply wouldn't see it. She really dreaded him making a fool of himself in print. It was probably some cynical reporter who would find the prayer letters at First Church a cause for wry, tongue-in-cheek reporting that would go over the heads of most church members and make them the laughingstock of town. What good would come of an interview? Nothing. Newspaper profiles were never fair.

Unfortunately, just as she was filing the message away in a neat pile beneath a request from a stockbroker hoping to interest the pastor in a mutual fund, Bob passed by her desk on his way to the men's room and picked up the message.

"When did the *Herald News* call?" he asked.

"A few minutes ago," she said. "You were on another line."

"Glad to know they're interested in us." He slipped the message into his pocket. Five minutes later, upon his return to his office, Lurlene knew he had called the woman. She could hear him going on at great length about the importance of prayer in his life and what it meant in the corporate life of the congregation. He would never get his sermon done if he insisted on this flirtation with the press. She despised the way everyone stopped everything simply for a taste of media attention. First Church got enough attention as it was. Pastor Bob's sermons were broadcast on a local radio station every Sunday morning. Wasn't that fame enough?

Turning this over in her mind, she returned to her typing at the computer. She felt a little better when she noticed that Bob had hung up. Then to her irritation, he closed the door to his office. There was no apparent provocation, no confessing parishioner at his side, no top secret colloquy with a trustee or board member. The light on her phone went green, indicating that he was back on the phone. She hesitated for a moment, tempted to lift her phone and listen in. It could be easily done–she'd done it before. But there was always the possibility that someone would slam a door in her office, and the noise would resonate in his receiver along with her gasp. Besides, Pastor Bob had clearly made the effort to exclude her from this conversation. Her conscience was such that she could still feel guilty for spying on something that had been purposefully withheld from her. It was different when the secrets were being kept from someone else.

Stepping away from temptation, she stood at her desk and

picked up her coffee mug, a large ornate angel leaning out from the handle, its wings wrapped around the lip. It was one of Jonathan's creations from a pot-throwing class. She walked past the closed oak door and paused at the coffee machine right outside. She heard her name. "Lurlene . . . our Mrs. Scott . . . working too hard . . . been here a long time."

Her worst nightmare had come true! He was going to fire her! Appalled, she listened carefully. There was more mumbling, then a guffaw. It was terrible—that he would laugh about her. How incredibly rude! That he would treat her so lightly. Had he no sensitivity to her feelings? Did he not even care about her after twenty-two years of service? After all the extra work she had done, staying late and not even asking for overtime because it was, after all, a church, and the place had better things to do with their money! In the meanwhile, she was earning a lot less than she was worth and sticking around out of some ridiculous notion of loyalty. She could have gone to a law firm and made money hand over fist typing legal briefs, but no . . .

She slammed down the coffee urn, almost breaking the glass. A trickle of hot liquid sloshed down the side and sizzled on the heating coils. *I'm being paranoid*, she told herself. *Jumping to conclusions.* It was all in her mind. He was not firing her, was *not* dumping her. Just because he was discussing her didn't mean a thing. . . .

She knew firsthand how hard it was to find qualified people. She herself had interviewed secretaries for other positions in the church. Some of these young ladies could hardly spell. They barely knew the difference between a colon and semicolon. They were unable to determine when to use single quote marks or double ones. How would an inexperienced airhead handle the intricacies of Bible attributions and proofing the accuracy of chapter and verse? How would she know when to capitalize the deity and when to leave the pronoun "him" lowercase? And how could a new girl be trained in the fine points of handling the prayer letters and all the possible responses?

Lurlene was no dummy. She had made sure she was indispensable in case such a thing happened. Patting her coif, she congratulated herself on her strategy. If her employer so much as mentioned a demotion or changeover, she could list the tasks that made her uniquely qualified for her job. The years of accumulated history, the encyclopedic knowledge, the sheer know-how. Not to mention her uncomplaining, cheerful demeanor. She could not be replaced.

Sighing with relief, she returned to her computer and was staring at the screen when the door to Pastor Bob's office swung open. He walked to the bookshelf and picked up a dictionary, humming "A Mighty Fortress Is Our God." Making a sudden stop, he took out a ten-dollar bill from his wallet and flung it down on Lurlene's desk.

"Take yourself out to lunch, Mrs. Scott," he said.

"What?" she asked in disbelief.

"Treat yourself to a nice lunch. It's on me. You deserve it."

Before she could protest and explain that she had some cottage cheese and sliced carrots in the refrigerator of the Fellowship Hall kitchen, he was gone, the bill looking as lonely as the ten-dollar bill a street musician puts in his empty guitar case in hopes of attracting similar donations. Stewing, she picked up the money and shoved it into her purse.

She had driven to work that morning, though she didn't

know why. Maybe it was the clouds in the morning. Now the sun was shining and no rain threatened. At any rate, she had her car parked in front of the church. She could drive to lunch and be back without missing too much time. The cottage cheese and carrots would wait another day.

Saving the document on her computer, she slipped her heels on, hoping to get outside before she burst out with some ungrateful remark. At the office door she turned around, strutted back to her desk, pushed the button on her intercom, and leaned into it. "I'm taking you up on your offer," she said tremulously. "Thanks."

"Have a good time," he said.

"I will." God willing, she would be able to hold back the tears until she reached her car.

In the privacy of her Pontiac, she took a sheet of Kleenex out of a travel packet in her glove compartment and gave in to her tears. She sat there for a minute, hiding herself from the world, then dabbed her eyes with a new tissue.

What was wrong with her? She hated herself for crying like this. She never thought of herself as highstrung or overwrought. She was practical, pragmatic, even-tempered. She lowered the cosmetic mirror above the windshield and stared into it. Maybe Pastor Bob was right. Maybe she *did* need a long break. She had always prided herself on keeping things in perspective, keeping a good head on her shoulders when others were losing theirs. For a moment she had panicked. Her instinct to flee had been right. She needed to get out of the office.

She would treat herself to a nice lunch. There was a popular soup and salad place on Sycamore Street where the fortunate ladies who didn't work "outside of the home" ate in their linen suits, sipped iced tea, and talked in voices that sounded like tinkling silver. She might even have a glass of Chardonnay. She knew Pastor Bob would not approve, but she was feeling a bit rebellious after overhearing him talk about her on the phone. Besides, she would feel better if the lunch cost more than ten dollars because it would prove how out-of-touch Pastor Bob was with the real cost of eating out.

By the time she pulled up to a ficus tree in the parking lot, her tears had dried. She reapplied her lipstick and stepped out of the car. As she sat at her table beneath latticework profuse with pale purple wisteria, she decided to enjoy herself. It was a lovely sunny day, and everyone else seemed to be enjoying themselves. Gazing out over the top of her menu, she recognized no one in the small patio. A Mexican busboy poured her a glass of water, and she smiled magnanimously at him before returning to her menu. When the young college-aged waitress came to her table, she had made up her mind. A Cobb salad.

"Do you want anything with that?" the girl asked.

"Yes," Lurlene said. "I'd like a glass of Chardonnay. Thank you very much."

"No problem."

It irritated her that this phrase had crept into the language and was now considered an acceptable answer to thank-you. Whatever happened to "you're welcome?" No problem! That was not good manners. She barely restrained herself from correcting the young woman.

The wine gave her a slight buzz as it bypassed her empty stomach and went directly to her head. She was sorry she didn't have anything to read. She usually sat down with a novel at her desk during lunch. It gave her a break. Now she felt awkward being by herself with nothing to do but stare at the other ladies and wonder if they were looking at her when she wasn't looking at them. She set her eyes off into the middle distance, where people were parking their cars and taking the sidewalk to the post office or the town's only bookstore. If anyone who knew her saw her, they would say, "There's Mrs. Scott from church, Pastor Bob's secretary. He must have given her the afternoon off. How kind of him."

Reflected glory! That's all she had. People didn't know and little realized how much she did for the popular preacher. Without her he would have been nothing. Ideas, speeches, sermons, books, articles, the radio show. All those things happened smoothly and without a hitch because she made sure he was in the right place at the right time. He could be free to dream up the clever words and winning anecdotes because she handled the business of running his life. His wife didn't do it. Mary Lou had her own job to handle. Instead, she, Lurlene Scott, was the great woman behind the great man. And in the rare instance that someone did pay attention to her, it was because that person wanted something from *him*.

Feeling sorry for herself as she stared into the distance, she spotted a battered tan Toyota. It pulled up and a figure dressed in black jeans and a T-shirt got out. Of course she recognized immediately who it was, but for a moment she gazed on him as though he were a stranger. The wavy dark hair, the piercing blue eyes, the shy smile, the long legs in their loping gait. The sex appeal of a Gary Cooper, gentle, tender, sensitive. When had her son become so handsome? It was as though the image of an awkward high school kid had stuck in her mind's eye and she hadn't revised it or edited it. But here, on a sunny February afternoon, sauntering through the parking lot off Sycamore, her son had the dusky allure of an artist. Irresponsible, daring, kind. What woman wouldn't go for him?

She ducked her head behind the wisteria-covered latticework.

"Yo," he said.

He had seen her! No. No, he was greeting the waitress, waving at her over the wall.

The waitress smiled. "Hey, Jonathan!"

They were friends.

"Catch you later," he mouthed the words. Then he walked on to the post office.

Just then the Cobb salad arrived. Lurlene attacked it in big forkfuls. She didn't want to be seen by her son when he came out of the post office. For some reason she felt as though she were imposing on his territory. She had also become self-conscious about being away from the office for more than a half hour. Swallowing a large bite, she flagged the waitress down and asked for the check.

"Something's come up. I need to hurry," she said. Burying her head in the salad when Jonathan came out of the post office, she stayed that way until she heard his Toyota disappear.

"Excuse me," the waitress said, arriving with the bill on a small plastic tray. Lurlene checked out the numbers. With tip and tax, it was over ten dollars. Good. Just as she thought, it was more than he'd given her. Not to be small-minded, she wouldn't even mention the price to Pastor Bob unless he asked. No, she'd be as silent as a tomb.

Pastor Bob wasn't in when she returned to the office. She

glanced at his calendar. A one o'clock lunch date. Invariably his lunches lasted at least two hours. Especially if he were trying to hit someone up for a fundraising campaign or a mortgage burning party or the annual pledge drive. If he were particularly successful he would say, "God loves a cheerful giver, Mrs. Scott" and do his own victory dance.

Ten minutes later he ambled in. No dance to make or report to give. Instead he plopped himself down in the chair next to hers again and asked exactly what she ate. His eyes narrowed earnestly, his face wearing the same strained look of compassion that it had when he greeted church members on a Sunday morning.

"A Cobb salad," she said.

"A Cobb salad!" he exclaimed as though he were considering an amendment to the Augsburg Confession or the Apostles' Creed. "That sounds delicious."

In twenty-two years he had never once asked her what she ate for lunch. In twenty-two years he had never once commented on her diet. What had gotten into him?

"It's been decades since I've had a good Cobb salad," he said. "Did it have lettuce, peas, sour cream, and bacon in it?"

"Yes, it did."

He smacked his lips. "Sounds mighty good, Mrs. Scott. I'm glad you enjoyed yourself. That's what I like seeing around here." Oblivious to her agitation, he left her desk and entered his office, closing his door behind him. Nap time. Lurlene stood abruptly and poured herself a big cup of twice-brewed coffee to keep herself from falling asleep or from giving him a piece of her mind. Work was her only consolation.

Cancer. Financial Troubles. Divorce. Death of Spouse. She was going through the prayer letters—she had given up hope of sending out the Sunday morning program in time—when another call came from the woman reporter.

"I'll get Pastor Bob for you," Lurlene said.

"Thanks, Lurlene," the woman said. *Lurlene? A first-name basis already?* Lurlene hated undue familiarity from people she had never met. It was unseemly and manipulative. People wanted to sound like your friend and then worm some favor out of you. No, she would not be coaxed into being buddy-buddy with this reporter. No doubt the lady was after some classified information. Her story would contain an exposé on First Church and its unsuspecting minister. Lurlene was fed up, just fed up. The bad morning, the strained interest of her boss into her affairs had her feeling out of kilter and at the end of her rope.

Just then, as she read the next prayer letter, she was inspired to do something completely unprofessional, something so out-of-character that it would have appalled her if someone had accused her of it. Maybe it was the glass of wine at lunch, maybe it was the fear that she was being let go or downsized. For a moment she faltered from her strong code of ethics. She pictured her handsome son jauntily waving to the black-clad waitress at the restaurant. And she looked again at the way the letter was written. *Six foot two, dark hair, a love of laughter, great sensitivity, midtwenties to early thirties. Pray that I don't become bitter and small-minded.*

Was Lurlene small-minded? Not for a moment. She was a woman who did her job. She continued reading. *Pray that I don't become desperate either, like some women I know. And pray that I'll recognize this Prince Charming when I meet him.*

"I know the man for you," she said under her breath. "I

know how you won't become desperate or bitter. I know the happiness you're looking for."

For the first time in twenty-two years, Lurlene diverted from the established script. For the first time she amended the form letter by adding a personal note.

> *We thank you for your heartfelt request for prayer. And with this promise of prayers, we also want to make a practical suggestion. We think we know of a young man who would be perfectly suited to your qualifications. Please send a letter to "Prince Charming" in care of Rev. Robert Dudley Jr. at First Church. We will forward it to the gentleman in question.*

That would work. That would be dandy. No problem. Lurlene opened all of Pastor Bob's mail. No one would be suspicious. Pastor Bob received dozens of unusual letters, many of them with dubious propositions. Everyone would assume that a letter addressed to Prince Charming was meant for the senior minister. No doubt about it.

She looked at the return address. A decent street, an apartment building. Probably young. Maybe attractive. The woman had only given herself a first name, but that wasn't uncommon. If the young lady was interested, Lurlene would match her up with the most eligible bachelor around. *P.S.*, Lurlene typed. *Be sure to include your telephone number and the best way to reach you.*

It was perfect. Enough of prayers. No more holy nonsense or mumbo jumbo with a verse from the Bible. This was practical help. The woman would be only too pleased to find a church in the matchmaking business. Some people used to say it was a marriage mill anyway, all those young single groups, all those good-looking unmarrieds talking about God and checking each other out. So here was a method more direct than Bible study and mountain retreats. This was better than a church dance or a church volleyball game to link the opposite sex in a like-minded pursuit. Here was faith in action.

Lurlene folded the letter and put it in an envelope. She would walk it to the mailroom herself, send it through the postage meter, and see it stamped with the message that went on all First Church letters: "Putting First Things First." First things first. Maybe this would be her last deed for Pastor Bob, but it would be a good one.

CHAPTER 6

"I CAN'T BELIEVE THIS!" Janice told her roommate, Shelly, on Thursday night in their apartment. "This is really amazing."

"What is?" Shelly looked up from the magazine she was thumbing through. She was lying on a folded-up futon, her jacket draped over the back of a chair, her shoes abandoned in the middle of the floor. She didn't really want to be interrupted in her reading, but when someone makes an exclamation and you're the only other person in the room, you're expected to respond.

"A dating service," Janice said. "A church providing a dating service."

"Who is?"

"The church. The one I was interviewing for that story on prayer. You remember the piece I was working on?"

Shelly had listened to all of Janice's descriptions of her big stories and vaguely remembered them. "Yes."

"They're trying to hook me up with some guy."

"Why? The story wasn't about the dating scene, was it?"

"I sent them a letter."

"Oh yeah." It was coming back to Shelly.

"They wrote me back."

"I thought you said they write everybody."

"They do. But not like this. I knew they'd pray for me, and I figured they'd send some sort of form letter or something. I just didn't think they would make a practical suggestion."

"A suggestion?"

"Check this out." Janice took two steps across the room—it was such a small apartment that she could cross the living room in three steps—and handed the letter to her roommate.

Putting down her magazine, Shelly began scanning the page, trying to find the crux of it. The sort of speed-reading she did all the time at work.

We thank you for your heartfelt request for prayer. And with this promise of prayers, we also want to make a practical suggestion. We think we know of a young man who would be perfectly suited to your qualifications.

"The man of your dreams," Shelly observed. "Found by a church."

"They can't do this with all their prayer letters. They would never have time."

"Who else is looking for a husband?"

"Think of the things people must ask for. Money, jobs, a new home. They could never provide all that."

"They're not giving you a guy."

"But they're making a suggestion."

"It's not a hoax, is it?" Shelly handed the letter back.

"No. It looks absolutely serious. I'm pretty sure it was mailed from the church. Look, it says 'First Church—Putting

First Things First' right on the front. It had to come from their postage meter. Nobody could fake that.''

''Nobody would bother.''

''And the stationery looks right, unless someone stole their letterhead.'' In a Nancy Drew mood, Janice held the letter up to the light.

''Watermarks?''

''It must have come from First Church.''

''You shouldn't be surprised. You told me that the people who pray there take these requests very seriously.''

''I assumed they would. But I didn't think they'd go this far.''

''Doesn't this mean that your letter was shared around and read by a lot of people?'' Shelly asked. She could picture gossipy ladies clucking their tongues about the fate of a young career women in this day and age.

''Only a few, from what I understand.''

''Enough to start a stampede of lovesick, church-going men knocking at our door or phoning us at all hours.''

''All the people who pray are women,'' Janice said crisply.

''They'll match you up with their sons.''

''It could be worse.''

''They'll find kid brothers or ugly cousins or their husband's geeky friends.''

''You might like them.''

''I can see a bunch of pimply church boys moping around outside. Waiting only for you.''

''You're jealous.''

''The landlord will have to hire a special security guard.''

''There are a lot unattached guys hanging out here already.''

The building had gone up in the seventies. It had a lima-bean-shaped pool in the back, illuminated banana plants in front, palm fronds and bird-of-paradise landscaping, and white sparkled flocking on all the ceilings. The landlord made a point of renting to single working women in the hope that there'd be a greater turnover as they married and moved out. He was often stressing the security advantages of the place. The front door was always locked, and the building was only a block away from the police station.

"To tell you the truth, I'm touched they prayed for me," Janice went on. She sat back down in the plastic chair at the Formica-topped table.

Shelly rolled her eyes. "What are you going to do about their offer?"

"I don't think I have a choice."

"Which is?"

"Write back. Or call."

"You're shameless. You'll do anything for a story."

"I'm serious. I've got to take them up on their suggestion."

Shelly looked across the room at her roommate. Janice was rereading the letter.

Dark-eyed, dark-haired, and fair-skinned, Janice had only recently discovered that she turned heads. It still came as a surprise when a construction worker whistled at her or when a truck driver honked while she was putting quarters into a parking meter. She would look behind to see who had attracted his eye. It had to be some other woman. They weren't looking at her, were they? Maybe Shelly was right. Perhaps she had become shameless in this new-found confidence in her appearance. She was discovering her looks could work in her favor.

An English major in college, she'd gone into newspaper work without any of the hunt-and-peck ambitions to be a journalist. She liked to write, and reporting was a way to do it regularly. She was glad for the job. In just a few months she had learned the basics, and then to her surprise she'd developed a passion for newspaper work. She could call people up cold and ask them questions without fearing immediate rejection. She could crank out a few paragraphs on any subject at the drop of a hat. She had discovered the pleasure of working her heart out on a feature piece even if it faded into oblivion in another week's time. There was always a new one to tackle the next day and the next. What pleased her most was that she excelled at reporting.

Janice could go to a meeting at the town hall and ask a dozen questions of a hard-edged, leering politico and watch him melt in her hands. At first she tried an aggressive, no-nonsense demeanor. Then she discovered that with her looks, it was better to appear helpless and vulnerable. While other reporters raised their voices to be heard in the ruckus, she lowered hers. Interviewees leaned forward, straining to hear her words. After issuing a formal press release, they were only too glad to answer her questions. Even when they'd discovered themselves framed in hard cold print, they still returned telephone calls from "that pretty young reporter." Guys like that confirmed her worst suspicions about men. It didn't matter what you said, they only cared what you looked like.

Many times she had earned the envy of her colleagues. "How did you get that scumbag to say all those nasty things in print?" a fellow reporter at the *Herald News* once asked. Janice shrugged her shoulders, laughed, and tucked a loose strand of dark hair behind her ear as she returned to her computer screen. The few women reporters on staff attributed her success to her extraordinary good looks. The men were a little too vain to do so. Admitting that an attractive face and a great pair of legs turned guys into blathering idiots was more than most men could face.

For a time Janice felt it was dishonest to use her good looks to her advantage. It didn't seem fair. After all, wasn't beauty on the inside what counted most? Somehow she thought her beauty–her recently realized and acknowledged good looks–would dissipate if used for profit. Shy and naturally modest, she had felt that her treasure would be greater if preserved to itself. Then practicality took over. She had a job to do, and all was fair in love and war . . . and newspaper reporting.

"Don't you think it was dishonest to write that letter?" Shelly asked.

"I've been wondering about that," Janice answered.

"Would you get in trouble if anyone at the paper found out?"

"Probably not."

"What about at the church?"

"No."

"Don't you think you were leading them on?"

"Not really. I was simply testing the mechanism."

"But you have a hidden motive."

"Not a nasty one. I couldn't write a story that was unkind, unless there was a real scandal afoot. People don't want to hear bad things about churches. They want someone to trust.

They want to see a few saints at work. Faith is such a rare thing it's heartbreaking to disturb. The press has decided it's best to leave well enough alone."

Shelly smiled. "I know you. I know your writing. Even if you don't go for the jugular, you'll make your objections in a subtler, swifter, deadlier manner. You'll be so dry that every cynic this side of Simi Valley will know exactly where you stand."

"That is only if I have objections."

"Every story needs its Doubting Thomas," Shelly replied.

Janice wondered if that were true. So far everyone at the church had been so nice and sincere. She picked up the form letter the minister sent out along with the specific response to her own situation. She scanned Pastor Bob's letter for objectionable phrases. "Dear Friend," it began. At least it didn't start out, "Dear sir." Give them credit for that. First Church was sensitive to its prayer petitioners, most of whom were undoubtedly women. Who else would take the time to write? She made a mental note to check that out. What percentage of the requests came from men and what percentage came from women? It would be good to include those figures in her story.

Dear Friend,

Thank you for sharing your need with us. We take intercessory prayer very seriously here at First Church. Of course we hope and believe that our prayers will help you, and we ask you to join us. We have found over the years that our prayers for you and others also help us. When we as a church look at ourselves and our needs, we become narrow-minded and not the generous souls God would have us be. But when we open ourselves up, sharing your pain, being sensitive to your struggles, we become bigger and greater. We become a true body of Christ.

There is no charge for our work. You will not be sent an appeal for money. The only thing we ask is that you join us in prayer. Every weekday morning, a group of our prayer warriors gather in what we call "the room upstairs." They read and pray for the hundreds of requests we receive. Some particular needs are posted on the bulletin board or sent by email throughout the church and to select members of our congregation. Sometime during the day would you close your eyes for a minute and join us? I promise that any concerted effort at prayer will make a huge difference in your life. Pray every day, and you, too, will change.

"For where two or three are gathered together in my name, there am I. . . ."

"And lo, I am with you alway, even unto the end of the world."

God bless,
Rev. Robert F. Dudley Jr.
(Pastor Bob)

Janice could hear the voice of the man she had interviewed over the phone. A friendly, earnest, slightly modulated baritone. Southern-sounding but not southern. She had the sense that when she was talking to him he was smiling to himself on the other end of the line. Not at her but with her, or with some other pleasantry beyond her.

She reread the letter with disappointment. It wouldn't be very good for excerpts. There wasn't one line that stood out for its egregious promise or money-grubbing proposition. In fact, it was a kindly, self-effacing letter. She wondered if Rev.

Robert F. Dudley Jr. had actually written it himself. There were some religious-sounding phrases and clichés, but overall it was the work of a thoughtful, articulate person.

"Prayer warriors," "true body of Christ," "sharing your need." What did these terms mean to Janice? What would they mean to the newspaper readers? Not much to an agnostic. She put down the letter and wrinkled her nose. This story was going to be a little harder to write than she thought. The "who" she had, and the "what, when, and where"—but what on earth was the "why"?

Why would people pray for perfect strangers? Why would perfect strangers ask to be prayed for? And why did the whole idea appeal to her so much?

By Friday Lurlene had heard nothing. She reminded herself that she needed to be patient. She had to be realistic. Correspondence didn't necessarily go across town overnight. It could take two days for her "dating service" letter to reach the young woman on Elm Street, and the return letter wouldn't arrive until the next week. The church office was closed on Saturdays, and Mike, the messenger boy, brought in mail late on Monday mornings. Lurlene wouldn't get a letter at least until then. But it didn't prevent her from wondering. What had the woman thought of the answer to her prayer letter? How would she react? Would she take Lurlene up on the offer?

The phone rang often that day. Dozens of callers inquired if Pastor Bob would be preaching on Sunday and what his topic would be, for the weekly church advertisement wouldn't appear in the newspaper until Saturday morning.

"Money and Power," she said crisply, repeating herself slowly if there was a long pause. Whenever a caller had a young female voice, Lurlene wondered if this was the one who had requested a man six foot two, dark hair, a love of laughter, great sensitivity, midtwenties to early thirties, nice singing voice, stable in career, willing to travel. Her son fit the description to a T.

Sometimes she thought of a catchy phrase, "Coincidence is when God remains anonymous." She had typed that quote in several of Pastor Bob's sermons and had heard it repeated at church. Now she wondered if it applied to herself. Was it a coincidence that the woman had requested a man just like her son? Was it a coincidence that the letter had come right after Lurlene had made such a wish to the stars?

"How ridiculous!" she told herself. She wouldn't harbor the thought. The qualities described were as general as the advice in a horoscope. Anyone could have written that letter. It was simply a matter of several arbitrary things happening at once. Nothing remotely out of the ordinary.

Pastor Bob refused all invitations to go out on Saturday nights. Early in his ministry—what he insisted on calling "their" ministry, although Mary Lou never indulged him in this matter—he used to go to the occasional dinner party, Christmas, or bridge party. But now he was afraid of becoming muddle-minded on Sunday morning if he stayed out too late the previous night.

He preached without ever looking at his text. Sometimes he took a few steps away from the pulpit, making the church sound engineers grateful for his clip-on mike. Often it seemed as though he were improvising his sermons, as though his words were not his own but those of the Holy Spirit. He was God's vessel and felt as such he didn't need a written-out, structured sermon of three points supported by anecdotes. Open to God's inspiration for time and place, he addressed his listeners with an intimacy that was both powerful and compelling.

Only once had he ever lost his place. Only once had he ever drawn a blank, and that was the morning after a dinner party to celebrate a friend's birthday. Sunday morning he had looked up at the half-moon balcony and across to the stained-glass window of Moses receiving the Ten Commandments. He had regarded the clock on the far wall—his reminder of when to wrap things up—and nothing came to him. He had turned to the choir that surrounded him on either side of the chancel. Their faces gazed at him with the utmost trust. His mind was void of all thought. Didn't anybody realize what a bind he was in?

He had picked up the glass of water that always sat on the first shelf of the pulpit next to a hymnal and Bible. He took a big gulp of water, and still nothing came to him. He couldn't tell where he had been in his sermon or where he was going. The only thing he could think to do was ask everyone to bow their heads for a moment of silence—it must have been agony to the radio engineer.

"I was praying for you," one of the congregation's most stalwart members said later.

"God bless you," he had responded. In the silence, emptier than such silences had ever been before at First Church, he had found a way out. But ever since, he had made sure that he never, never went out on Saturday nights. He needed to be fresh for church on Sunday mornings. It was one of his few rules.

This evening Mary Lou had gone to see a movie by herself. They had already received telephone calls from two of their four offspring. Their children knew Saturday was a good day to find Mom and Dad home. One son claimed he wanted to learn how to skydive and asked what they thought of that. A daughter said she had been away on a ski trip for a week, in case they wondered where she was. They had wondered. Adult children could run as hot and cold as adolescents, one moment asking permission and the next claiming surprise that their parents wanted to know their whereabouts.

Passing up the movie, Bob instead watched a basketball game at home with the sound off. He didn't stand up and practice his sermon. He certainly never looked into the mirror on the wall to practice any corny gestures. The mirror was deadly. Once you started watching yourself, you no longer looked natural but started to take on the blank gaze of an aerobics instructor admiring her abs. He relegated his vanity to less external matters. That's what was on his mind now.

He saw himself on Sunday mornings after the service greeting people at the back of the church. One bear hug after another. When he knew a parishioner was in the midst of some turmoil, he cocked his head to one side and asked, "How *are* you?" He had a capacious memory for the trials and tribulations of his congregation, even though he often couldn't remember their names. Their warm embraces were his fuel. He hated to admit that, but it was true. As much as he told himself that he was loved by God, he needed interaction with people to confirm God's call on his life.

What bothered him at the moment was how extraneous

his family or his closest associates could become to this fueling process. He often dropped everything to rush to a hospital bedside or to call on a grieving widow, but how attentive was he to those people he saw every day? For instance, he was never as upbeat and positive with Lurlene as he was with his flock. Did he listen to her with as much concern as he did to some lost soul he was counseling? Did he hear her troubles? How deep was he really? How thoughtful? How loving?

Looking at the basketball game, he tried to put these concerns aside. Nevertheless, he felt himself sink into a blue funk.

What would his congregation think if they knew he stared into a silent TV on Saturday nights and questioned his capability of leading them? He, the famed pastor of First Church, could barely muster the energy to throw into the trash the cardboard container that had held his supper.

CHAPTER 7

SUNDAY MORNING LURLENE woke up with the idea of going to the 9:45 service. Although she wasn't a member of First Church, she occasionally attended services. She went to worship the way someone might go to an amateur community concert because the second violist happened to be the boss's secretary or the tuba player was a regular customer. Lurlene wanted to be supportive of Pastor Bob, and she needed to be well informed.

For instance, if George, the organist, complained on Monday morning about how the basses sang in the anthem, she would be able to tell him that as far as she was concerned, they had pulled off their part rather well, especially in the quieter passages. Or if the lighting technician said he had to make a special appointment with Pastor Bob because he felt one of the spotlights cast a weird shadow over the pastor's face in the chancel during worship, she would be able to say that she knew exactly what he meant, but really, the shadow was so imperceptible it didn't bother her and probably didn't bother anyone else.

Or even if Rocco, who ran the homeless shelter, asked if the announcement for more volunteers was effective, she could say yes, indeed, Pastor Bob gave it a big push.

One of her jobs was to be a gatekeeper for the boss. It always amazed her how some people cringed before authority, even authority as mild as Pastor Bob's. It was in her best interest to be on the congregation's side. "I'll do what I can," she would say to her colleagues, though the doing might be nothing more than squeezing in a pastoral meeting between a telephone appointment and a hospital visit. "He's very busy, but I'll find a time when you can talk to him," she would say reassuringly, thereby assuring everyone of her power of access.

In truth, the Reverend Robert F. Dudley Jr. was putty in the hands of anyone who asked him for a favor. He had trained himself not to say yes right away unless it was a request for money from a desperate person. Then he had a biblical basis for instant charity. When challenged, he would quote Jesus. " 'Give to him that asketh thee, and from him that would borrow of thee turn not thou away.' " Otherwise he would say "I'll have to refer that to the right committee," "I'll have to ask our business manager," or "We'll have to bring that up in a meeting." Then he'd ask Lurlene to put it on the agenda.

Because he was a persuasive, attentive, and charming man, he succeeded in getting things done without ruffling feathers. How he did it confounded Lurlene, but he managed to pull it off. Like pulling rabbits out of a hat.

In her drawer at the office, in a special file, she had collected letters of thanks that came to her from people who were grateful for her work as gatekeeper. "My ego boost file," she called it. She would turn to it whenever she needed cheering up, when she felt her work had been for naught. Would the Narcotics Anonymous group be meeting on Thursday nights in the basement if she hadn't set up the appointment for the nice young man who requested it? Would the young working mothers have their weekend play-and-share group if Lurlene hadn't urged them to talk to Pastor Bob on a Monday, when she knew he would be in a good mood from his Sunday triumph?

Sipping her coffee, she decided that she could be pleased with what she had accomplished as a secretary. She'd overreacted earlier in the week. Things were going to be fine. She wasn't going to be fired. It was all in her mind.

Glancing at her watch, she put a finishing flourish on the Sunday crossword puzzle. As always she did it in ink, an achievement she downplayed. Some people could spell, some could add large sums in their head, some could do crossword puzzles. It was nothing to be overly proud of.

On this clear winter's day she chose to walk to church. She locked the front door, leaving her son asleep inside, and took up a brisk pace. One dog walker and two joggers passed her. Otherwise she was the only one on the sidewalk. As she approached First Church, she began to notice the cars parked along the wide streets, which were shaded by California oaks and palms. The vehicles never ceased to amaze her. Black shiny sedans, flashy sportscars, gold station wagons. Most cost more than her husband had paid for her house. Out of a minivan worth a fortune stepped a family of five: mom, dad, a son, two daughters. The boy wore a white long-sleeved shirt and a tie. The girls were in party dresses and grabbed their father's hand as they crossed the street.

"Good morning, Lurlene," the father said.

"Morning," echoed the wife.

Lurlene recognized the woman as a Sunday school teacher. She'd been in the office the other day picking up permission slips and insurance waivers for a field trip. Even churches have to worry about liability suits.

"Beautiful day," the husband commented.

"The mountains look like you could touch them," the wife added.

"They sure do," Lurlene said, smiling her brittle smile.

There were some poorer people who attended First Church. Lurlene had reviewed enough church camp scholarship applications, and she'd heard enough hard-knock stories to know their needs. But on a Sunday morning as the cars pulled into the wide parking lot and stacked up one behind the other along the tree-shaded curbs, everyone looked rich.

These were the people who gave thousands of dollars to the church. A realist, Lurlene knew how expensive it was to keep up the place. Bricks and mortar were always threatening to crumble. Heating, lighting, and air conditioning didn't come free. Because First Church hadn't built a new sanctuary, a large portion of their funds could be set aside for outreach. People gave to the health clinic in a Hispanic neighborhood, the halfway house for recently released criminals, the soup kitchen, and the homeless shelter.

Hoping to buy their way into heaven, Lurlene thought. Weren't the big donors looking for divine approval? It was an idea as old as the magnificent cathedrals of medieval times. If an election could be bought through political donations, why couldn't the good Lord be swayed?

The electric chimes in the bell tower played a few phrases of "How Great Thou Art." George controlled them from his organ console. The date palms next to the bell tower shivered in sympathy. Lurlene looked up. Bats made their homes in the dead branches. They flew out at night alarming more than a few June brides at sundown. No bats this morning.

"Good morning, Lurlene."

"Nice to see you this morning, Lurlene."

The line outside the west entrance was slowly making its way into the church. It was a good crowd today. She sized them up like a Broadway producer checking out an opening night audience. Most of them would be seated in the sanctuary. Those behind would be too late. Not to worry. Lurlene could sit in the sound booth in the back if she had to, a glassed-in cage that once had been reserved for crying babies and their mothers. Now fussy infants could go into Fellowship Hall, where a closed-circuit TV broadcasted the service. Some worshipers preferred the TV broadcast to the real thing. "People who don't like to get dressed up," an usher had explained, "feel more comfortable in the Hall."

Stepping out of the bright February light, Lurlene ducked into the vestibule with its mosaic-patterned floor. An usher wearing a white carnation in his lapel shook a stack of programs in his hand, fanning them against his other hand. Standing in a corner under the balcony, he beckoned Lurlene with a curling finger. "I've got an empty seat in the front row on the right in the balcony," he whispered. "We always save one in case someone important comes at the last moment."

Who was he expecting? The president?

"Thanks, Hubert," Lurlene said, never missing a name. "I'd appreciate that." She preferred to sit with the congregation, and the balcony would be perfect for studying everyone gathered today. She thought that maybe the writer of the prayer letter—the one she had so boldly answered—would be in church this morning.

No amount of carpeting could mask the creaking sound of the stairs as she mounted them. The organ was playing a fluty tune in the prelude. When she looked down on the congregation, Lurlene envied their faith, their families, their wealth. She didn't condescend to them or feel superior to them, but what they did Sunday after Sunday was a mystery to her. The heart of religion said nothing to her. The Crucifixion narrative was a good drama, the Resurrection something out of science fiction. Even the story of Jesus' birth—one that attracted the most churchgoers with its promise of angels, shepherds, and worshiping wise men—gave her nothing more than the sentimental twinge she felt during a heart-tugging TV commercial. She had heard the Bible stories countless times, mostly through Pastor Bob's sermons, and they had no more effect on her than the Paul Bunyan legends.

Taking a front-row seat, Lurlene felt for a moment like someone who had been given the red-carpet treatment for the State of the Union Address. She was not beyond enjoying the perks of her longtime position.

George played a few notes of the trumpet stop on the organ, and the congregation rose en masse, hymnals in hand, for the singing of the processional. There had been a movement by some parishioners to install video screens up in the front and post the words of hymns so their voices would go up and out instead of down into the pages as they praised God. But certain traditionalists objected to the intrusive big screen up front. Lurlene was relieved. When she went into a church, she wanted it to look like a church: pews, hymnals, robes on the preachers, stained-glass windows, and candles.

The procession snaked its way down the center aisle, veering left and right as the choir stared at their hymnals. There were white curly heads, well-coifed heads, bald heads, and heads teaming with blond hair that hung down the backs of women singers. George, who also directed the choir, had done a good job with his talent. No wobbly voices stuck out. No screeching soprano or rumbling bass ever succeeded in cutting through a near-perfect harmony for a moment of stardom. This group sounded as one.

There was also a youth choir made up of fifth through eighth graders. More girls than boys, of course. Sweet-looking children. Until his voice had changed, Jonathan sang in the choir. He even did a solo one Christmas, his bright soprano voice ringing out through the sanctuary. Lurlene had been so proud of him. Nervous but proud. Perhaps she had failed in her attempts to make him well-rounded. So he hadn't been a sports star. At least singing was one thing he had done well.

The first part of the service moved briskly through the pastoral prayer, the choir anthem, Bible readings from the associate minister, and the announcements—including one for the shelter. Another prayer followed, leading up to the sermon. When Pastor Bob stood in the pulpit and clicked on the lectern light, the congregation leaned forward in their seats. Many took out note pads or pens to write down pertinent thoughts in their programs. Because Lurlene was sitting to the side in the balcony, she could check out faces and profiles.

A flurry of laughter rose from the listeners like birds thrushed from a field. First a few chuckles here and there, then honest-to-goodness laughter careened up to the redwood beams. Bob made a few self-deprecating remarks and told a real joke. She would skip it when she typed up the text on Monday, transcribing the tape. The jokes were never funny in print. But at the right moment, in the context of the service, they worked. And Pastor Bob was showman enough to ad-lib them.

Lurlene's eyes scanned the rows of rapt listeners. What brought them here week after week? It startled her how the same themes were repeated again and again. Forgiveness, love, patience, prayerfulness, acceptance. Bob had once told her that all preachers have only one sermon. Love seemed to be basic to the faith—a given, as far as she could tell. How forgetful people were that they needed to hear the same message week after week! Comforting perhaps, but was it really necessary? Lurlene was a quick study—a crossword-puzzle-in-ink person. If she heard something once and it agreed with her, she would remember it.

There were no hats in the congregation. Ladies used to wear gloves and hats to church when she was a girl. She and her mother went for a time to a big city church, a pale neo-Classic one with Doric columns. She could remember running up a long flight of low stairs in her Mary Jane shoes, her gloved hand on the rail. There was a sweetness to the stories the Sunday school teachers had told. But then there were the disappointments she'd faced in her life. What could sweet stories say to them?

There. That looked like her. The young woman she would match up with her son. Lurlene knew she was making a wild guess, but the woman's appearance went with the picture Lurlene had in her imagination. She wore a nice silk dress, on the conservative side, her brunette hair was pulled back, she appeared pert, perky, what men would call a looker. Unthreatening. Lurlene watched the young woman take notes on the sermon. Not on her program, but in a little spiral-bound notebook. She was organized. She had come prepared to the service.

Why would someone so pretty need any help finding a mate? Why would she ask others to pray for her? That part confounded Lurlene. Of course that's what people did at First Church, but it seemed such a violation of privacy. Lurlene could never imagine sharing a secret with total strangers. Revealing her longings in an open letter? Never.

She listened to the sermon. "God knows what's in your heart, but God also wants to hear you say it. Ask and it shall be given. Speak up. Make your needs known to Him. Be bold, and mighty forces will come to your aid." Hearing the words, she found her fingers unconsciously typing them as they would on Monday morning. "Be specific when you pray," Pastor Bob said. "Make it very clear what you want. In this way you will become a co-laborer with God. The two of you working together to fulfill His kingdom here on earth."

The young woman yawned, one hand over her mouth, then smiled and kept writing. If this was the girl, she would be perfect for Jonathan. All that a young man could wish. Pretty, alert, smart. It would have to work.

"This morning before I close," Pastor Bob was saying, "I'd like for us to take a moment of silence to speak to the Lord and reveal to Him our desires. If you wish, you may speak your petitions aloud, praises as well as intercessions. Or you may prefer to be silent. God knows your deepest thoughts better than you know them yourself. . . ."

The difficulty would be, Lurlene thought, to get the two of them together without anyone else at the church finding out.

"God wants to help you more than you'll ever know," were Pastor Bob's final words.

CHAPTER 8

"SHELLY, IT'S ME, Janice."

"Why are you calling me at work?" Shelly lowered her voice.

"I wanted to ask you something."

"Did I forget to take out the trash?"

"No."

"Did someone break into the apartment?"

"No. It's nothing about home. Don't worry."

"But your voice. You sound like something's wrong. Is it your work? A bad assignment? A story not coming together?"

"I've got to make that call," Janice said. "I'm dreading it."

"Since when have you been timid about interviewing people? I thought you'd gotten over that."

"My prayer letter."

"What's that?"

"You know, the one I wrote for the story I'm doing."

"Ah . . ." Shelly said. She was at her desk at the bank, poring over a dozen prospectuses from companies in the petroleum business. For this she had majored in French literature at college. How did *The Red and the Black* or *Madame Bovary* connect with the millions of barrels of oil pumped from beneath desert sands or North Sea oceans? They used to say in college that if you could concentrate on one field and master it, you could use those same skills to master anything else. Some justification for a liberal arts education. When she had trained to become an analyst, Shelly wished she'd taken a few more economics courses.

"I was thinking about what you said. I'm having some second thoughts. I'm worried that I might be wandering into a gray zone for a journalist," Janice said. "I don't want to get myself into trouble."

"Were you honest about yourself in the letter?"

Janice hesitated, then answered, "A part of me was."

"What part?"

"The part of me that reads Georgette Heyer whenever I feel crummy."

Shelly stopped scrolling the document on her computer. "Now you're telling the truth."

"Wouldn't you like a sensitive guy about six foot two with a good sense of humor, a nice singing voice, and willing to travel?"

"So you really meant all that stuff?"

"At first I was just putting it down as it came to me. You do that when you write sometimes. Stream of consciousness. Whatever you come up with you put down. But when I think about it, maybe it was true."

Janice was calling from the office of her newspaper. In the background Shelly could hear a colleague ask if she wanted any coffee or café latte. The one time Shelly had visited Janice at work, she was disappointed that the newsroom didn't have teletypes and green-shaded journalists pounding out stories for deadlines. The tapping of computer keys was a mere clicking, like fingernails drumming on Formica.

"I told you you were in the market for a guy," Shelly observed. And this after Janice had sworn off all men for months. "It was only a matter of time."

"Give me a break."

"You're the one who wrote about the six-foot-two paragon."

Janice hesitated. "Maybe it was just an abstract idea."

"Sounds like you were very specific."

"I didn't want to be vague. Letters without any specifics to them are dull."

"And you can't write a prayer request that isn't just a generic request for help? You have to doctor it up with your romantic imagination?"

"I'm just wondering if I should leave this part of the story alone. I'm wondering if it would be better for me not to respond to the letter I received. I don't have to write about it in the article."

Shelly's boss was passing by the cubicle. No matter how tolerant and supportive the woman was, Shelly didn't want to appear to be a slacker. Whenever the woman appeared, Shelly always hoped she gave the impression of being hard at work. How many times in a day or a week did she see Shelly? If Shelly was always gabbing on the phone, what would the cumulative impression be?

"What do you mean?"

"That it's not necessary—what I wrote and asked for."

"You said the prayer request was honest. Follow up on that."

"As a journalist?"

"As a person."

"Okay." Janice sighed.

"Do it."

"Thanks. I'll think about it." Janice hung up.

Janice wished that she had an office with a door that could be closed, so she could make the call where no one could overhear. Of course she'd had to make other personal calls from her desk. Anyone could hear her saying all sorts of things as they passed by, but after blushing a few times, she learned that people tried not to eavesdrop. Once she had caught a nearby colleague getting up from a desk and making a trip to the water cooler just to give Janice some privacy.

She practiced lowering her voice. "Hello. I'm calling about a note I received from you." Who would she be speaking to? How would she address the person? She looked again at the letter. Whoever it was didn't expect her to call. She was supposed to write, but she didn't have time for that. If any of this would be helpful to her story, she needed to find out now. Personally, she was interested in the church's response. And she was interested professionally. Which was more important?

She glanced at the file on her desk that contained all her contacts for the story on prayer. She looked for the number of the pastor's secretary. That would be the place to start. Not a general switchboard number but a direct call to someone in the thick of things. She would use her own name and identify herself as a reporter.

No, that would never work. She would hate to be recognized as the reporter from the *Herald News*. She would lose all dignity. She wanted to appear as a young professional woman responding to an offer for help.

"Hello," Janice spoke to herself again. This time she made the voice a little higher. Lighter, breathier. Not a dingbat but someone a little ethereal. Smart but otherworldly. She'd used a voice like this for a play she'd done in college. An ex-hippie with transcendental notions, dangling earrings, and a batik-print skirt, saying "Wow" a lot. Her friends said she was very funny. If she were an ounce less practical, she might even have tried the theater. But with her college loans to repay and the impatience she felt with theater types, she was glad that she had found a job on the newspaper.

"First Church," said the woman who answered the phone. It sounded like the pastor's secretary. Janice remembered the name from the week before. Lurlene. Of the old devoted-to-the-boss school no doubt. Would Lurlene recognize Janice's voice? Maybe not if she made it more languid and less forceful than the reporter doing a story.

"Pastor Bob's office. May I help you?" Lurlene sounded attentive, efficient.

"Yes." Janice jumped right in, keeping her voice high and ethereal. "I'm calling about a prayer request I wrote. I received a letter back. It was a form letter from Pastor Bob, and someone else wrote me a note."

"Oh."

"I was supposed to respond in care of Rev. Dudley's office, but I don't really have time to write a letter." Janice's story was due tomorrow for the Wednesday Lifestyles section. "That's why I called."

"Yes?" Now the voice was a little less businesslike. More earnest, sincere.

"The letter I got back had some practical advice in it."

"Prayer *is* practical," Lurlene said, trilling like a soprano soloist. "We consider all prayer practical at First Church."

"Well, this letter offered some direct assistance."

"You mean financial? We have soup kitchens and food pantries and support groups. You can make an appointment for counseling if you wish."

"It wasn't like that. In the note someone wrote that you might introduce me to the perfect mate. I mean, that was my prayer request, to find a husband or at least a boyfriend."

The silence on the other end of the phone lasted so long that Janice wondered if she had been put on hold. Then she heard breathing.

Lurlene finally answered in a lowered tone, just the way Janice had lowered hers so that no one would hear this private telephone conversation. "You mean Prince Charming?"

"Yes." Janice laughed. It was so absurd. "Yes, Prince Charming, if he exists."

"I'm sorry. I haven't been very sensitive to you. It's terrible to have to talk about this private matter on the phone. And I have to admit this is highly irregular. I don't want you to think that First Church has started a dating service or something like that. We don't do that. I mean, not normally. We have a singles group that you might want to join. Lots of women and men meet their future spouses at that group, although that's not what it's set up for, of course. It's for fellowship."

Lurlene was talking very fast, the words rolling off her tongue, tripping not trilling. Used to interviewing subjects on all sorts of sensitive topics, Janice thought she sounded nervous. Out of her normal scope of affairs.

"I'm not really interested in joining a group," Janice said.

"I know what you mean. I was never one for groups when I was your age either. I don't think people are at their best when they're in groups. I didn't really have that in mind when I wrote you that note."

"You wrote the note?"

"Not the form letter from Pastor Bob."

"No. The note of advice. The practical suggestion."

"Yes. It just came to me when I read your letter. I don't usually do that when I respond to letters. It tends to be business as usual, but your request hit me. It was so frank. You sounded like such a nice woman, and the description was so apt. The minute I read it, I thought, 'I know someone who fits the bill exactly.' "

"Are you one of the . . . uh . . . prayer warriors?" Janice was in her newspaper reporter mode. Checking a story out. One that she just happened to play a major part in, but she was trying to overlook that for the moment. "Are you one of the women who volunteers in the room upstairs?"

"No, not at all. I don't want to give you the wrong idea. They're lovely ladies. A few men join them too. They're very serious about what they do. They work very hard at it. You can find some of them praying here almost every morning. I like them. I'm just not part of them."

"Who are you?" Janice knew who she was, but she wanted Lurlene to identify herself. For the record.

"I just work here. I'm Pastor Bob's secretary."

"I assumed that, but I wondered how it works. Do you also volunteer to pray?"

"No, not regularly."

"But you prayed for my letter?"

"I'm not part of the group that prays regularly. I see that answers get sent to everyone who writes. All the requests are prayed for, then the letters are sorted to make sure the writers get a proper response."

"Did you also pray for me?"

There was a slight hesitation. "Yes, I did."

Now it was Janice's turn to be surprised. She was touched. Of course in the past when she had heard people say "I'll pray for you" or "I'm keeping you in my prayers," she tended to think of such phrases as clichéd promises like "I'll give you a call sometime" or "Let's get together for lunch." She remembered when her mother had a bout with cancer and people called or wrote notes, the religious among them promised prayer. *That's all very nice*, Janice had thought then, *but a casserole or a ride to her chemotherapy appointments would be more useful*. It had almost seemed as though the phrase "I'll pray for you" was a way for people to get off the hook. Here, with Pastor Bob's secretary, she had the opposite impression. The woman seemed to be right on the hook.

"That was very nice of you," Janice said.

"That's what we do here. We're a praying church."

"I'm impressed."

"Pastor Bob is very serious about it."

"Evidently."

"So is everyone else."

"I see."

"Now that we've prayed for you, would you like to meet the man I had in mind?"

Janice swallowed hard. Did she want to meet him or not? Was she ready to face the consequence of her request? She hedged for a minute. Did she really want to meet the man of her dreams? Or was she doing this to get a good story? "I guess so. . . ."

"It's embarrassing for you?"

"It is."

"It's embarrassing for me too." They both laughed.

"Is it?"

"I won't tell him beforehand what this is about."

"I think you should."

"Then I will."

Of course, that was it. She had a story to write, a deadline to meet. If she was going to find out anything useful for her piece, she should meet him soon. And she had to sound very aggressive. "How about tonight?"

Another hesitation. "I might be able to convince him. What did you have in mind? The two of you meeting for dessert?"

"Sure."

"About nine o'clock?"

"That would be cool."

"Where?"

Janice thought for a moment. Someplace big, someplace fairly hip. Not too intimate. She didn't want him to get the wrong idea. "Do you know where Rene's is?"

"Yes."

"We can meet there."

"His name is Jonathan. He's six foot two with dark hair. He's got a good sense of humor, and he's very sensitive."

Lurlene laughed. So did Janice—at the description that was

coming right back at her like a boomerang.

"My name is Janice."

"If there's any problem, can I call you back?"

"No. That wouldn't work." She didn't want this woman calling the newspaper. "Just leave me a message at Rene's."

"Will do," Lurlene said.

CHAPTER 9

LURLENE BROKE OUT in a cold sweat when she got off the phone. It could have all worked out so badly. She was horrified at what could have gone wrong. What if she hadn't answered the phone? What if the call had bounced to the switchboard and then back to the business office and another assistant? What if it had landed upstairs with one of the prayer warriors who would have had no idea what to do and would have suspected Lurlene immediately? "What might have been." These weren't just sad words. They were frightening.

She'd never done anything this unprofessional in her entire life. She couldn't remember ever having been caught so unprepared and then having to admit what she had done. That was the right thing, of course, to say that she had indeed written the note. And yes, she would like to introduce the woman to a perfectly delightful young man who would probably be delighted to meet her. Lurlene imagined the two of them talking at Rene's, a steak and fish place with bright-colored Haitian art on the walls. The food came in little dishes and the clientele could linger over it for hours, trying this or that and ordering a bit more of whatever they liked. She'd gone there for another secretary's birthday.

If only Lurlene could go along to introduce her son to this young woman. She would give the maître d' a twenty-dollar bill, the check would be covered, and they'd leave after hours of fascinating conversation, unaware of how fast the time had passed.

Then the next day Jonathan would come down to breakfast. "Did you have a good time?" she would ask her laconic son, and he would respond, "Wonderful!" She'd fry him some eggs and heat up bacon in the microwave, the smoky flavor wafting through the kitchen as he told her all the things he and Janice had talked about.

She thought again about what she had done. She had lied. She had told the woman a bold-faced lie. "Did you pray for me?" the woman had asked. "Yes, I did," Lurlene had said. Yet she had done no such thing. Her response represented just the sort of shallow faith she abhorred. All those parishioners passing through her office, making promises to pray for each other when she could never believe they spent a second—let alone half a minute—on their knees supplicating the good Lord on anyone else's behalf. It appalled her to think that to protect her story and keep the young woman interested she had lied. Faith made people do that. The sentimental wishing for goodness and peace turned folk into feel-good junkies. Liars.

I would pray for you, she thought, *if I prayed. But I don't pray, and I don't see what good praying can do. To my mind you're deluding yourself. It's a placebo. All those scientific tests seem to show that.*

She'd read about a test in a hospital where a skeptical doctor had two groups of patients, one that was prayed for and one that was not. Amazingly enough, the group that was prayed for experienced fewer complications from their operations, had a quicker recovery rate, and were less likely to have relapses. Unconvinced, Lurlene saw grave error in the survey. True praying people would never participate. They would see the fault in a test where they were asked *not* to pray for needy people. It was ungenerous, exclusive, prejudicial. Nothing remotely Christian about it.

But what a hypocrite she was! How could she have lost such a hold on her senses? For twenty-two years she had maintained her dignity at First Church by refraining from being caught up in the empty promises of the place. Not that such promises ever came from Pastor Bob. There was something authentic about his faith, however mysterious it was to Lurlene. But she had seen hypocrisy in the assistant ministers who came and went, trying to match Pastor Bob's enthusiasm and coming up flat with false zeal or pretentious psychobabble. They stayed for a few years, leading retreats, teaching classes, counseling, and then off they went to places where they could pastor churches of their own.

Some of the assistants she had liked—the earnest young men with beards and sandals who wanted to change the world. They led the youth on mission retreats to Mexico and building projects in the inner city. But most of *them* left the ministry altogether, exchanging their motorcycles, leather jackets, and clerical collars for three-piece suits and better paying jobs.

Did any of them have a hint of what Pastor Bob's sincerity and convictions cost him? Had they ever glimpsed his inner struggles? Lurlene could feel her boss's anxiety, sense it week after week as he gave of himself to his congregation and brought them to a personal understanding of the Scriptures. If he succeeded, it was because he himself had been led to new spiritual truths. Lurlene had noticed that during those weeks when he had thought himself hopelessly inadequate for the task, he preached the most powerful sermons.

No, she did not feel like a hypocrite in her relationship with Pastor Bob. She served him well, but she had always stayed aloof of the words she typed up for the prayer-room ladies. The notes were harmless, perhaps, sincere, well-meaning, but they had no more depth than a children's wading pool.

Had she really said "Prayer *is* practical"? Had she started to spout off the lines that she had typed and downloaded and put into letter after letter? She was no better than the women who thanked her time and again for the tireless work she did at First Church. "I'm paid for it," she always wanted to say. "It's my job." Of course it was nice when they asked about her son and exclaimed over the photos of his latest projects. It's just that she couldn't believe they went upstairs and prayed, really prayed, for complete strangers.

Maybe I should be fired, she thought. *I have been here too long. After being a mouthpiece for all the things I mail and print and type, I'm starting to say stuff like that on my own accord. I have lost my integrity. My convictions have been cast aside.*

For a long time she sat at her desk, her head in her hands, looking as if she were praying. She didn't notice the click of the clock on her desk or the blip of the screensaver as it changed from a brilliantly colored fall scene to one of snow-covered Sierras. She didn't hear the beep of her watch saying that it was eleven o'clock, nor did she hear the door opening from Pastor Bob's office or see the large man standing there.

"Mrs. Scott," he said in a soft voice. "Mrs. Scott, are you all right?"

Startled, she looked up. "Yes. Yes, I'm fine, Pastor Bob. I was feeling a little dizzy."

"Do you need new glasses?"

"I suppose I should have my eyes checked." She slipped a finger into her auburn hair and massaged her temple as though she had a migraine.

"You can take the afternoon off."

"No," she said forcefully.

"As I've told you before, a vacation might be in order."

"Not just yet . . . I have so much to do."

"That's a good time for a vacation. I've done some of my best work after a vacation. I always come back reinvigorated."

"No, thank you."

"What I wanted to tell you," he went on, "what I came here to say was that I'll need your help Saturday after next. We'll be having a small conference at the church—a group of other ministers will be here to discuss leadership. It will be very informal. I'd like you to take notes in the afternoon. Is that okay?"

She flipped the pages of the desk calendar. "Yes. I'm free. I'd be glad to come in." Even as she grabbed a pencil to write the information down, she thought how typical it was of him to say she needed a vacation and then to ask her for help on her day off. "What time?"

"After lunch. Around two o'clock."

"I'll put it down."

"Thanks, Lurlene. I knew I could count on you."

Always dependable Lurlene. "How late will it go?"

"Into early evening. We'll break for dinner. It'd be nice if you could stay for that too. To help things go smoothly. You won't have to plan the meal. Just talk to some of the out-of-town guests."

"A Saturday . . . I'm surprised you won't be planning your sermon."

"It's the exception that makes the rule. I don't want to be a Pharisee. Occasionally I break my doing-nothing-on-Saturday rule so that I won't get too stuck in a rut."

Even despite herself, Lurlene said, "I'm flattered to be in on the occasion." She liked being helpful, and she liked Pastor Bob.

"Thanks again." He winked at her and then returned to his office.

When Lurlene got home that evening, she found Jonathan hard at work in his basement studio, the smell of glue and paint rising from the room that had once housed a washer and dryer. His radio was tuned to a classical station, and in between dabs of paint, he wielded the brush like a baton and conducted a few measures of Mahler in the air. Clutching the rail at the top of the steps, Lurlene felt for a moment that she'd walked into a private moment. It was as though he were a teenager and she had entered his bedroom with a folded stack of laundry to find him performing air guitar in front of his mirror. Elvis. She wiped her feet on the step to make a little noise.

"Come on in, Mom," he said, not looking up. "I want to

put on one coat of paint before dinner."

"Who is it?" Lurlene asked, studying the tall, lanky marionette.

"I don't know. I'm still trying to figure that out."

"He looks like a young man from a hundred years ago."

"Maybe he is. That's why I've dressed him like a dandy."

"I'd say 1900. Did you take him from a story?"

"I think so. From a picture I saw in a book."

"Which one?"

"*Seventeen.*"

"Booth Tarkington."

"Yes."

"Where on earth did you find that?"

"It was on our bookshelves."

And then neither of them said anything, for she suddenly remembered that it had been part of her ex-husband's collection, one of the few things that remained of his that had been absorbed into the house. A frontispiece from his boyhood or maybe his father's boyhood was still on it—a silhouette of Peter Pan and *ex libris* with the name not filled in. The two of them shared this information, mother and son, as they shared much of the knowledge of Jonathan Sr.: silently, unacknowledged, too weighty to banter about. The bond of an unuttered secret. When he was younger, Jonathan had asked many questions about his absent father, but he rarely spoke of him now. Neither of them did. For Lurlene it was too painful to bring up, and when Jonathan realized that, he left the subject alone. But she wondered if he didn't brood about it on his own.

"I don't think I've ever read the book," she said, "but it enjoyed great popularity in its day. There was an ancient librarian who tried to foist it on me, along with *The Winning of Barbara Worth*. She probably thought those books safer than Ian Fleming.'' Lurlene settled herself on a stool next to her son's workbench.

''With some luck I'll win a grant from somebody for rescuing forgotten tomes of American literature.''

''Booth Tarkington, I'm afraid, is not on anyone's list.'' Where did he get this habit of going against the grain? It would be one thing to rescue some forgotten minor poet who had mastered a Georgia island dialect, but to bring into the limelight someone who had more than his share of popularity in his day—he would score no points with that. If he was going to look for the neglected, why couldn't he go for something trendy? Was he never going to move out of his childhood home?

''That's half the fun,'' Jonathan said. Squinting his eyes, he brushed a thin stripe along the crease of the puppet's pant leg. ''To keep people guessing.''

''I really wanted to talk to you about something,'' Lurlene said. ''I have a favor to ask of you.''

''Go ahead. Shoot.''

''I'd like you to meet someone.''

''A prospective patron of the arts? Or someone who will give me a job in something practical like advertising or marketing?''

In her defense, she never did that. In fact, she was proud of his career and the independence with which he pursued it. She had realized it took more guts and imagination for him to make his way as an artist or craftsman in this world than working at a corporation with a regular salary.

''No,'' she said, steeling herself for his reaction. She was meddling, no doubt about it. Not at all fair. "A young woman. Someone who would enjoy a young man like you."

"Mom!" he said. "I can't believe you've turned into a matchmaker. You and the rest of the world."

"Others are doing it?"

"All the time. Especially the parents of my students. They always know some girl who would be just perfect for me. When I arrive at their homes for dinner expecting to entertain their kids, I find a woman, as embarrassed as I am, sitting on their sofa. Once our hosts are out of the room she tells me she has a rock-and-roll singer boyfriend in Pismo Beach. We end up going through the whole charade of exchanging phone numbers even though we know we'll never call each other."

"This is different. This woman *wants* to meet a young man."

"How do you know?"

Lurlene considered evading the question altogether. Then she changed her mind. She'd had too much lying for one day already. Wincing slightly, she dove in. "She prayed for it."

"She prayed for a boyfriend?"

Lurlene nodded.

"What is she? A Sunday school teacher? A holier-than-thou type? Is that what you've got planned for me? Someone from First Church?"

"She doesn't teach Sunday school, and I don't think she usually goes to First Church. She didn't seem that familiar with the place."

"How do you know her?"

"She wrote to the church. She wrote to Pastor Bob and the prayer ladies."

"What did she say?"

"She said she wanted to meet a man. She was very specific. She wants a man who is six foot two, has dark hair, great sensitivity, and loves to laugh. He should have a nice singing voice, be stable in his career, and willing to travel."

"I'm six foot one and a half."

"Close enough."

"And I'm not stable in my career."

"You have a nice laugh."

Demonstrating it, he asked, "What are you running at church? A dating service?"

"No, Jonathan. It was a prayer request."

"A prayer request? She prayed for these things?" He sighed.

"She wanted the church to pray for all these things. She asked them to pray."

Jonathan put down his paintbrush and looked at his mom. "This doesn't sound like you, Mom. You've never really gone in for that prayer stuff."

"That's why I suggested she meet you. I wanted to do something practical." Even as she said it, she could hear herself say *"Prayer* is *practical."* She cringed at the words. What on earth had gotten into her?

"What made you want to help her?" Jonathan asked.

"I wanted to help you."

"I've got plenty of friends."

"I know, I know. But this is different."

"How so?"

"It would be good to meet a different girl. Somebody who's serious about meeting you."

"Can't you get in trouble for this? Those letters are confidential, aren't they?"

"Yes," she said, massaging her temple.

"How did you even manage to read her letter?"

"I see all the prayer requests. I have to send out the responses, the ones that relate to their problems."

"I remember you telling me you did that."

"We have sixty-two topics with a different response for each. The letters suggest Bible readings and advice, plus a personalized message from Pastor Bob. The prayer ladies select what response they think is appropriate, and I supply the letter."

For a moment the look of concern left Lurlene's face. She was in her element when it came to organization. She'd always been a whiz at it. When Jonathan was a boy she planned birthday parties for him that were masterpieces of organization: games, prizes, puzzles, food, favors. She would have the whole afternoon mapped out, from treasure hunts to mazes, from pizza to cake, with a few extra activities up her sleeve in case any parents were late picking up their kids. One year each kid's paper plate was personalized, another year it was the party bags. The expenses weren't great, but no effort was spared.

"Over the years I've organized an elaborate database," she continued, "so that I know if a person has already received one of the form letters. Then I send a second or third on the same topic. We have Financial Needs A, B, C, D, and E. Jobs goes up to G."

"A lot of people looking for work?"

"Lots of people writing us about it. It's a high stress

moment. Like moving. We have three or four form letters relating to selling a house."

"I guess that's a time when people want prayer."

"They sure do. They'll write us several times until things are okay."

"Any one-letter categories?"

"Forgiveness. Not many people request help for it."

"Forgiveness is never popular."

"And the death of a pet. It doesn't happen very often."

"What did the boyfriend request get?"

"A letter about Relationships and Love Life. We get lots of that sort of thing."

"Have you ever suggested a match in the past?"

"No."

"What came over you this time?" He took out a rag to wipe off his fingers.

Lurlene knitted her brow and looked across the basement room to the spot where the washer and dryer had been, their shadows still imprinted in the linoleum. How could she make him understand? Would he be able to see it her way?

This was the life she had known for twenty-two years. The two of them against the world. The two of them making their way bravely against larger forces. This house was their retreat, their sanctuary. She prided herself on not being overly protective. Other women in her situation might have been. She had been generous with curfews. When Jonathan was in high school plays, she let him stay up late for the cast parties. She had encouraged him to go away to college and live on campus if he wished. That he had decided against that option was not her fault. She had thought of herself as too practical to be clingy.

"I guess I want you to be happy," she finally said.

"Mom, what makes you think I'm not happy?" He put down the rag and picked a spot of black off his fingernail, then looked right at her.

"I'm sure you're happy. But I want you to have . . . everything." There was so much she couldn't say. *I want you to have a wife and kids and a nice house and a normal life shared with someone who adores you. I want you to know what it is to mean the world to another person who will support you in every endeavor.* She didn't see how she could say it without sounding judgmental or without obliterating the myth that theirs had been a fulfilled life.

"I *am* happy, Mom. I have my work. It makes me happy. I have a couple of good friends. I have my students. And there have been girlfriends in the past. Some worked out, some didn't. I'm in between girlfriends right now, okay?"

Lurlene smiled. "So wouldn't this be a good time to meet a new one?"

Jonathan looked at her closely, searching her face. He then flashed a boyish grin, the one that broke the hearts of his adolescent girl students. "Would it get you off the hook?"

"You would be helping me out a lot."

"For that reason, then, I'll do it," he said.

"I really appreciate it."

He turned back to his puppet. Lurlene paused on the stairs. "One more thing," she said.

"What's that, Mom?"

"Don't tell her I'm your mom."

"I wouldn't dream of it."

"She'll probably find out eventually, but don't start out with it."

"Sure, Mom. No problem. Guys never talk about about their moms on a first date."

"I guess not."

CHAPTER 10

NOTHING COULD HAVE PREPARED Jonathan for the beauty of this woman. He had been expecting a wholesome type like the high school girls who helped out at the church nursery. Nice, squeaky clean, but not the kind of girl a guy wanted to take out on a date. In his mind's eye he saw a round, shy blonde with a bad complexion and a slight limp. She probably wouldn't be wearing any makeup, and she would be sitting in the last booth of the restaurant, hiding behind monstrous Coke-bottle glasses, terrified of the pick-up scene the place was known for.

Walking into Rene's, Jonathan stood for a moment at the entrance waiting for his eyes to adjust to the dim light. Only once had he ever tried to meet girls here. He'd been coaxed into it by a friend. And very soon he discovered that "puppeteer living at home" was a very unappealing tag line. When he started to describe making paper-mache heads, their gazes frantically searched the room for someone else to talk to, like a stock analyst or budding banker or anyone. Once he realized he was such unpopular fodder, he would expand his description, making wildly perverse claims about the joys of stringing marionettes or sewing costumes on half-size stuffed figures. *Get me out of here,* his listeners' eyes said.

Now as he was surveying the scene, he decided that if he had claimed to be a rock-and-roll singer or attorney he would have had much better luck. According to his mother, the woman he was supposed to meet today would be seated at one of the tables in the back. He looked that way.

Small blue flames burned in colored glass lamps covered with netting. The tables were raw slabs of wood varnished in so many layers of resin that the wood grain was obliterated. Cups of peanuts sat in the center. On the walls, as his mother had reminded him, were bright Haitian scenes, palm fronds, sunsets, and small figures harvesting sugar cane in magenta fields. Most of the revelers sat in groups. Groups of guys, groups of girls, groups of guys meeting the groups of girls. It reminded Jonathan of the early stages of a high school dance with the sophomore girls standing against one wall, the sophomore guys against the other. In fact, some of the girls and guys here were probably people Jonathan knew from high school or college.

Then he saw her. She was sitting alone. Dressed in black that set off her fair skin, she was studying one of the colorful wall scenes. He couldn't fathom why a half dozen guys hadn't surrounded her, desperate to introduce themselves. She was so stunning he couldn't take his eyes off her. Every other man in the place must have had the same reaction.

Then he remembered what happened to beautiful girls. In high school and college they intimidated the jock types and the macho boys. Guys like that usually chose the tomboyish, party-hearty girls, the ones with big laughs and field hockey legs. The truly remarkable princesses were left alone for the very brave.

He was not one of the brave. He had never been a romantic risk taker. He had learned that his best card to play was friendship. Unlikely to inspire swooning awe, he could evoke interest and concern. Enough to make a start. Probably because of the easy banter he had with his mother, he was comfortable talking with most women. Curious to hear what was on their minds, he asked questions. He could make conversation. What he had not yet discovered was that he was also handsome in a way that did not coincide with his bookish self-image. Perhaps that was just as well, because there was little narcissism to his persona. When a woman looked in his eyes, she got an honest reflection of herself. He gave her back the pleasure of her company.

"You must be Janice," he said, reaching the table where she sat.

"You must be Jonathan."

"I guess I am." He blushed, imagining her thinking *"Six foot two, dark hair, sensitive, nice singing voice, loves to laugh, willing to travel."* Was she comparing the real goods with her own classified request?

She stood up. "Have a seat."

He took off his jacket and flung it over a chair. "Thanks."

"The woman at the church spoke highly of you."

That's no woman; that's my mother. He wanted to break out laughing. "She has a higher opinion of me than I deserve," he said.

"We could all use friends like that."

"She had a high opinion of you."

"I don't know what she could tell about me from the letter I wrote."

"It must have been what you said." The description of the perfect mate.

"She was confident that I would like you. How did you meet her? Have you known her for a long time?"

He squirmed inside. He was not a good liar—never had been. When he had to fib, he usually found some way to tell the truth and leave out some essential details. "Yes," he said. "I've known her for a long time."

This was terrible. Flustered by the contrast of what he expected her to look like and what she really looked like, he was thrown off balance and didn't know what to say. He dug his hand into the bowl of peanuts and put a handful into his mouth, asking between chews, "Do you want something to eat?"

"Sure," she said.

"Dessert?"

"I guess so." They both looked at the menu, then Jonathan flagged down one of the waiters who was dressed in a multicolored tropical shirt, a fellow who was no doubt working his way through college. She ordered a slice of lemon meringue pie, and he asked for apple pie a la mode.

"Anything to drink with that?" the waiter asked.

"Some herbal tea," she said.

Jonathan stared at her eyes, searching for her own reaction to him. In the dim interior her eyes were so dark it was hard to know what she was thinking.

"Herbal tea," he said to the waiter, "and a cup of coffee." Then he turned back to Janice. "What do you do?" *Never pick up a girl by asking her about her work. It's deadly.*

"I write," she said.

"A writer?" he said. "What kind of stuff do you write?" *Get her to talk about herself. Show her that you're interested in her.*

"Articles," she said evasively.

"About what?"

"All kinds of things."

"Would I have read any of them?"

"Maybe. I don't know. It depends on what you read."

This isn't working. I'm out of my league. She's wondering why she agreed to this. Say something. Anything! "What do you like to read?"

"Different things."

"Like what?"

"Novels."

That got them started. They talked about books, going from Booth Tarkington's *Seventeen* to murder mysteries. Janice was partial to psychological thrillers but had no patience for any movie versions if they showed much blood. When the drinks and pie arrived, they were comparing movies to books.

"Did you ever see the movie version of *The Age of Innocence*?" Janice asked.

"Some of the scenes looked a little fake, but it was really good."

"Not as good as the book," Janice said.

All the while Jonathan stared at those dark eyes and the charcoal eyebrows above, and he wondered why it didn't make her self-conscious to have men stare at her, as he was doing.

"I've only read two Edith Wharton novels—*The Age of Innocence* and *The House of Mirth*. And of those two I preferred *The Age of Innocence*."

"I haven't read it. Do you write fiction?" he asked.

"No, I don't."

"What about poetry? Do you write that?"

"No. That's much too hard. I need cold hard facts to put down."

"Facts scare me."

"How so?"

"I like making things up," he said.

"Like what?" she asked.

And he was off on a description of what he did, the puppetry and the off-beat scripts he wrote and of his dream to someday do a museum installation of puppet characters from works of early twentieth century American fiction, both known and unknown. He looked away as he talked and then focused his eyes right back on her, searching for signs of boredom. He saw none.

"You must read a lot," she said.

"No." He laughed. "Not really. A few paragraphs of description is enough." He sounded shallow and pretentious to himself.

"What museum will you put them in? The puppets, I mean."

"I don't know. Any place that will accept them. It's not a practical project—there's no money in it."

"Why puppets?"

"Because I like making things with my hands. I started making them when I was a kid. I've always made puppets."

"What kind?"

"I started out with hand puppets." Suddenly he found himself telling her about the puppet shows he put on when he was a boy, the grand theatrical productions with sets, scripts, programs, music, and lights. When he was ready with a performance, he would put on a sandwich board and parade around the block, announcing the show and selling rolls of tickets.

"I put them on in our living room," he said. "A big painted refrigerator box was my theater, set up near the fireplace with two rows of folding chairs I borrowed from the church. Other kids were never allowed to play in their living rooms. I was."

"Your mother was very tolerant."

"I'd say encouraging."

"Did you make any money?"

"I charged ten cents a ticket. I'd wear a top hat and collect the tickets at the front door, then rush around to the refrigerator box to put on the show while my mother helped me."

"Were you any good?"

"I don't know. I thought so. I used a cassette tape recorder for sound effects and recorded background music from records. The plots were usually taken from fairy tales so that the same puppets could be recycled—the prince and princess, the witch, the king and queen, a dwarf."

He popped a few peanuts in his mouth and looked at her just to make sure she was still listening. When he saw she was, he continued.

"I wished I had a best friend or a little brother to be my assistant but could never find anyone who liked to do it. The few neighborhood kids who volunteered usually dropped out after the second or third rehearsal. So Mom pulled the curtain and moved the backdrops. I moved all the puppets."

"Do you still perform?"

"At the schools where I teach I perform with the kids. I have to do that, or the parents won't pay. They want to see what the kids can do. They feel much better about paying me when they get their kids on video. What about you? Do you do anything besides writing?"

"I took piano lessons for years when I was a kid," Janice said. "From the time I was in first grade all the way through high school."

"Do you still play?" Jonathan asked.

"Sometimes after work. To relax. I've only just started up again." And then she told a story about her senior recital when she was in high school. How she had spent months rehearsing. Her teacher had rented a small auditorium, a program was printed, and she invited all her friends.

"I wore this great dress," she said, "and a really serious pair of high heels. I was psyched."

Jonathan could see it: a more sedate version of the performances his students put on. The teacher making announcements, the moms bringing cookies for afterwards, the dads falling asleep during the Polonaise.

"But on the last piece, a difficult Chopin ballade, I had a disaster. As I was playing, my mind flew a thousand different directions, just like it always did. I was thinking of the prom, my stockings, the weird mustard color of the curtains and how it reminded me of the counters in our kitchen at home, and then I had a memory lapse. For a split second I had no idea what was coming next in the piece. I couldn't see it. I couldn't feel it in my hands. I was petrified, but I don't think I stopped playing. I got through all right, stood up, bowed, and walked off stage. But after that my confidence was dashed. I didn't want to play again. I certainly never wanted to perform. It was too nerve-wracking."

"That's really sad."

"It was enough to scare me off the piano for a long time."

"Until recently."

"Just recently."

By now the pieces of pie had disappeared, and Janice and Jonathan had ordered second cups of tea and coffee. The pickup scene at the restaurant had quieted down. People had either found who they wanted to meet or they had given up. All that time Jonathan had been staring at the one woman he was certain was prettier than all the others put together. He berated himself for rambling on too long but was so flattered by her apparent interest in him that it had made him slightly giddy. When had he ever talked so much to a woman? Certainly never to a stranger.

They successfully managed the who-should-pay-for-dessert gambit by neatly dividing the check down the middle, although he claimed his pie was more expensive because it came with ice cream. She said her two cups of herbal tea made up for that—they didn't charge for Jonathan's second cup of coffee. He picked up his jacket and walked her outside.

A thin drizzle had started, and it made the reflection of the restaurant's lights glow on the asphalt in a blur of red, green, yellow, and glaring white, like the bright colors of a child's picture that has been covered with black crayon and then scratched out to reveal the pigments underneath. Jonathan felt all soft and blurry inside, yet at the same time his senses were pinprick sharp. He suddenly saw things he hadn't noticed before—the chirping neon chicken on a barbecue restaurant down the block, the camellias and azaleas in the parking lot divider, the pattern the parking lines made.

"This is my car," Janice said, standing outside a turquoise blue Honda.

"I love it when it rains, don't you?"

"It smells good," she said, nodding. "Like damp mulch and wet charcoal."

"There's a song about that," he said, launching into the lyrics of a song from an old musical. Smiling, he grabbed the lamppost, becoming Gene Kelly for a moment, although it wasn't a Gene Kelly song. He let himself look silly, his voice crossing half of the empty lot. Then he stopped and rolled his eyes.

"I know that one too," she said. "It's from *Guys and Dolls*."

"Name it."

"Marlon Brando sang it in the movie. . . ."

"Good."

"And Alan Alda's dad did it originally on Broadway. . . ."

"That's right."

"I know! It's the lead-in to 'I've Never Been in Love Before' by Frank Loesser."

"Perfect. I'm impressed."

"Don't be. I've got a flypaper mind." She got into the car.

"Okay, Miss Flypaper, what's your last name?"

"Ascher. And yours?"

"Scott. I'm Jonathan Scott. Can I call you again?"

"I'm in the book."

"I'll call."

The last thing she said before rolling up her window to the falling raindrops was "You've got a nice voice."

He was left humming "I've Never Been in Love Before."

CHAPTER 11

PASTOR BOB DID NOT LIKE praying on rainy mornings nearly as much as he did on temperate days when he could sit outside.

Tuesday morning it was raining. He had to eat his breakfast inside, where he couldn't squeeze his grapefruit into his mouth and let the juice drip down the sides of his mouth. Instead of staring mesmerized at the water in the swimming pool, he drank his tea studying the bulletin board his wife had put up when their children were young. Back then it had held announcements of school plays, field trips, permission slips, Little League schedules, and summer camp forms. Now it wore a collage of yellowed newspaper clippings, photos from magazines, and notices of church meetings. Finishing his grapefruit, Bob retreated to his home office. Staring out the window, he couldn't see the mountains through the gloom, but he knew they were there. He turned to the Psalms. *I will lift up mine eyes unto the hills, from whence cometh my help. My help cometh from the Lord. . . .*

The narcissism of some Christians troubled him. In the past few days he had seen several church members who had claimed to hear God's voice. He had no reason to doubt them, but he was bothered by the arrogance of their assumptions. They seemed to think that getting a certain directive from God was enough, and they didn't need to do anything further. He was tempted to tell them, "God helps those who help themselves," although it wasn't an aphorism he believed in. God helped the helpless.

But for goodness' sake, the Lord could use a little cooperation once in a while! Three women he had recently counseled expected God to do all the grunt work. One believed God wanted her to become a midwife, another a writer, and the third a television actress. From what he could tell, they each had some aptitude for their callings, but they remained stuck at the bolt-of-lightning stage. Didn't they know that following a vocation took work? Look at how life had worked out for Robert Dudley Jr. God had called him to become a minister, and he'd been working his tail off ever since.

He flipped a page in his Bible, the thin paper whispering in accord. The young woman who wanted to be a writer was diligent about writing, it seemed. She claimed to be putting hundreds of words to paper every day. But she had no notion about nor any desire to do research about where she might sell her matchless prose. It was as though God, who had given her this vocation, was also expected to do the marketing, agenting—and even make the telephone calls. If she ever sold an article, she had better give God his ten percent.

The actress had come to Southern California from Oklahoma to pursue her God-inspired career in television. So far she had only been doing part-time typing in a production office in Studio City, and it had nothing to do with stardom. She was beginning to understand that this bit of heavenly guidance could have been the perfect motivation for classes, photos, hustling, waiting, phoning. But it was as though such mundane work would have been an insult to the divine.

The would-be midwife simply sat there in his office and told him that surely God would show her where to go to fulfill her dream. Yes, but surely not from the cocktail lounge where she worked an evening shift.

God, please be with all those people who have come to me, trusting in my ability to give them guidance in their lives. Help me give them the advice they need. Help them to hear what I'm saying. Give me the patience to understand their dreams, for indeed it is true that sometimes you speak through our dreams.

Sunday after Sunday he was expected to inspire his flock with anecdotes of faith, and he was ever on the lookout for tales of modern-day saints. He had a huge file of volunteers flying Latin American children north for life-saving operations, eye doctors operating out of trailers in the rain forest, and high school kids taking puppet shows through the inner city. What he really wished for were examples of quiet good works. The businesswoman who silenced the office gossip. The remedial reading teacher who never raised her voice. The man who once explained he had never lost a friend. Bob wished he could tell stories about people like his own tireless, unperturbable secretary.

Lord, I promise to be more appreciative of the people I work with. I will thank them for what they have done with little notice, little recognition, and little praise day after day, year after year.

He loved Lurlene's no-nonsense attitude. He appreciated her realistic outlook on life. She would never go dewy-eyed and sentimental on him. She watched the women come and go from his office, their light hair piled on their heads like a nimbus, and the young bearded men with sandals who told him that God was urging them to preach. Someday he wished an accountant or a banker would drop by and say that God double-checked their budgets and balanced their books. Mrs. Scott inspected the steady stream of visitors and gave him an indulgent smile when one appeared flaky in the extreme. God bless her.

God, bless Lurlene Scott. If anyone deserves a miracle, she does. Grant her heart's greatest wish.

Lurlene found her umbrella in the back of the closet. She hadn't used it since last winter, but the rain was coming down now in such big drops that her raincoat would not suffice. It was a lovely umbrella that a member of the congregation had brought back from Venice. It had large flowers on a vine that kaleidoscoped into the center of the umbrella. Definitely more expensive than anything she'd buy for herself.

She hadn't waited up for her son. She'd given up doing that when he was a senior in high school. By then she had realized that even if she fell asleep before he came home, she always knew when he was in the house. A mother's sixth sense. When she looked back on her parenting, she decided that feigning sleep when he came home was one of the best examples of trust she could give her son.

The night before, he hadn't been home when she turned out the lights at 11:00, and when she woke up at 2:12 to go to the bathroom, she knew he was in. No need to walk down the hall and check. That gave her a large window of time to consider. Say he had come home at 11:05, a fairly perfunctory conversation would have passed between her son and Janice. Enough for both to part ways knowing they had been polite but hadn't risked any signs of extraneous encouragement. But if it was 2:10 . . . what an occasion for her to imagine a budding romance! Think of all the things they could have talked about.

Lurlene was disappointed that it wasn't a Saturday so she could cook Jonathan a big breakfast of bacon and eggs and sip coffee while he described his blind date. The date she had set up. Instead, she lingered for a few moments reading the *Herald News* at the breakfast table, hoping he'd wake up. Then at the sound of stirring in his bedroom, she grabbed her umbrella and headed out. She didn't want to seem overeager for a tidbit of gossip. She didn't want him to think she was prying. There was such a fine line between interest and prying.

As she walked in the rain, she wondered if she had overstepped her bounds—not as a secretary but as a mother. Now that the professional crisis had been solved, she was feeling guilty about dragging Jonathan into it. She had a sense that a disaster in the making had been averted. The young woman had agreed to meet her son. Lurlene was the only person she had spoken to at the church. No scandal there. No grave error. But had Lurlene done well by her son?

The rain came down in Q-tip-sized drops. The gutters were running with raging streams that raced to the storm drains. Lurlene stood back from the curb as a passing car splashed a rooster tail of spray across the cement. She crossed San Anselmo a block before her usual intersection to avoid one of the biggest storm drains.

With some qualms she thought about her attempts to push her young son into activities that he hadn't been interested in—volleyball, baseball, basketball. Every time she saw a father playing catch with his son, she felt an ache in her heart. If she had been able to throw a good overhand pitch, would Jonathan now be a businessman or a banker? It pained her to think that she might not have given him some skills—however mysterious they might be—that would serve at the negotiating table or make him a boardroom team player.

Then she felt bad that maybe she *hadn't* allowed him to pursue his natural gifts. Had spending weekday afternoons with the junior varsity basketball team deprived him of time he could have used developing scripts? Had the team spirit of Little League infringed on his imaginative individuality? Had success at volleyball robbed him of piano practicing time? And when he had said rather wistfully one day that he wished boys could take ballet, should she have marched him up the flight of stairs to the local studio above the town's Chinese restaurant and demanded that the imperious grandam take on her son?

The problem was, the only place you couldn't push your child was in relationships. She had arranged for other children to come over on Saturdays when she wasn't at work, but she couldn't make friendships happen. She could check his homework and his fingernails every night, but she couldn't check his crushes.

Of course Lurlene could remember every girlfriend Jonathan ever had, even back to the perky blonde who came to his birthday party in fifth grade and then didn't answer his letters that summer. He had searched through every stack of arriving mail for weeks. Nor would she ever forgive the lively headstrong girl who served as class secretary when they were both high school juniors. She was attractive and self-involved and always insisted that she and Jonathan were "just friends." Jonathan had asked her to a big school dance. The girl seemed to be stringing him along, never saying yes or no until she chose to accept a second, more attractive invitation. Lurlene had refrained from saying "I told you so." It took all of her resistance to stay out of that emotional quagmire. Why had she inserted herself so aggressively in this one?

Because boys need to be pushed. Because she had observed Jonathan becoming less sociable, more wrapped up in his work. Because . . . because the opportunity had presented itself.

Her shoes were getting wet. Not her best shoes, but nothing for the church rummage sale either. She stepped quickly across the flagstone patio to Pastor Bob's office. She opened the door to be greeted by the cool, musty smell of a closed-in space. There was nothing colder than California on a rainy midwinter day. This was what Liverpool in autumn was like, she imagined, or Tuscany without sunshine. Mildew creeping up the walls. She shook off her umbrella and set it over in a corner to dry. Making a pot of coffee, she flicked on her computer and transcribed the phone messages that had accumulated overnight on the pastor's voice mail. Then she sat at her desk and waited, working as she waited for the phone to ring with the one caller who could set her mind at ease.

When would her son call?

"Janice Ascher, how could you?"

"How could I what?"

"How could you agree to go out with this guy the day after you met him?"

"I'm twenty-four years old."

"That's no explanation."

"I'm interested in him."

"You've been interested in other guys."

"They never knew as much about me after the first date as this guy does."

"You never told them as much."

"They never asked."

"But you haven't even had a date with him."

"That's why we're going out tonight. To have a date."

Shelly sighed. She was in her cubicle at work, and Janice was calling from her desk at the newspaper. This was no time to have a revealing conversation, but Shelly was surprised by her roommate's throw-caution-to-the-wind attitude. Janice was the sort to pay her rent precisely on the first of the month, to balance her checkbook whenever she wrote a check. She was the only person Shelly knew who had never overdrawn her bank account. Janice promptly put her dishes in the dishwasher after every meal, emptied it first thing in the morning, and wouldn't leave the house without making her bed. She wouldn't encourage a guy unless she was really interested, and she never before had displayed this much interest after only one meeting. At the very least, it would be wise for her to play hard-to-get.

"What do you like about him?" Shelly asked.

"He's kind of goofy. He sort of stoops when he walks, hanging his head out in front of him, and you think, 'Dork City.' But when you sit with him, he looks at you with these deep, penetrating blue eyes and listens to what you say. Can

I tell you what a relief it was not to have one of those business school types giving me a recap of his resume and his ambitions in the direct mail business? Remember the marketing whiz who talked and talked and talked, and then suddenly said, 'If you have anything to say, just jump right in'? Remember him?"

"Only vaguely."

"Well, this guy isn't like that."

"If you did all the talking, how do you know anything about him?"

"He spoke too. We talked about his puppets—he makes puppets."

Shelly sighed. "Dork City is right."

"And we talked about books. He reads stuff. Knows stuff."

"Did you tell him what you do for a living?"

"Not exactly. I said that I write."

"Nothing about your career as a journalist?"

"No."

Shelly clicked her tongue. "You're digging yourself a big hole. You didn't say anything about the article that you're writing for a newspaper for publication? I can't believe it! Don't you think he deserves to know why you wrote that letter to the church, that you're not really sure you believe in prayer, but you took a gander on it for the sake of a news story?"

"I was sincere about the letter. I've decided that."

"Only after the fact. An act of desperation or self-justification."

"No. I was sincere. A big part of me was sincere."

"Like the person who prayed for you. I think you need to tell this guy—"

"His name is Jonathan."

"I think you need to tell Jonathan that you are a newspaper writer, and that you originally got interested in the church because you were writing a story on it. You'd better alert him to the fact that you are not necessarily the girl of his innocent Christian dreams."

"I think it was because of that letter that we were able to get to know each other so fast. We had some common ground. He knew what I liked. It was easier to cut to the chase. I can't remember when I've felt so comfortable so fast."

"Evidently."

"I'm serious."

"You'd better be, or you'll have one very disappointed guy on your hands."

"Trust me."

"Will you at least let me meet him?" Shelly asked.

"If you're home."

"When's he coming by?"

"Seven."

"Tonight?"

"Yes."

"I wouldn't miss it for the world."

"I've got to go now. We'll talk later. I thought of a great lead for the story about the prayer letter and the church responding by matching me up."

"You're putting yourself in there?"

"Not by name. It's too good an example to lose."

"I don't know, Janice. You seem to want it both ways. Hard-nosed journalist by day, incurable romantic by night. Better make your choice."

"A story is a story."

"This story has only just begun."

Jonathan was proud of the way he had handled the call to her. He knew he could have come up with a thousand different pretexts for calling Janice Ascher on the morning after he had first met her. He could have started out by saying, "I'm sorry to be bothering you so soon after we met, but I just happened to get this pair of great tickets for a concert this weekend. . . ." Or he could have said, "I just read about this fascinating new restaurant, and I want to check it out before the crowds get to it." But he didn't fall back on any pretexts. Boldly he had put it to Ms. Ascher straight: "I really liked meeting you last night. I know it's nervy of me to call you today, but I'd like to go out with you again. Soon. Could I take you out for dinner tonight?"

He had called her apartment first. That was the only number he could find in the phone book. The only listing for a Janice Ascher. The message on the machine sounded like her voice. *"We're not in right now, but leave a message after the beep, and we'll get back to you as soon as possible."* So he followed with, "Hi, this is Jonathan Scott calling Janice Ascher. I hope this is your line. Give me a call when you can. I enjoyed meeting you last night, and I hope we can get together sometime."

After leaving the message he went down to his basement shop to work. He was scheduled to be at an elementary school in the afternoon. Mornings he spent working on his own projects. While he mixed some paper-mache, he avoided rehearsing what he would say to Janice when he got her on the phone.

With other girls he'd practiced for hours so he'd sound casual and nonchalant. He'd wished he could be the macho, strong type, all the more irresistible for appearing reticent and gun-shy. In the past it had taken him hours to dial, carefully calculating when his call would arrive and what the woman in question would be doing. Not too soon after work because she would just be getting home from the office, changing clothes and going through the mail—not ready for hearing an attentive male caller. Not at dinnertime, which was tough to calculate and basically kept him guessing. The call couldn't be after ten-thirty if he expected the girl to be an early riser. Then the TV schedule had to be taken into account. Sometimes he studied the TV listings in the newspaper and imagined what shows the girl might be watching and if he'd possibly be interrupting anything. *"I hate to call right now because I'm sure you were watching the same movie I was watching . . . I called just in case you weren't tuned in to the hockey play-offs."* And it made him particularly jumpy to call a woman at work. Like many free-lancers, he found office schedules a complete mystery, and he could only assume he was interrupting a top-level meeting.

This one was a writer, although she didn't say exactly what for, and he hadn't asked. Maybe she hadn't left for work yet. Writers sometimes worked flexible hours. Even so, he didn't expect to hear from her until early evening.

Lifting his hands out of the paper-mache, he turned to his volume of Booth Tarkington. *Seventeen* was a ridiculous choice, with the lovesick language of a seventeen-year-old at the turn of the century and the Amos 'n' Andy dialogue of a loyal retainer. "No wonder there was a civil rights movement," he told himself. A wonder there wasn't a revolution. Some books were well deserving of their neglect.

He had picked this book up because it had belonged to his father. No surprise there. *Ivanhoe, Ben Hur, Robin Hood, Kidnapped* and *Treasure Island* were the only other books on his mother's bookshelf that bore the Peter Pan ex libris: Jonathan Walter Scott. Those were familiar. He wanted to pick something unusual. Besides that, before he read it, he had been entranced by the pen-and-ink sketches that accompanied the story. A dandified hero walking down a small-town street in the Midwest. Several turn-of-the-century men surrounding a Gibson Girl beauty making kissy faces to her lap dog. The hero escaping the clutches of his all-too-embarrassing sister. The hero's father trying on his old tuxedo and discovering it doesn't fit. Tarkington was a writer as far removed from Jonathan's own experience as he could imagine.

Jonathan had read enough psychology to know that he should be curious about his father, but he had so little information that he didn't know where to begin. He had only the vaguest recollections of the man. He'd seen pictures, of course, and had heard some of his mother's stories. "*The handsomest man I'd ever seen,*" his mother described him. Jonathan could not connect this depiction with the smiling man pictured in a plaid coat holding a baby in his arms. Friendly, with an open face, but hardly movie-star handsome.

Sometimes Jonathan felt the stirrings of sorrow at the thought of this man who had dropped out of their lives. Perhaps he could dredge up unspeakable rage. Mostly he just felt bewildered. Why had his father left them? Why had the man never come back? Jonathan gazed at the snapshots in the leather photo album, turned the pages to his third birthday, by which time his father was completely out of the picture. There the story ended. He had nothing more to go on but memories. And he had finally concluded that what he remembered about his father was an animated version of the few stills he had seen over the years. That and the few things his mother said about him.

"Your father was charming, so charming he could sell ice to the Eskimos," she had said, and he took it as a warning that he should develop more substantial character attributes, because charming people were not responsible. "He loved to tell stories–oh, how he could go on," she had said, and he thought that meant it was okay to spin out an anecdote but better not embroider it too much. "He loved you," she had told him. This he tried to accept at face value, but then what did she really think love was? That you could leave the object of your love after a few years? That love never lasted? That devotion was short-lived?

Jonathan turned to one of the illustrations in *Seventeen*. He was wondering if the courtship notions of Booth Tarkington's era were what had captivated his father or if his father had even read this book, when the phone rang. He had left the door to the basement open, and he could hear the *rrrrring* upstairs in the kitchen.

Dashing up the flight of stairs, he reached the phone on its third ring. It was she. That his wish could be fulfilled so fast was startling to him. It left him almost speechless.

"Hi, this is Janice Ascher. . . ."

"I can't believe you're calling me," he'd said.

"I can't believe I am either."

"You didn't give me your work number."

"You didn't ask."

He could hear the noise of other people in the background, so he assumed she was dialing from her office. She must have phoned home for her messages. That was a good sign. He hoped it meant she was checking because she hoped he had called. Where did she work? He had carefully avoided the mundane sizing-up questions like "Where do you work?" and "How long have you been there?" Too often they were a means of measuring salary and rank. Might as well say, "How fast have you moved up the corporate ladder?" Might as well ask to see her pay stub.

"I really liked meeting you last night," he had said. Asking for a date was the most natural thing on earth. He didn't even feel he needed to preface it with banter. "So would you like to go out?"

"That would be very nice. I'd love to."

That was that.

CHAPTER 12

LURLENE FINALLY CALLED her son before lunch. She could wait no longer. She had matched the two of them up and had set up their meeting. If it were a failure, she would have only herself to blame. A quick report—any report—would put her mind at ease.

"Hi, Mom," Jonathan said, as though he expected her call. Had he purposefully not dialed her at church just to keep her on pins and needles? Her punishment for meddling.

"How was it?"

"What?"

"Oh, come on, Jonathan. You know, the date. How'd it go?"

"It was okay."

"Okay?" She was crestfallen. *Six foot two, dark hair, a love of laughter, great sensitivity, midtwenties to early thirties, nice singing voice, stable in career, willing to travel.* After all that, just *okay?*

Jonathan laughed. "I'm teasing you, Mom. It was much better than okay. She was great, really great.

We had a great time."

"Great?" Lurlene couldn't believe it.

"That's what I said."

"She's really great?"

"Absolutely."

"What's great about her? Smart?"

"Yes. And interesting. And really beautiful."

"I didn't really know that when I suggested she go out with you." Although Lurlene wasn't surprised. She'd gained theories about people over the years in Pastor Bob's employ. You could tell a lot by a voice. Even pretty.

"She's gorgeous."

"Jonathan, I've never seen her before in my life. Honestly. I just thought the two of you might like each other. What color hair does she have?"

"Dark brown. Almost black."

"Eyes?"

"Brown, I think, with very fair skin. Beautiful coloring."

"I'm glad." Relieved, really. "She sounds very nice."

"You did right, Mom."

Lurlene felt flushed with a sense of triumph. For once disaster had not struck. Just the opposite. "Thanks."

"We had such a good time we're going out again tonight."

"Oh," Lurlene said, worried. "Don't you think it's rather soon?" Jonathan could blow it all by rushing things. He could seem too aggressive or naive. A rube without any wiles. "Slow and easy wins the race."

"Don't worry. She agreed. I left a message at her home this morning, and she called back from work. We like each other. That's all."

"Okay, dear." Suddenly Lurlene didn't want to appear as

though she was prying. It was enough for the day. "I'll see you at home." She put down the phone and felt wonderful. She wanted to get up and do a little dance. She was vindicated, victorious. She had done something completely out of the ordinary, and it had turned out absolutely fine. Maybe better than fine. Maybe fabulous.

She picked up a stack of prayer letters and glanced at them thinking, *What all these people need isn't prayer but good, practical help.* The financially desperate needed loans and advice on keeping a budget. The lonely could use good friends and visitors. The people messing up relationships required psychological counseling. And the lovelorn needed a matchmaker. Never would she impose again. Never would she intervene. Lightning could not strike twice in the same place. But this one time, for her own son, she'd done the right thing.

It was in this happy mood that she walked out of the office and to the church kitchen where there were some leftovers from the week before. She spooned out a dollop of applesauce with the cottage cheese and buttered two slices of toast. The rain was still coming down, splattering loose flower petals onto the flagstone walk, plastering them down like papermache.

Lurlene took her lunch back to her desk and ate there. Pastor Bob had a lunch date, as usual, and Lurlene enjoyed listening to the radio in the office alone. The reports of flooding in the foothills and landslides at the beaches made her feel safe and secure in her office.

In the afternoon, she had a meeting scheduled with several of the prayer ladies. They wanted to get her input on the system and how it was working. The meeting was in the upstairs room above the organ pipes, and she could hear the rain's steady patter on the roof as she walked up. New slate tiles had been put down after the last capital campaign, and with a proprietary air she observed to herself that the roof was holding well. Money well spent. Getting capital for a new building or something that would be named for a parishioner was relatively easy, Pastor Bob always said, but fundraising for a new roof was a colossal bore. Who would want a plaque titled "The Julia Shaw Memorial Roof"?

"Mrs. Scott, I might as well be a civil engineer," Pastor Bob had told her. "We pastors go to seminary because we love God and the Bible. We learn theology, Greek, church history, and Old Testament. And what do we find we need when we get the job? A knowledge of plumbing, painting, electricity, and drainage."

"Lurlene," Helen Bradford said in greeting, "I'm so glad you could make it to this meeting."

"I'll do whatever I can to help." Meetings. Churches ran by meetings. If Jesus returned to earth today he would hardly be noticed because the Christians would be too busy attending meetings. Lurlene was grateful that she wasn't a member of First Church. Her meetings were usually over by five o'clock, but the congregation couldn't escape them. Their yearning for the divine took them to meetings.

"It's good for us to check with you every so often to see if you have any suggestions for us," Doris Matthews said from her seat at one end of the table.

"I appreciate that," Lurlene said, seating herself. There were three other women there, part of the newer crop, women who'd come to First Church's prayer ministry in the last few years, revitalizing it. One of them had extensive computer experience, and she was busy updating the system and making it as efficient as possible.

"I'm a little out of my depth with computers," Doris said, looking fragile in her birdlike way.

"Me too," Helen said, strong enough to admit to weaknesses.

The two of them were classic volunteers of another era. Lurlene had once resented their ability to give their lives over to worthy causes. They had no need to work "outside the house." No demands for money.

When she was a young mother dropping Jonathan off at day care or school and scrambling through her workday to be able to pick him up, she would see Helen or Doris walking through the courtyard to the business office or sanctuary or back to their cars. She envied the flexible, unburdened shape of their days. They had nothing more important to do with their time than sit around a walnut table reading letters and meditating over them. It looked easy compared to the constant grind of single parenthood.

But by now Lurlene had come to admire their constancy. Freed from the most basic struggles for survival, she could appreciate the choices they had made to continue in their little-noticed, unrewarded volunteer positions. Their photos weren't in the paper's society pages as "prayer ladies." They couldn't be seen posing with coffee cups and planning a benefit that would bring in money for cancer or kids or the opera. Helen and Doris worked anonymously, as did all the prayer volunteers. They could have retired to Cambria Pines or Cardiff-by-the-Sea and passed their mornings polishing their crossword puzzle skills. Instead, they kept coming to First Church to pray.

"How are we doing?" Helen asked. "What were our numbers for the last few months?"

Lurlene opened a Manila folder and looked up the numbers. "I've sent one hundred fifty letters this month so far, and two hundred thirty the month before. And December, as usual, was slow with eighty-seven letters for the whole month. Many people are too busy to ask for prayer during December, although generally the subjects we get are very serious. Those who need help need it most then."

"What sort of problems did you notice?"

Lurlene gazed down through the bottom half of her glasses. "We had ten letters from people threatening suicide."

"Is there anything we do about that? Can we intervene?" asked one of the newer prayer warriors, unacquainted with policy.

"They were all referred immediately to the suicide hotline. That's our standard procedure. Whenever possible, suicide cases are contacted, especially if they can be traced," Lurlene explained.

"We've always done that," Helen said.

"What about cases of extreme loneliness?" the same novice asked. "Are they ever contacted?"

"Lurlene sends whatever helpful brochures we have," Doris said, "and a letter suggesting appropriate Bible verses."

"But there are no handwritten notes?"

Lurlene thought of her own note amended to the official response and Pastor Bob's prayer letter. She blushed at the memory and answered quickly. "No. I don't have time for that." God willing, they'd never suspect her of such outlandish behavior.

"We don't expect it of you, dear," Doris said. A generation older than Lurlene, Doris could get away with the occasional "dear" or "honey" and not sound patronizing. "You have a lot on your plate."

"This is very exciting," said the second newcomer, flush with the enthusiasm of the initiate. "What an extraordinary ministry. We must publicize it more. Get the word out. I think we could organize a very effective marketing campaign. We could double the number of prayer requests First Church gets. We could triple it!"

There was silence around the table. *And who would do all the work?* Lurlene wondered. *How many more letters am I to mail? How much more can I handle?*

"I don't like having to pray for too many people a day," Helen said in her husky contralto. "It's not stinginess. Rather, I need to feel for the people I pray for. After a dozen cases of cancer, heart troubles, and financial ruin, I sometimes find I'm depleted. I can't pray anymore."

"I see," said the newcomer.

"We take as many prayer requests as the Holy Spirit brings us," Helen added. "If the Holy Spirit felt we could handle more, we would receive more. It's as simple as that. God broadens the back that bears the burden."

"God also tempers the wind to the shorn lamb," Doris said, giving the opposing viewpoint. "Besides, I have a confession to make. I pray for others not only for what I believe it will do for them, but also for what it will do for me."

She was silent, to let her point sink in. "It's rather selfish,

I'm afraid. When I come here to the upper room, I'm weighted down with my own problems. But after I read the letters, I feel much better because I realize how much I've been blessed. As I grieve for the people who trust us to pray for them, I'm taken out of myself. I would hate to see so many people writing us that I couldn't read my stack of letters carefully. I would feel like a machine. That's not why I pray."

Ever polite, the new woman suggested, "As the number of letters increased, we could get more volunteers."

"Yes," Helen said. "You're probably right."

But Lurlene didn't think she meant it. It was her observation of church meetings that people pretended to agree more often than they really felt like it, no matter what she'd said about God broadening the burdened back.

"I don't like the idea of a marketing campaign," Doris said. "It seems vulgar."

"I don't either. The Holy Spirit keeps us busy enough," Helen said, reiterating her earlier thought.

"But if we could reach more people, think of what a difference we could make."

"A reporter is working on an article for the *Herald News*," Lurlene said. "Evidently, the woman is interested in the prayer ministry. That will bring us some publicity."

"That's right. She talked to me," Doris said.

"She talked to me too," Helen said.

Lurlene began to worry. If the reporter had talked to both of them, what had she said? How much of the prayer ministry was she investigating? Would she see anything out-of-the-ordinary in Lurlene's work? *Don't jump to conclusions*, she told herself. *No one knows anything about what you've done.*

No one except her son and his date.

"You might discuss a marketing campaign with Pastor Bob," she said. "He probably has some ideas."

"That's a good idea," Doris and Helen both said. It was left at that. Moving on to their next item on the agenda, they turned to Lurlene and asked, "What do you think about our response letters? Are there any improvements you'd like to see in them?" The neatly timed interest of the two women made Lurlene blush again. Had they found out about the note she wrote? Is that what they were thinking of? Were they trying to catch her in a trap?

"No, absolutely not," Lurlene blurted out.

"Do you think our letters are personal enough?" Helen asked. She had a touchy-feely side ever since a brief stint with group therapy, which was prompted by her daughter who had become a therapist.

"Helen, you worry about that too much," Doris said. "If we get too personal, our anonymity will be compromised. It's not as though the people who pray are a group of nuns in a cloistered monastery hundreds of miles from town. We prayer warriors are members of the church and community. So are the people we pray for. Like as not we run into them at the mall, the gas station, or across the tennis court. We might know their most intimate secrets, but we keep them—or with God's help, we forget them. That's why our correspondents often don't sign their names. We must not get too personal."

"What about people who need urgent help?" a newcomer asked. "Other than the suicidal."

"If the need is great, the letter is referred to Pastor Bob."

"Through his secretary," Lurlene said gamely. She wanted to reassert her control.

"Through his secretary," Helen reiterated.

"Through you, dear," Doris added.

Lurlene heaved a sigh of relief. She had the group's support. "Thank you," she said. She had panicked unnecessarily. Why on earth had she worried?

If Lurlene had been four stories down and on the other side of the sanctuary in the antechamber of Pastor Bob's office where she usually sat performing her secretarial duties, she would have found a whole new reason to worry. For at that moment her position was being covered by a new, young, and not entirely capable administrative assistant from the business office. Because the senior minister's office was isolated, it was necessary that a person be in the outer room for security reasons. A person who could greet any unexpected visitors.

When Lurlene was present she was ever vigilant about monitoring whoever appeared, doing everything short of passing out numbers like a vendor at an ice cream store on a hot day. She had a near photographic memory of faces and could quickly size up cranks and kooks among the vast visiting horde of parishioners. She never made a mistake.

But that afternoon Lurlene was not present when a bearded man—looking like an aged John the Baptist—walked down the flagstone path to Pastor Bob's office and entered the antechamber. Because it was raining, he was covered by a black plastic raincoat, and on his head he wore a rather fine black beaverskin hat protected in a plastic bag. He was tall, like Abraham Lincoln, and he spoke in a commanding voice.

"I'm looking for Pastor Bob." Instead of greeting the ever vigilant Lurlene, his eyes met those of a young, inexperienced secretary. She looked up from her computer, where she wasn't typing addresses or proofing a document but playing a game of solitaire. Her expression was one of guilt.

"Pastor Bob's taking a nap," she said. She had been told that Pastor Bob did not like his employees to lie for his benefit. He'd said he was taking a nap, so she repeated the information.

"I'll let myself in," the stranger said.

"Oh no. You'd better not," she said. "He won't like that."

But before she could stop him, the tall man in the black raincoat made his way into Pastor Bob's office, where he found the senior minister of First Church—the popular radio preacher—sound asleep on his ratty Naugahyde sofa. With his feet aloft and his mouth open, he lay with his hands on his chest. A book lay opened on the floor, abandoned. Never was a man more vulnerable. Never was a busy man more at rest. Giving into a late-afternoon bout of mental fatigue, he had sacked out on the couch.

Lurlene's substitute leaped up from her game and peeked in over the stranger's shoulders. "Oh no," she whispered, a hand covering her mouth. She decided that she would be better off if Pastor Bob did not spot her when he awoke, so she returned to solitaire.

"Excuse me, sir," the stranger said.

"Yes," Pastor said, rolling open a lazy eye, as though he had been faking sleep.

"I would like to see the pastor of First Church."

"You're looking at him." He made no attempt to rise.

The stranger peered at him closely. "Yes, it looks like you. It even sounds like you."

"Glad to hear it."

"I came here to talk," the stranger said. Water rolled off his raincoat and dripped on the gold shag carpet.

"I'm meditating," Pastor responded, unmoved.

"I thought you were sleeping."

"I was contemplating it."

"I'll wait for you to be finished." The stranger did not budge. He would have stood there until midnight, waiting for the pastor to rise from his Naugahyde couch. It was this look of determination that made Pastor Bob think the man might not be playing with a full deck. He looked to the senior minister like a bag person without the bags.

Well acquainted with homeless people, Bob made regular visits to the men in the church's shelter, usually to perform a short worship service. Afterward the men liked to talk about religious subjects. Many were well read in the Bible and could quote chapter and verse. But generally they fixated on one aspect of the Gospel that overshrouded all others until Pastor Bob found himself at a loss of words. This man reminded Pastor Bob of a homeless guest. Where was Lurlene? Why had she let this man in?

"What can we do for you?"

"I'd like to tell you my story," the man said, never moving from his damp patch of carpet.

"Okay."

"I can't tell it to you here," the man said.

"Why not?" asked Pastor Bob, still lying on the sofa, holding out for his nap.

"I'd prefer to talk to you someplace private."

"This place is very private," Pastor Bob said.

"She can overhear us," the stranger said, gesturing to the paneled door behind his shoulder, which was still open. The new administrative assistant had resumed her computer game.

"I can close the door."

"I'd feel better outdoors," the stranger said. He had long eyelashes and blinked them slowly. "I'm not used to closed-in spaces. I've lived for a long time out-of-doors in big places. I don't know how to handle myself in offices."

"It's raining outside," Pastor Bob said. "The biggest storm of the winter so far."

"I know. I like rain. It cleans the air and washes away the dirt. There must be someplace here where we can speak without getting wet."

In his slow, laconic way, the man had a force of personality that was impossible to resist. He practically willed the senior minister of First Church off his sofa.

Pastor Bob's day was always full of interruptions, but this was one of the worst sorts, partly because he didn't have any idea how long it would take. He'd leave a note for Lurlene to come fetch him—he had other appointments later in the day—but he knew he needed to give this man a few minutes of his time.

He was well aware of the biblical injunction to entertain strangers, for he could be hosting an angel, but that alone didn't motivate him. What he had recognized ever since his sermons were broadcast was that hearing kooks was part of the price he paid for his fame. It was his job to listen to whomever wanted to talk to him.

He brought his feet to the carpet and stood up. "Let me

tell my secretary where we're going."

In the vestibule, he found the young woman from the business office. "Where's Lurlene?" he asked.

"She's upstairs in a meeting with the prayer group," she said, looking up from her computer game.

"Tell her when she comes back that I'm out in front of the church with this gentleman." He gestured to the dripping stranger. "What's your name?"

"People call me Doc," the man said, as though that were name enough.

"I see." It irritated Bob to be without Lurlene. She would know exactly what to do in a situation like this. She would save him from any interminable discourse. "Tell Lurlene to come get me when I'm needed," he instructed the young woman. He pulled his beige raincoat off its hook on the back of the door and headed outdoors.

CHAPTER 13

PASTOR BOB COULDN'T REMEMBER if he'd ever sat on the bench beneath the awning in front of the church. The only reason he'd ever spent much time there was posing for wedding photos, when a bride or groom wanted a shot of the wedding party outside the church, the ladies in chiffon and the men in tuxedos. On a damp day like this, a photographer would need a golf umbrella and a plastic drop cloth to stay dry. Cars sloshed past on San Anselmo, surging through the water in the gutter. Pastor Bob sat down on the redwood bench. Doc sat next to him, a little too close for easy social banter, but then, that wasn't what this man had in mind.

For a homeless fellow he didn't smell bad. In fact, he was neatly groomed. His white hair stuck out beneath his hat in rows of trimmed straw like the mane of a Halloween scarecrow. His salt-and-pepper beard showed no brown patches of nicotine stains. His fingernails were long, but they wore no half-moons of dirt. As he sat down, his overcoat opened to reveal a white shirt, clean but unpressed. The tie was a paisley pattern and frayed at the end. The piercing blue eyes were unclouded by alcohol. His breath was clean.

From experience Pastor Bob knew it would be best to wait for the man to speak. No questions, no friendly chitchat. The silence was filled by the steady patter of rain falling on the roof and splashing on the flagstone in little crowns. Rivulets flowed from the drainpipes through the grass next to the sidewalk, spilling over the curbs and into the gutters.

The Holy Spirit is the Lord of my time, he told himself. It was a phrase he used in his sermons and in his life, a reminder to himself that interruptions could have a godly purpose. He could resist this man, frustrated by the thought of the work that needed to be accomplished back at his desk, or he could accept that this homeless man had something important to say. *Be in this moment, Bob. Be with this man.* After all, he told himself, he was only giving up his nap.

"I listened to your sermons a long time ago," the man began. "I used to have an old transistor radio, and I could tune in to you. I discovered that the station broadcasted your messages a second time late on Sunday nights. When I lay in bed, I held my radio up to my ear. I kept your voice so low that my wife couldn't hear you. It was like your voice was inside my head. Other ministers made me feel like a loser, but there was something different about you. I felt better hearing you talk. And when I was far from you, I could still hear things you said. Other people said the same things, but the voice I heard was yours."

Bob resisted the temptation to say he wasn't worthy of such adulation. He was troubled by ministers who went on about their failings, competing in the sinfulness arena, trying to show how flawed they were and how amazing it was that God could forgive even "a wretch like me." Bob saw the sin of self-righteousness in such grandstanding. *It's not me you responded to. It was something other than me*, he thought.

"Sometimes I wanted to get away from that voice," Doc continued, "times when I resented the cheerfulness of that voice. I might have looked successful, but I was already on a slippery slope. 'Do this. Do that,' your voice seemed to say. 'Be good. Be honorable. You are loved. You are valuable. You are important.' Somehow those words made me feel worse, not better. Yet I couldn't shut off your voice."

The stranger looked at the rain-slicked street, then turned to Pastor Bob. "You were too good."

This time Bob raised his hand to protest. "Perhaps you were projecting something on me that I didn't deserve."

"You were the one I heard," Doc went on. "Other people gave me pamphlets or shoved a Bible into my hand. Between binges, I went to a mission on skid row and listened to sermons—a free sermon for a free lunch. You were the one I kept thinking about while others preached.

"By then I didn't want to have anything to do with religion," the stranger continued. "I thought it was a waste of time and energy. I hated churches. I hated the well-dressed people singing songs, praying, and listening to a preacher talk about how blessed the poor are, the poor in spirit. I knew well enough that when a man in a dirty crumpled suit showed up on their doorstep smelling of booze, they would hurry past as though he had the plague. Or they would give him a pass for a free meal at McDonald's and a bag with some toothpaste, a toothbrush, and a comb—for the streets. I didn't want to have anything to do with them. They weren't real Christians."

"They might have been trying," Pastor Bob volunteered. *God save me from self-righteousness*, he thought.

"You were the only good man, the only holy one. I began asking people, 'Do you know Rev. Robert Dudley Jr.?' 'Have you ever heard of Pastor Bob Dudley?' It was my test. If someone came up to me with a pamphlet and said, 'Do you know the Lord Jesus Christ?' I asked back, 'Do you know the Reverend Robert F. Dudley Jr?' "

"A lot of good that must have done," Bob said.

"By this time I was back East. People didn't know me there. Well, my conclusion about people who give out pamphlets is that they really want to convert lost souls. Some of them were genuinely nice people."

"Yes, it's a legitimate calling."

"Most had come into the city from comfortable, well-to-do homes. Some of them had lots of money. Many of the kids were going on mission trips, and coming to skid row was good preparation for them. Drunks and bums like me were their goal. I loved the kids and felt sorry for them and let them convert me. I wanted to make them feel good. Sometimes I was converted several times a week. I got born again—again and again."

"The Spirit can be rediscovered again and again."

"The most times I can remember being born again was four times in one week. I tried to make sure the proselytizers came from different groups, so they wouldn't figure out that I had already been converted. At least they could go back to their air-conditioned churches and say that they had saved a soul. They had one victory. Was that bad of me?"

"Four times in one week? That might have been a little dishonest," Pastor Bob suggested.

"It wasn't entirely dishonest," Doc went on, disagreeing. "The more I heard the story and pretended to say the prayers, the more I liked them. I think I was born a little bit at a time. Each time my heart opened a little bit and part of the message sank in."

"That can happen," Bob said.

Doc looked directly at the preacher. "It's the lucky ones who get Jesus all at once in one full swoop. Some of the rest of us are late bloomers." He turned back to the street before continuing.

"The funny thing was, when I accepted Jesus it wasn't through the ministrations of any evangelist. There wasn't even a person involved. By this time I happened to be in New York, living in and out of homeless shelters. I'd get a little money so I could sleep in some fleabag hotel with a girlfriend, and when the money gave out, I'd go back to the shelters. They were nice shelters too. Church-run. I stayed out of the city-owned shelters. They were too dangerous, too many criminals around. But at the church shelters, I felt safe. The rules required lights out at nine o'clock and everyone up at six. No booze, no drugs. A disciplined life. It was like being back in the Army.

"At one shelter they had a little service before we went to bed. I didn't mind going so much. It seemed a reasonable price to pay for a cot, a cup of coffee, an army blanket, and a good night's sleep. At this church they led us out of the basement shelter to the sanctuary above. It was a beautiful chapel with stained-glass windows. The pews had comfortable velvet cushions on them, and there were flowers at the ends, as though someone had just had a wedding. There was organ music, candles on the altar, and a very handsome minister in a black robe. The fifteen of us bums were thrown in with a handful of regular people. I had to share a hymnal with a lady who looked like a banker. I was glad I had taken a shower that morning."

"I'm sure she was glad too," the pastor mused.

"We sang a bit and prayed, and I watched the minister closely. He was the spitting image of you when you were young, the way I remembered you. Big football-player shoulders and a swagger in his walk. A face that had been sculpted out of granite. He could have been a college athlete. He looked like a statue of one. Holy, good, and pure. He made me feel the way you made me feel. That I could never measure up."

"That wasn't my intention," Pastor Bob said.

"I used to think that God liked only handsome, pure, Eagle Scout family men, and that he really had no use for low-down guys like me. So I was feeling pretty sorry for myself until I saw this minister do something really funny.

"Just before he got up to preach, he looked sideways across the chapel at a closed door that had a little window on it, and because it was dark on the other side, that window became a mirror. He glanced at it, and I saw him stare at himself with a look of pure vanity. It was just for a moment, but long enough for me to notice. He was making sure he looked all right. Seeing if he measured up. He was one handsome dude and just as vain and pompous as the rest of us.

" 'Amen!' I almost shouted. 'You and me, brother, we're just the same. You're no better than I am, and I'm no better than you.' I thought about how Jesus loved this guy. Jesus gave him a beautiful church and a beautiful speaking voice. When he preached he sounded smart, not vague or rambling.

He had a good-looking congregation and a busy soup kitchen. We ate well there. He probably had a beautiful wife and four beautiful kids. In the middle of a service thanking Jesus, he had looked at himself in a mirror, loving himself. He was good and talented, but he also had flaws."

"Some of God's most gifted preachers are flawed," Bob said, silently including himself.

"That's when Jesus spoke to me," the stranger went on. "The goodness of the Lord flooded into my heart and made me warm all over. 'Jesus Christ, I'm a sinner,' I prayed like all those evangelists had taught me. 'Jesus Christ, forgive me for all my sins. Take me as I am.' I figured if Jesus could use a guy like that minister, he could use me, as rotten as I was. 'A wretched wretch like me.' The way he used you."

"So you've found me out." Pastor Bob smiled wryly.

"No, not you. Me!" Doc raised his voice and pointed at himself, then he gestured back at the minister. "I don't know what your sins are. You don't look as vain as that handsome minister did, but I'm sure you have something you're hiding. Something you and God know about. If he can forgive you in your rich, comfortable church, he can forgive me. That's what I thought back then, and I still believe it."

"Is that why you came here?"

"I'm still trying to understand what God wants of me. All those wasted, lost years—I don't know what they were for. I want to make them count for something. I want to make my life worth something."

"Are you looking for a job?" Pastor Bob said. "Is that how we can help you?"

"Eventually. But first I have to set some things right. There are people I have hurt."

"Did you want to tell me about your sins?" Pastor Bob asked. Not that he wanted to play the role of a confessor, but sometimes these fellows had things they needed to unload—things to get off their chests and put their minds at ease.

"No, sir. I have nothing to confess to you. Jesus knows all my bad business. I don't need to tell you about it. I just want to do one thing with you."

"What's that?"

"To pray with you, Rev. Dudley." He smiled and the shy smile took years from him. No longer did he seem spent and wasted. It was as though the prospect of doing something for someone else revitalized him.

"Of course."

They closed their eyes, and Bob felt the man lay his large hands on his shoulder.

"Jesus Christ, bless Pastor Bob. Show him how much you love him. Fill him with the goodness that he gives to others. Let him know that he is yours." They stood up, and the stranger hugged Pastor Bob.

It was a curious sight for a rainy afternoon, a homeless man hugging the senior minister of First Church. Pastor Bob forced himself to relax in the embrace. He was warmed by it, comforted.

When the stranger backed away, Bob looked into his clear blue eyes. "There must be something we can do for you," he said.

Doc became timid all of a sudden, hesitant and fidgety. "Yes," he said. "I guess so. Do you have a shelter here?" It was as though he were afraid that his asking would make him suspect, discounting his story. A past master of the con job, he was struggling to prove that his motives were pure.

"Yes, we do."

"I don't want you to think I told you this story because I needed to find a place to stay. Not at all. I was serious. Everything really happened. I'm not faking it—like some of those times I was born again. I really experienced Jesus. I understood Him and accepted Him into my heart. Because of Jesus I'm a new man."

Pastor Bob smiled reassuringly. "I believe you."

"I'm sorry I misled some of those earnest evangelists who tried to convert me in the past. I'd like to tell them I really know Jesus now."

"We house twenty people in our basement every night," Pastor Bob said, moving on to practical matters.

"I want to be honest—I am homeless. I need a place to stay."

"I'll talk to Rocco. He's the man who runs our shelter. He should be able to find a bed for you for a few days. How long do you intend to stay in the area?"

"I don't know. I was going to say, 'Jesus will tell me,' but I'm not sure He goes that far with me. Does He with you?"

"Once in a while," Pastor Bob said. How could he tell this man all the ways Jesus spoke to him? How could he describe it? "Sometimes the Lord makes things very clear."

"That's a relief. I'm still new to this Jesus stuff."

"You've come further than most." *You had a long way to come,* he thought. *Like the prodigal son. Like the woman at the well. Like Matthew the tax collector. Like the thief at the cross. Like me at times.*

They walked back through the memory garden of azaleas, past a few lily of the Nile sticking their blue heads above the drenched sea of white and pink. The stranger clutched Pastor

Bob's elbow as though he were a blind man being led across a busy street. Bob smiled to himself. Homeless people were no different from the rest of the church members who came to him for counseling. He often opened some door inside them, and they wanted to be acknowledged by the man who seemed to possess the key to their spiritual awakening. They came to his office. He listened and prayed with them. Too busy to provide regular one-on-one counseling, he trusted in the wide array of programs provided at First Church. In this case, he would refer Doc to the church's outreach for homeless people.

His office was alert to his return. He noticed the two female members waiting in the anteroom to speak to him.

"Ladies, how good to see you," he greeted them warmly, wishing Lurlene were back from her meeting so that she could remind him of their names. She was known to go so far as to hold up a sign behind his conferees with their names.

"Pastor Bob, I'm so glad you came back. We have a meeting with you about Lurlene's surprise party right now," one of the women said.

"Of course. That's right. I had forgotten that." How would he have remembered without Lurlene to remind him? And she couldn't have reminded him because the whole thing was supposed to be a secret from her.

"That's one reason Doris and Helen called her to their meeting in the upper room. To give us a chance to meet privately with you."

"Of course. I knew that. First of all, if you'll excuse me for a minute, I need to take care of this gentleman."

Doc had backed into a corner of the office near Lurlene's

climbing philodendron. It was as though he wanted to be hidden by it. A few minutes earlier he had been animated and outgoing, and now he was a wallflower. He had apparently learned to make himself invisible from his years on the street.

"Could you take this man down to Rocco in the basement?" Pastor Bob said to his temporary assistant. "Rocco will know how to help him."

"You should be able to stay in our shelter tonight," he said to Doc.

"The party for Lurlene is supposed to be on Saturday, and there's not much time," one of the ladies interrupted.

"I know," Pastor Bob said. "I know. The sooner the better. She deserves all our attention." Then turning to Doc, he said, "I hope you'll be all right."

"Yes. I'll be fine."

"Come to me if you want to talk more," Pastor Bob said.

"Okay," Doc replied.

"God bless," Pastor Bob added, then returned to the two women, consummate party planners, who wanted to tell him all they had done to make this surprise event for Lurlene something to be proud of.

"Ladies," he said before they got down to the business of event planning, "sometimes I discover that I am pastor of a flock I don't even know."

CHAPTER 14

AS JONATHAN DRESSED that evening for his date with Janice, a vivid memory came to him. He was at the beach where he and his mother spent one week every summer. They rented a small one-bedroom clapboard shack at Balboa, surrounded by multi-storied stucco monstrosities. When he was really young, Lurlene would take him to the bay where he made sand castles on the little beach and swam in the safe, placid waters. But as he grew older, he was allowed to venture to the ocean side and swim in the turbulent waters as long as he stayed in front of the lifeguard. He had looked with longing at the older boys who took their surfboards out early in the morning and rode the waves. Lurlene wouldn't allow him a board.

At the beach he discovered a passion for body-surfing. Floating on the crest of a breaker, bobbing in the surf, he would paddle to the top, kicking with all his might, and then lead with one hand in the blue-green water, plunging down the mountain that kept rising beneath him. It was like skiing with your hands, head first. Often as not he fell over the crest before he had a chance to back out of a wave, and he ended up twisting and turning in the white water. Bashed into the sand, held under for a split second, he then would rise and spit out a mouthful of salt water, staring back up the beach to the lifeguard in his orange uniform and his mother under her umbrella.

Even a wipeout could make him laugh. He felt free. Lifted up and thrown back into the water where he always felt safe. When a late-summer storm far out in the Pacific brought with it devastating surf, the lifeguard station flew a red flag, and he stayed out of the waves. But even sitting on the beach, hugging his knees and gazing at the ocean, he had the same exuberant feeling of wild freedom and safety at once.

On the last day of vacation a great sadness always filled him. While his mother swept every inch of the rented shack, scouring sinks and bathtubs—knowing full well that a professional cleaner would come after her and do the same thing—Jonathan went back to the waves for a final swim. For one week each summer he owned a tiny stretch of beach, and he was loathe to give it up. He wanted to take it back with him, along with the sand that had collected in the hem of his bathing suit and the tan that would fade before school's start. Of course it was impossible. But for that week he felt like a hero conquering the unknown. Bold, courageous, strong. Then he would return to the world where he was a bumbling bystander.

All this came to him as he was dressing for his date with Janice. He felt as though he were riding the crest of the wave, feeling it rise beneath him, and instead of ducking under and letting it pass with all its possible dangers, he was swimming in with it, paddling, kicking, pushing forward to take it several yards into shore. He had never acted so decisively as he had with Janice. He had never before been so aggressive. He didn't like pushy, macho guys—he would never be one of them. But here he had discovered a style all his own, like the push of his hand through the water. And like those days at the ocean, it filled him with an awe that he didn't feel entirely responsible for. Bold but not proud. Sure of himself but not cocky.

Why would she like a guy like him? Why in the world would she go for him? He had no money, no great career prospects. He wasn't a knockout. He still lived at home, for goodness' sake. What did that say about him? That he had a mother fixation? That he was cheap? That he couldn't afford much better? He wouldn't have recommended himself as a prospective husband. But he was absolutely sure he had a lot to offer this girl.

As he stared at himself in the bathroom mirror while combing his hair, a tremor of fear passed through him, the same fear he felt at the top of a wave he was about to take, not certain if he would be smashed into the sand and held under by the passing white water. It was a sensation that he found strangely comforting, reminding him that he had something to overcome, some reason to show courage.

His mother was unusually silent as he walked through the living room on his way to the door. He imagined that he was heading down to the beach to catch some waves and that she was distracted, staring at her sweater pattern, trying to figure out where she had lost a stitch.

Then another comparison with those summer vacations came to him. Something akin to the sadness that hit him on the last day. After they moved out of the rented shack, he always took one last wave and then dried off in the sun, savoring the salt that would dry on his body. As he and his mother drove down the peninsula, going against the crowd on a Saturday, he resisted the temptation to crane his head around and take one last glance at the beach. He knew what he would see—a final glimpse of the water as the car climbed the hill, the sunlight scattered on the sea behind him, the wind blowing out the surf in a thousand whitecaps. He would be filled with a painful ache over "the end of things."

That was how he felt now. This beginning could also signal an end of things. He was traveling forward now, and he felt an ache for the relationship he had outgrown.

"Night, Mom," he said.

"Good night, dear. Have a good time."

"Don't wait up," he said out of habit. Did she ever wait up for him?

"I won't."

The windshield wipers slapped at the window of his little Toyota, 142,000 miles on the odometer and still going strong. He was driving to pick up his date. Not since high school had he been so conscious of going out on a date. There were other girls he went out with—a would-be rock singer who waited tables at a restaurant in town and an old friend who wrote copy for an advertising company. He'd go to movies with one or hang out at a coffee shop with the other, sitting for hours with only one cup. He'd listen to music at their apartments or watch TV, but this was a date. This was special. The last time he'd taken a girl out on a date was to the senior prom—65,000 miles ago, when the car was his mother's and only his to borrow.

He knew of a restaurant in one of the canyons, a woodsy place beneath native sycamores and eucalyptus, built from boulders that had washed down the mountains over the centuries. There would be a fire in the fireplace and candles on the tables. The kitchen would smell of rosemary and garlic, and the host would make lascivious glances at the two of them. It was odd enough to be driving to pick up a girl, but to have every minute of the evening fully planned in his head reminded him of high school, when nothing turned out to be what you imagined it. The difference now was that the stakes were higher.

He parked in front of her building and took the steps up to her apartment two at a time. No parents to meet here, but he expected to be checked out by a roommate.

Sure enough, a young woman answered the door, still in her work clothes with her shoes off and a sizable run up the back side of her sheer navy blue stockings. A short blonde, she held a jar of nail polish in her hand. "You must be the date," she said. She was blunt too.

"Yes," he said, putting out a hand. "Jonathan Scott."

"Can't shake," she said. "My nails are still wet. I'm Shelly."

The apartment was a starter unit with hand-me-down furniture, Formica bookshelves, and some overgrown poinsettias left from Christmas. Against one wall was an upright piano with a pile of music on top.

Shelly sat down at the table in the corner and resumed painting her nails. Jonathan walked over to the bookshelf and studied the titles. He was confused by the collection of business school textbooks and volumes of nineteenth century French poetry.

"Don't worry," Shelly said. "Those are my books. Janice's are in the bedroom."

"Were you a French major?" Jonathan asked.

"Yes, although I can't remember much of it anymore."

"What do you do now?"

"I analyze oil stocks for a bank," she said with cool efficiency.

A line she'd no doubt delivered at countless parties. If it was meant to impress, it had its effect.

"What do *you* do?"

Jonathan cringed. "I make puppets."

"Cool," Shelly said, barely looking up. "Is there much money in it?"

"Some. I teach classes and lead workshops at schools. I'm working on a project for a museum right now. That's where the real money is, if someone will start thinking of me as an artist. That and movie or TV work."

"Did the musium commission you?"

"I wish. It's just something I'm amusing myself with now." He looked back at the books to change the subject. "I know nothing about business. I don't think I could even read an annual report."

"I didn't know much before I started this job either. Everything I studied was pretty abstract. You learn on the job."

Jonathan was about to ask what bank she worked for when Janice showed up. In the twenty-some hours that had passed since he'd seen her last, he'd wondered if his eye had served him well. He had tried several times to conjure up her face in his mind. And he hadn't quite succeeded, only coming up with a vague image of pale skin, dark hair, and dark eyes. If he'd had to take a test on their color he would have failed—

they were actually grayish blue. The lights had been dim at Rene's the previous night. Maybe what he'd remembered was an illusion fostered by the light.

But here in the incandescent glow of her apartment, she was still a knockout. Something eternal, undateable. There'd be a place for her in any wing of an art gallery. He wanted to look down at his feet and then look back up just to enjoy the element of surprise her face gave him each time. Like finding a rainbow at the end of a squall or hiking for hours on a tree-shrouded path to discover a waterfall in a clearing. Why should he be so lucky?

"Shall we go?" he asked.

"Sure," she said.

"Don't be too late," Shelly called.

"I won't," Janice said, mimicking a dutiful daughter.

They ran to the car under Jonathan's umbrella. At the Toyota, he opened the door on Janice's side and then waited for her to be settled before he closed it, a surfeit of chivalry that seemed to amuse her. Next thing he'd be walking on the street side of the sidewalk so his lady would not be doused by splashing water—on a rainy night, not a bad idea. *If you thought you could close your own door, think again. You're going out with one of the last of today's gentlemen.* He slid into his car seat and slammed his door. He turned off the radio so they could talk.

Then he froze. What next?

For that brief moment he thought the date was going to be a disaster. They'd gotten this far, and both seemed to be overcome by self-consciousness. His fingers fumbled at the gearshift as he started the car and headed down the street. Stopping at a red light, he watched the colors reflected in the pavement and still didn't know what to say. "Where'd you meet your roommate?" "How did you find your apartment?" "Are you a vegetarian?" They all seemed like dopey lines.

"Sorry I was late," she said, finally breaking the silence.

"No big deal. I enjoyed meeting your roommate." He laughed. "I thought she was going to give me a real going over. Worse than any parent."

"Give her time. She'll check you out with a fine-toothed comb. Shelly looks out for me. That's why we're roommates."

Yes, Jonathan thought. *Say what's on your mind. That's why we're together*. Not just because he loved the way she looked, but because he was delighted to hear her talk. The night before, without any risks to worry about—no great stakes except maybe disappointing his mother—they had said whatever came to mind. Unafraid of the most commonplace chatter. Even the weather.

"I love California in the rain," he said.

"Me too." The car in front of them slowed to a stop at a gutter. "Except for driving in it."

"Do you enjoy driving?"

"Not really. If I could live without a car, I'd be completely happy. One summer I did an internship at a magazine in San Francisco. I sublet an apartment near the office and walked to work every morning. That was ideal."

"What was the magazine?"

"A trade publication for hardware stores and suppliers."

"Why did you do it?"

"To get some writing experience. I had other offers, magazines that you've probably heard of, but I was afraid I'd end up answering phones and filing. I wanted to be sure I had a job where I could write. They promised me that I would write, so I went to *Hardware* magazine."

"Did you like it there?"

"They were nice people. I was really proud of all the stuff I learned about nuts and bolts and screws. I thought I'd be able to impress my friends back at school. But a few months after the job ended I forgot everything I knew, everything I researched—plumbing, piping, hammers, paint stock. That's what happens when you write about forgettable subjects. You forget the information."

"To make room for new stuff."

"I don't know. I've never bought that line about the brain having more room than we can possibly use."

"We only use three percent of our brain. Something like that."

"That's because three percent is the only part that's worth using. The rest is hard-disk stuff for tasks we never want to accomplish, like all the extra features on a computer."

Jonathan was charmed. Janice could have been reading out of the telephone book, and he would have been fascinated. She'd say one thing, and it would prompt a new question in his mind, which would lead to another avenue for discussion. Filling up the silence so that they no longer noticed it was there, so that they no longer found any mental barrier stretching between them, they made their way to the firelit restaurant in the canyon.

"I read somewhere that people lose their powers of memory once they start reading," he said.

"Look at those long epic poems people use to memorize," she said. "Like the Odyssey. Or the Iliad."

"Or the Bible, for that matter."

Jonathan parked beneath a live oak that dropped a few swirling leaves on the windshield. He held up an umbrella for Janice, and they hurried inside where they found that they were one of the restaurant's few customers.

"Californians are such wimps about the rain," Jonathan observed. "They never go out in it." The maître d'—the same one who'd been there when Jonathan had come to the place in high school—raised his plucked eyebrows several times at Jonathan and seated them at a secluded table by a window overlooking the now rushing river.

Normally the river was a thin stream fed by the runoff from lawn sprinklers. The water usually tumbled placidly over the rocks and boulders, so it was hard to believe that once every few decades a torrential storm brought down the boulders and rocks from the foothills and mountains and the water rose up the canyon walls, threatening any homes in its way.

For Jonathan and Janice this was a once-in-a-lifetime evening, but not because of the rising water in the canyon. They had hardly noticed the orange striped barricades that the police had erected on the side streets. The wind had picked up and blew the rain in sheets down the plate glass window, but they were comfortable, warm, and so wrapped up in each other that the weather hardly mattered.

"When did you first start going to First Church?" Janice asked.

"As far back as I can remember. One of my earliest memories is of the huge mural of Noah and his ark in the church nursery. I tried to copy it with my crayons and paints. I didn't do a bad job either. When I got older, I graduated from classroom to classroom around the Sunday school courtyard. I can remember singing songs with autoharp accompaniment and watching videos about the Holy Land and building Judean houses out of popsicle sticks. We made water jugs from clay and stained-glass windows out of tissue paper."

"Did you make puppets there?"

"I did my first big puppet show at First Church. One summer at Vacation Bible School we made puppets from Styrofoam and paper-mache. I ended up doing Joseph and his brothers, all twelve of them. I directed the rest of the class in a play about Joseph being thrown into the well, then being rescued and taken to Egypt. I'm not sure what the teacher had in mind, but she let me run with it."

"She was probably relieved that someone was going to entertain the class," Janice proposed.

"I had a pharaoh, a sphinx, and a couple of pyramids in the background. Everybody had to participate in the scene where the brothers come down to Egypt to meet the brother they thought they'd bumped off. I delivered Joseph's best line, 'What you meant for evil, God meant for good.' I think I was jealous of anyone who could be so lucky as to have twelve brothers. I would have given my eyeteeth to have just one brother."

"It sounds like you learned something."

"Maybe not the things that I was supposed to learn. I don't really remember much about the Ten Commandments or the books of the Bible or what Jesus said in the Sermon on the Mount. But . . . I guess I did learn something."

"What?"

They paused for a minute while a waiter approached them and gave them the menu, reciting the specials of the day.

When they ordered, he bowed stiffly and hurried off to the kitchen.

"So what did you learn?" Janice repeated her question.

"Well, that a church can have some decent people in it. Caring people. Later, when I was in high school, I was part of the youth group. We marched against hunger, raised money for poor people in South America. We'd have meetings downstairs in the church basement and talk about our feelings for each other and for the kids who felt left out. It wasn't nearly so preachy and sanctimonious as it might sound."

"It doesn't sound so bad."

"We had swim parties and camping trips up in the mountains and dances once a year that got pretty rowdy—the church was always full of guys looking for girls, and I guess girls looking to meet guys. But I think they came away with the same thing that I did—that church was a warm, welcoming place. I know we prayed together and read the Bible, but it was the caring that made the biggest impression on me."

"Did you go to a church when you were growing up?" Jonathan asked Janice.

She smiled. "Not one that provided a matchmaking service."

"This was totally irregular, you know," he said quickly.

"Am I complaining?"

"I just don't want you to think they do that all the time."

"I don't," Janice said. "But I don't really know much about churches. My family slept in on Sundays. I went to Sunday school for a little while with a girl who lived next door. My parents thought that was okay. They didn't disapprove of church. In fact they said it was very helpful for a lot of people."

"But not for you."

"That's what it seemed."

"So what brought you to First Church?" Jonathan figured that at some point they would have to cover the sticky religious questions. Now was as good a time as ever.

Janice blushed. "I was looking for something," she said vaguely, "or maybe someone. I really should tell you . . ."

Just then their waiter arrived with one large ceramic dish carrying the appetizers, which he spooned onto their plates with a flourish.

"What were you looking for?" Jonathan asked.

"It's a long story."

"People come to the church for all sorts of reasons," Jonathan said. "I think my mom actually took me there because she wanted to enroll me in the day care program. That's what she once said." As he spoke he became aware that his voice echoed in the restaurant. Looking around he saw the place was remarkably empty. Granted, it was a Tuesday night. He could spot only one other couple, and they were rising from their unfinished meal, the dinner plates not even cleared. At that moment the kitchen door swung open, and Jonathan heard water pouring into a bucket, which he assumed was the sound of a pot being washed, and then he began to wonder if there was a leak in the ceiling. It sounded like a lot of water falling into water.

"Did you hear that?" he asked.

"What?"

"The water in the kitchen."

"Like a fountain."

"Yes, or water running into a bucket. There must be a leak somewhere. You were saying something about why you went to First Church."

"You know," Janice said, "it's awfully quiet in here."

"I noticed that."

"Do you think there's something wrong?"

At the front of the restaurant the maître d' was conferring with their waiter. The two of them were speaking in lowered voices.

"It's hard to tell, but I'm sure they'll let us know if it concerns us."

If Jonathan had been thinking clearly, he would have remembered that the old sycamores and live oaks outside were usually illuminated from their rock-ribbed bases. But no artificial lights glowed from them now. The lights had shorted out. In fact, it was so dark that he couldn't see the raging stream. They were dining next to a torrent but didn't know it.

Jonathan was preoccupied. He had something on his mind he felt he'd better let Janice know sooner rather than later. He needed to say it to clear the air. He didn't want there to be any misunderstanding between them.

Spreading cheese on a piece of bread, he shoved it into his mouth. "Janice, I have a confession to make," he said, still chewing.

Janice looked worried, furrowing her brow.

"You know the woman at the church who set you up with me?"

"The one I spoke to?"

"Yes, the one who works for Pastor Bob." He had a terrible fear that revealing her identity would mess things up.

"She seems really well organized."

"She is. Incredibly so. She does everything for Pastor Bob. He wouldn't be able to get anything done without her."

"The voice of authority."

"Yeah. I should know," he said. "She's my mom."

Janice looked at him, amazed. "You mean your mother is the one who wanted us to go out together? *She* matched us up?"

He cringed. Somehow it was unsavory to have to bring up your mom on a date. It gave all the wrong impressions. "Yes, it was her idea in the first place," he said. "I wanted to tell you. But I don't want you to get the wrong idea. Mom got inspired when she read your prayer request. It was all spontaneous. She read what you wrote and thought of me. She figured we'd be perfect for each other."

Janice laughed. "I can't believe it! That's exactly what Shelly said. That the only person who would match me up at the church would be a mother anxious about her unattached son."

He looked concerned. "She didn't mean any harm by it. She did it out of the best intentions."

"Who else but a mother?"

"She worries about me sometimes. She wants me to be happy, and whatever you said in your letter made her think that we might get along. I hope you won't blame her."

"No," Janice said, smiling. "I'm kind of touched. I'm even more amazed that you went along with it."

"I didn't want her to get in trouble."

"How would she get into trouble?"

"For meddling on the job. Those prayer letters are supposed to be kept confidential. No one should ever think that they're read by dozens of church employees or members. People need to feel free to write whatever they need prayer for. Mom is just an employee of the church, a secretary. She's not supposed to make big decisions like recommending dates for anonymous single women."

Janice put down her fork and looked grave. "Would she really get into trouble?"

Jonathan answered. "I don't think she'd lose her job or anything like that. She's been there so long she's almost indispensable." A note of pride entered his voice. "But she would be humiliated. She tries to keep herself apart philosophically from what goes on at First Church. You know, she's not really a member. For her it's just a job."

"Jonathan," Janice said. "I've got to make a call."

"What's wrong?"

"I've . . . I've got to see if I can catch anyone at the office." She rose from the table, clutching her purse. "It's urgent."

"There's a pay phone near the entrance."

As she walked toward the cloakroom, Jonathan wondered what had come up. Why had she become so distressed all of a sudden? Something he's said had triggered it. But what? Almost immediately she returned to their table.

"The phone's not working," Janice said. "The lines must be down."

"Do you want to leave?"

"Yes, I've got to go to my office. I've got to see if I can stop a story. Or if I can change anything in it. I'm afraid it's too late, but I've got to try." She dropped her napkin on the table so that it fell into the pale pink sauce that swirled over the cheese.

"What story?"

"One I've been writing. One that's supposed to appear tomorrow. We've got to go right away. Pay the bill, and let's get out of here."

He stood up and grabbed her arm. If she wanted to go, he was ready to leave. Something was wrong, and he would gladly help her correct it. They could come back another time and have the rest of their dinner. Anyway, the spell had been broken. Outside the sound of the water had grown louder, there was the splashing in the bucket in the kitchen, and the look on Janice's face convinced him that whatever she was talking about was serious.

"Hurry," she urged.

CHAPTER 15

THE HOMELESS SHELTER at First Church closed its doors at eight o'clock in the evening. The men—it was an all-male shelter; women and children slept at St. Mary's down the block—ate dinner at six, prepared by a once homeless chef who made excellent meals when he was on the wagon. They were served by a group of volunteers. After dinner the guests could sit at the card tables in the basement and talk with the volunteers, play games, read, or prepare for bed. There was an earnest youth who wanted to quiz them on their quality of life, urging them to unite and picket for greater government benefits. Sometimes the discussions led to spiritual matters, issues in which the homeless were well versed. In fact, one schizophrenic described going into a full sanctuary on Easter morning, declaring that he was the Son of God, and asking the congregation what they were going to do about it. It was startling for members of First Church to discover that the recipients of their charity knew more about the church or could quote more Bible verses than many of them could.

That Tuesday night of the great rainstorm, the men were jumpier than usual. Because of the weather, most of them hadn't been able to stay at their outdoor haunts. Instead of sitting on park benches or rattling a cup of change on the post office steps, they had lingered inside the library—fighting sleep over volumes of the *Waverley* novels—or had sat near the indoor fountain at the shopping mall, earning the glare of the security guard. Some had nursed cups of coffee for hours inside McDonald's. Southern California, cooperative for the fresh-air bum, was inhospitable in a drenching winter rain.

Because of the weather, the guests of the shelter arrived at their pickup spot near the bus station wearing plastic garbage bags over their sodden clothes. At First Church they were invited to recycle their garb for free. Clean, dry clothes were available in a small room next to the bathroom, where Lurlene brought many of her son's garments if they hadn't been recycled into puppets' costumes. Alas, few of the guests checked out the shelter's wardrobe. Most of the men clung to the clothes they were wearing because they were familiar. When you have very few material goods, it's hard to let go of the things that have been your friends for weeks. So added to the normal shelter odors of Pine-Sol, floor wax, coffee, and mothballs was the stench of damp wool and body odor, much like a wet dog coming out of a rainstorm.

Doc, the newcomer, was greeted with some suspicion by the regulars. Was he a psycho? A schizoid? Did he knock back a flask when lights were out? Would he steal a shopping cart if given the chance?

The smokers hanging around outside eyed him warily. The

coffee drinkers setting up a game of dominoes made no attempt to lure him in. A young advertising executive from the church—the nightly volunteer—was eating spaghetti and meatballs with the homeless men. He already had his hands full with one old fellow who kept dropping his meatballs into a cup of coffee and dishing them out with his spoon. Rocco, the ex-homeless man who ran the shelter, was sorting towels and sheets. He felt that he had done enough by offering Doc a bed at the last minute. God only knew what riffraff Pastor Bob would send down next.

Doc didn't need much guidance. He had spent enough nights in church shelters to know the drill. Pulling his cot into a dark corner under a vaulted stone arch, he spread the clean rough sheets on the mattress, tucked in the corners foursquare like a military veteran, fluffed up a pillow, and took off his shoes. He put them under his bed, along with a handful of small change in the toes. That way if someone tried to steal the shoes, he would hear the jingle of coins. His few bills he kept pinned to his underpants. He took off his coat and his wrinkled white shirt and hung them from the back of a chair. When he stretched out on the cot, his feet stuck out over the edge at the bottom and his spine sagged in the middle. He lay there listening to the domino players, the radio, the grumbling smokers, and the evangelists at work. It would take him time to become attuned to the natural rhythm of the place. For now he lay low.

One by one the guests went to the bathroom and brushed their teeth. They made their cots and lay down. The lights went out at nine o'clock. He could hear his roommates tossing and turning, some already snoring. It amazed him how much homeless people slept—ten, twelve, fourteen hours a day. On a park bench, under a bridge, in an alleyway—cat naps merging into fitful sleep in shelters with a half-dozen cups of overbrewed coffee under their belts. That he was one of their number he had only lately accepted. Not just a man temporarily down on his luck, not a fellow between jobs, not anything as picturesque as a hobo or skid-row bum. He was a street person who depended on charity for survival. No poster boy for fundraising appeals, no newspaper profile subject. If he was going to change, he had to start by accepting the truth of his current situaion.

He had always liked church shelters, even before his spiritual awakening. The food was decent, the sheets clean, and there were usually non-homeless people around, sometimes even church families serving meals or chaperoning. He could perform magic tricks for the children. He liked to smell the sweet scent of their hair when he made a quarter appear out of their ears or when they leaned over to pick the right pea from under a walnut shell. At one church shelter the families and homeless men stood in a circle and sang "Kum ba ya" before bedtime. The memory brought tears to his eyes in the darkness of his cot and reopened the wounds of loneliness, reminding him of all that he had when he left his family behind.

He listened for the sleeping sounds of his neighbors. Breakfast would be served at six o'clock. Most of them would wake up at five. He knew if he were to get any sleep he would need to knock off now, but he couldn't turn off his mind. Outside the rain fell in torrents on the flagstone courtyard. A drainage pipe from the roof emptied into a larger drain near a low basement window, and the sound of the flowing water was like a toilet continually being flushed.

Doc admired church buildings, especially old ones. He enjoyed seeing the signs of church activity around him. Stacks of Bibles and hymnals, choir robes and starched cottas, scissors and crayons from nursery schools, framed biblical scenes. Was this what his son had studied in Sunday school? From his crypt bedroom, he listened for creaking floorboards as members from the church above carried out their liturgical worship. Once he had gone upstairs to a nave and watched a wedding rehearsal from a back pew. The bride carried a bouquet made of ribbons and bows, and the groom kept pretending that he would forget the ring, clowning around with the groomsmen. He had even watched a funeral that way. It was the death of someone much loved, with long eulogies, dark suits, a crying widow, and flanks of bewildered mourners. His own funeral would have no such trappings. Certainly there would be no grieving wife nearby.

Now he put a hand against the wall behind his bed. He could feel moisture in the plaster. The room was dark except for the portable heater plugged into one wall, which cast a dull glow in one corner, doing little to dry the air. He heard coughing at the end of the row, a smoker's hack. Emphysema? Lung cancer? Tuberculosis? Shelters were full of diseases, but Doc had convinced himself that fewer germs would be passed in a church basement than elsewhere. Here he imagined he was in a germ-free bubble of protection, like one he'd seen in a magazine article about a man with an immune deficiency who lived in a plastic bubble. As long as he was in God's house, he thought he would be safe.

He raised himself on one elbow and peered in the dark. A sliver of light from the bathroom shone down the hall, traversing the linoleum like a laser. Doc brought his feet to the floor and padded toward the light, stopping to pick up one of the Bibles from a shelf. Better to read while waiting for sleep than to strain his eyes counting ceiling tiles from his bed. The hall stretched behind the shelter sleeping area to a ramp that reached the back of the sanctuary. Rocco, the caretaker, was sleeping closest to this passage, perhaps to guard it. Doc passed beside him and walked upstairs.

A streetlamp glowed through the stained-glass windows, illuminating the blue-and-green panes as though they were seen from underwater. A fluorescent night-light came from somewhere beneath the pews. Doc stared through an open doorway. The place was empty and yet full, maybe fuller than when it had a crowd of people inside. Waiting for his eyes to adjust, he gazed at a plaque on the wall commemorating the dead of the Great War. The war to end all wars. And then a second plaque for the dead parishioners who fought in the Second World War.

The church was a place of lists. In his mind's eye he could read the lists of flower donors for the Christmas and Easter programs. He could see the lists of children who received their Bibles after memorizing the Twenty-third Psalm. In the dark he found the posted list of hymns sung for the last Sunday, the numbers on a wall. Everything passed through this place, consecrated, sanctified, verified. Baptism, marriage, death. Even people who didn't believe in church felt the need to do one or all three there. The event wasn't real unless it happened within these walls.

He felt sorry that he had ever ridiculed the activities of this place and called the members hypocrites. Back then he had told himself that he was above such weakness and dependency. He would go it alone, a rugged individualist. His life had been a quest for freedom, freedom from everything that would tie a man down. The irony was that he ended up deeply dependent in predictable ways. Any preacher could have pointed him out as an object lesson. Free to travel? His trips took him as far as a park bench and a bottle of wine. A narrow, miserable end. If he could have reversed anything, he would have started here in this place. He would have been one of the hypocrites at worship—a sinner but earnest and trying.

Doc was careful not to move too far inside the church. By his calculations he was standing someplace above the bed where Rocco, the shelter chief, slept. Here the floorboards were creaky, and he didn't want to be interrupted in his contemplating. He sank gently to the floor and spread himself out flat on his back, staring into the wooden arches above the nave, which looked a little like the hull of a ship. Where was he going this time? How long had he been traveling? Could he never call a place, even this place, home?

Ever since he'd found Jesus, he'd had a yearning to go back home. He had longed to see the loved ones he'd once turned his back on, but how could he do that now? They would probably have nothing to say to him, or they wouldn't believe he had changed.

He had discovered that as a homeless person, people expected outlandish things of him. He could say outrageous things, make brazen confessions, and be responsible for none of them. Other men had mortgages, jobs, and families for ballast. If they wandered off course, people would notice, call to them, bring them back. If they wanted to follow Christ, they would be guided in proper paths.

But if you were a homeless man who had just found God, well, bully for you. Give up everything? What a laugh! What was there left to give up? He'd already sacrificed his life for a spot of tequila in a weedy park behind a baseball backstop. It occurred to him that in all those conversions he kept making—born-again again and again—no one was really fooled. What else did they expect of a homeless bum? Conversion came cheap to gutter types. What did bums have to give up?

Everything! He would lose everything he had built up in his mind to hide behind. The illusion of purpose, this pretense of freedom, his imagined dignity. He would have to say out loud that he was wrong, admit that he'd been hopelessly wrong for all these years. It had been easier in that church hundreds of miles away where there was no one specific to apologize to, no one to say "I'm sorry" to. He had no history there. He was nothing more than a smell lingering in a crowded elevator or an unappealing sight seen from a passing car window. Motorists rolled up their windows, afraid that he'd harangue them for a donation.

He'd come here to make himself known. He'd made this pilgrimage to seek forgiveness. He didn't dare hope for acceptance. Not yet. He'd endlessly practiced the speech he'd give. In his head he'd started and restarted a thousand times the letter he would write. *Not a day goes by that I don't think of you* . . . but he could never get it down on paper. He thought it would be easier to go to a minister first and tell his story, to get some understanding, but he had scarcely begun. It wasn't that Pastor Bob wouldn't have listened. It was that Doc couldn't bear to go on with his story. The burden of his past and his deep feelings of remorse weighed so heavily upon him that he could hardly bear the distress of it all. How would he ever be able to express how sorry he was?

At that very moment in the restaurant, Jonathan was trying to flag down the waiter.

"Excuse me," he said, his voice echoing across the nearly empty room. "Excuse me."

Janice looked at her watch. The sound of dripping water could not now be escaped.

The waiter rushed forward. "Is everything is all right?" he asked. "Do you need anything? More pepper with your pasta? Some Parmesan cheese?"

"No," Jonathan said. "The food is fine. We just can't stay."

The waiter frowned.

"It's business," Janice said. "Something urgent I forgot. I've got to get back to the office right away."

"Could you bring us the bill, please?" Jonathan said.

At that same moment, the maître d', as though he were moving on wheels, arrived at their table. "I'm very sorry to interrupt, but we've just received some urgent news."

"They have to leave," said the waiter, adding up figures on his pad of paper.

"That's exactly what I was going to tell you," the maître d' said, apparently wanting to make the announcement himself. "You'll have to leave immediately."

"What's wrong?" Jonathan asked.

"It's nothing to be too concerned about," the maître d' said, lowering his voice. "These things happen from time to time."

"What things?"

"Mudslides. Rockslides. Avalanches. Flooding!"

"Is it the river?" Jonathan was worried now. "Will we be able to get out of the canyon?"

"Please, do not fret. One road is still open, but we were told that everyone should seek higher ground. You must evacuate."

At that moment the chef came from the kitchen and burst forth in a torrent of Italian, "*Acqua, acqua! Che miseria! C'é l'acqua dappertutto.* I cook no longer. Water is coming right to the door. My feet! My feet will get wet."

The maître d' turned to him and, as though trying to calm a child, said, "Pietro, I was just telling these people that the kitchen is closed."

Red in the face, the chef continued. "*La famiglia!* My daughter, my wife. They be drowned and I still at work."

"Pietro, there's no need to panic," said the maître d'. "We should all be able to drive right home."

"*Basta,*" he said. "I have enough!" He threw down his chef's hat and marched out of the restaurant, presumably to his car. At the same moment, the waiter ripped the bill from his pad and put it down on Janice and Jonathan's table.

"No, no," the maître d' said. He picked up the bill and crumpled it, dropping it on the floor.

"There will be no charge for your dinner. Please come back another time. We can give you a rain check." He snorted like a pug dog at the unfortunately accurate term. "We'd love to have you back in sunnier circumstances."

"Thank you," Jonathan said as Janice grabbed his elbow and they headed to the door.

Like a valet, the waiter appeared at their sides with raincoats and umbrellas. Jonathan remembered to stuff a couple dollars in his hand. Outside, huddling under the umbrella, they rushed to the Toyota.

The stream had risen almost as high as the base of the rock-hewn wall across the driveway, the same rocks that had washed down the river over the years, now smoothed and rounded like pearls under its force. The sky was still pouring down rain in torrents.

The only car on the road, Jonathan found that the headlights barely cut through the curtain of water. He drove very slowly, carefully keeping his eye on the broken white line in the center of the road. He could see little else.

Natural disasters rarely filled him with foreboding. He didn't feel fear, even in earthquakes. The ones he'd been through as a child gave him a sense of adventure. He would sit up in his bed riding the roll of the seismic waves. Forest fires provided light shows at night when the Santa Ana winds blew. Mudslides, rockslides—he'd experienced them all. This stretch of Southern California sat on a gently sloping plain built from the accumulating debris of natural disasters. The mountains rose through earthquakes, the vegetation covering them was destroyed by forest fires, the loose rocks and dirt washed down to fill up the land. The rising waters could be considered a beneficent act of God. He never thought for a moment that he and Janice wouldn't make it safely home.

What was uppermost on his mind was the conversation that had been interrupted. Janice had panicked when she discovered who his mother was. She had mentioned a story. What story? What was it?

"I don't think we're ever going to make it in time," she said, trying to read the dial on her watch in the darkness.

"I can't go much faster."

"It's all my fault," she said.

"The driving conditions couldn't be worse."

"I should have put it together myself. I should have thought before I did it."

"Did what?" Jonathan said, leaning into the steering wheel, hoping to see better.

"Keep driving. I'll try to explain. Just promise that you won't hate me for what I'm about to tell you."

"How could I?"

"Promise me that much."

"Okay," he said. "Whatever you say. Scouts' honor."

CHAPTER 16

PASTOR BOB DID NOT SLEEP very well that night. He liked rain—even these winter storms that wrought havoc for a few days and then retreated from the headlines. He had lived in California long enough to know that rain was needed. He had prayed for it often enough from the pulpit. For the skiers in the congregation, he would sometimes add a line about snow in the mountains "for those of you who worship God on Sunday from the slopes." Winter storms were necessary for filling up the reservoirs, dampening the chaparral, and providing snow that would sink into the ground and replenish the water table. But that night in his bed he worried about the roof over First Church. When he finally dozed off, hearing the sound of rain pattering on the roof over his own head, he saw so many buckets being filled up that he couldn't keep up with them anymore. And the water kept coming.

He awakened from his dream with a jerk, sitting straight up in bed. He glanced around him, seeing no pots or pans collecting drips. His wife slept unconcerned beside him, the covers pulled up over her ears. "*He sendeth rain on the just and on the unjust.*" The words from the book of Matthew didn't seem to apply at the moment. But when Scripture came into his head, he paid attention, for the biblical passage might have been triggered by a hidden desire. Was he the just or the unjust? Was he feeling guilty about something now? Was he one of the deserving or the undeserving?

Dreams were impossible things. Sometimes God meant them for a message. Like Joseph's interpretation of dreams. But other dreams were a hodgepodge of bizarre impulses, a synthesis of a day's diverse sights and scenes.

His dream tonight said that he wasn't keeping up. Work was entering his "in" box and not going out. His correspondence was backed up for weeks with letters that Lurlene had never seen. Notes of appreciation that he needed to respond to, questions that he had to answer. The letters he struggled over contained stories—like the one the homeless stranger told him that afternoon. People were moved by what he said and wrote. He wished he could be brisk and businesslike when he wrote back. He wished he could answer with a form letter, like the ones Lurlene sent out in answer to the prayer requests that came in. Instead, he'd put these notes in a coat pocket and agonized over the right words to use.

He always found himself praying when he took notes out of his pocket. He prayed for the senders. Maybe that was all that was needed. Maybe that was all people expected. But he wished he could do more. He felt backed up. The demands on his time kept coming in like an ever rising flood. The buckets had overflowed.

Perhaps the dream was telling him that he had a leaky

ship. The boat, the church—the metaphor was appropriate—was taking in water. The staff positions were not what they should be. People weren't performing up to their capacity. Their gifts weren't being fulfilled. They were doing futile tasks, emptying water right back into the places they had bailed. Year after year the church was married to a calendar—from Christmas to Easter to Vacation Bible School—but what new things were accomplished? What milestones had First Church passed? Perhaps the institution was sinking under its own worthy endeavors. . . . What a horrifying thought! This dream could be a nightmare.

Then he considered that it might be based on reality. A new roof had been put on the nave after an impressive fund-raising campaign. Was it holding? The janitor had seen no signs of leaks during the day, but perhaps they had appeared during the night. Maybe the buckets were overflowing right now. Sometimes dreams were painfully literal.

Pastor Bob got up from his bed and pulled a pair of jeans out of a bureau drawer. In the dark he fished his tennis shoes out of the bottom of his closet. He pulled a sweat shirt over his T-shirt and tied on his shoes without socks.

"Where are you going?" his wife asked, half-awake. She was used to him being called out at all hours of the night to a hospital emergency room or to the home of an unprepared widow. Usually the event began with an unexpected phone call, but tonight there had been no telephone ring or knock at the door. Pastor Bob had gotten up of his on accord, awakened by his dream.

"I'm going over to the church," he said. "I want to check on the roof."

"Okay," she said drowsily. In their marital division of

labor, she let him do the worrying. "Don't get too wet," she said before rolling over.

"I won't," he replied.

The manse was separated from the church by a wide parking lot, symbolic of the barrier between the pastor's private and public life. Most of the congregation respected his privacy. When his children were in high school, he would appear at Friday evening football games and sit in the stands rooting for the home team—rooting for his cheerleader daughter or benchwarming son—his neck empty of his clerical collar. Once a year he was asked to give the invocation at the annual awards dinner, but otherwise he was just another dad.

As he walked toward First Church, he hunched his shoulders against the rain. Water came in wide rivers rolling down the expanse of asphalt in the parking lot. The drain at one end of the lot was clogged so a small pond was forming, turning the curb around a carob tree into an island. Bob blinked his eyes against the rain. It wasn't that the drops were so large now, it was that they were constant. He lowered his head and walked on, dodging the deeper puddles.

If he'd been less successful as a preacher, maybe he'd have been a better servant of God. Was his public speaking an extraordinary waste of time? he wondered. When he took his annual summer vacation he'd make a resolve to refuse all speaking invitations that took him away from First Church. But then a parishioner from the Ladies' Guild or a big donor to the capital campaign would ask him to address the Daughters of the American Revolution or the Rotary Club. And in the back of his mind he knew that his buildings needed to be heated and his secretary had to be paid and the roof of the sanctuary had to be secure. So he accepted the speaking engagements.

He thought of the homeless man he'd spoken to that afternoon. Poor in material goods but seemingly rich in faith. Burning up with the newly discovered gospel. Why couldn't he have that same zeal? Had he lost it in all the works required of him? In all the responsibilities of the pastorate? *Father, renew the fire of the gospel in me*, he prayed.

The bald trunks of the palm trees were black from the rain that had soaked them on all sides. The wind from the storm had come from all corners. To Bob's irritation he noticed that one of the sprinklers in the side lawn was on. Either the pipe was broken or the timer had still gone off, regardless of the rainstorm. He made a mental note to tell Lurlene to have Harold check on the sprinklers near the third grade Sunday school rooms. What a waste of water. Water shouldn't be wasted. That was what stewardship was about. The careful marshaling of resources. Being careful with what God has given us.

Light from the sanctuary streamed through the stained-glass window at the front of the church. Lighting that window was one of the first things he had done at First Church. He wanted to have light shining from the church in the evening, even if no one was in the building. *"Our light shall be a beacon to this community,"* he had preached. Figuratively and literally. Lurlene could check, but as best he could remember, the sermon had been called "Beacon of Faith." As a practical demonstration he saw that the lights would shine there every night. *"People will know us for our faith. They will flock to us for our light. They will see us in the darkness of their needs."*

Standing under the awning at the side door, he escaped the rain for the first time. It splashed on the flagstone courtyard, spilling over the eaves. He thought he'd asked the janitor to make sure the gutters were clean. Or had more leaves clogged them up again? He felt as though he were behind a waterfall, watching the water tumble before him. Fishing in his pocket, he took out his set of keys. He turned the key in the lock and pushed open the door, flicking on the light switches.

He loved being alone in the church. Once again Scripture invaded his mind. "*Where two or three are gathered together in my name* . . ." Christ might have made that promise, but Pastor Bob felt His presence best when he was in the sanctuary on his own, alone. He walked up to the chancel and looked to the high wall over the altar. He craned his neck, gazing at the vaulted ceiling. He could see no moisture or drips. He felt his way to one of the choir stalls. Nothing was damp. He returned to the center of the chancel.

Here was the spot where he celebrated communion once a month. Here he stood over the small cups of grape juice and the bread cut into edible bites and said, "This is my body which is given for you; this do in remembrance of me." How could he ever complain about his vocation when it was his privilege to say those words? How could he not feel like the luckiest man in the world?

He turned now to the empty church and said those words to himself, holding his arms aloft. Spreading God's love. Feeling in his own body the sacrificial nature of God's love. Filling himself up with faith. *Thank you, God, thank you.*

That was when he saw the body.

It was spread flat-out on the floor like a corpse on a

coroner's stainless steel table. *A dead body,* he thought. *A corpse in the aisle. A murdered man on the floor at First Church.*

Then he looked again. No, the man wasn't dead. The figure was breathing. The hands were clutched at the chest like a bow on a package. The hands rose and fell as the man inhaled and exhaled. He was sleeping. He was actually sleeping in the sanctuary on a wet, stormy night. Who was he? How had he gotten in?

Pastor Bob walked down the steps and up the center aisle so he could look at the man's face. At once he recognized it. It was the homeless stranger, the same man he had listened to that afternoon. The man would have come up from the shelter. The door was open; there were no locks. He had found his way here. The tanned, lined, weathered face looked rested, relaxed, at peace.

Bob leaned down so he could whisper, "Wake up. You need to go back downstairs. No sleeping allowed up here." He was going to tap on the man's shoulder. But as he looked at the man's face, another image came to his mind. What was it?

He had seen this man before, many years before. In different circumstances. He knew this man. Liked him. Counseled him. What was his name? Where had they met? When Bob subtracted the deep lines and white hair, he saw a younger face, a more confident, unwearied one. But whose?

CHAPTER 17

FROM THEIR TRUNCATED CANDLELIGHT DINNER at the romantic riverside restaurant, Jonathan and Janice drove up the cliff on a narrow asphalt road and stared down into the now raging torrent. The sound was incredible, a roar like the rushing winds of an unleashed tornado.

"I'm sorry we had to leave so fast," Janice said.

"It's not your fault," Jonathan responded. "That restaurant was a bad place for me to pick on the night of a rainstorm."

"No, I'm thinking of what I did. I shouldn't have been so hasty. I should have put two and two together."

In her short career as a newspaper reporter, Janice had found herself in situations that seemed dangerous. Reporting a story about drug dealers infiltrating the schools, she had bravely knocked at the front door of a crack dealer in a rundown apartment building, then stood to the side so as not to get bumped off by an imagined hailstorm of bullets coming out through the door. The dealer had previously promised to give her some tips for a story. That day her heart had been pounding so hard she could hardly hear her questions shouted through the closed apartment door. Any minute she expected to be surrounded by a dozen semiautomatic weapons. Scared out of her wits, she had scribbled down a few sentences in her notebook. Finally she realized that the supposed informant was too stoned to give any reliable answers. Trembling, she had given up and returned to her car, sighing with relief.

That had been a life-threatening situation, but this felt dangerous too. Everything that came to her mind to say to Jonathan was emotionally dangerous.

"We're never going to make it in time," she sighed.

"This is as fast as I can go."

"I wish you had told me about your mother, that Lurlene was your mother. . . ."

"I didn't realize it was so urgent."

As they slogged through the rain, Jonathan decided he deserved an explanation, but it would have to wait. For now he concentrated on driving. He was grateful that he'd bought new windshield wipers and the car had good visibility. Hugging the inside of the cliff, he prayed they wouldn't hit a slick spot and fall off the edge. He couldn't remember how many miles he would have to go to get out of the canyon, but it was not a remote, untraveled area. Houses, some on stilts and others behind high retaining walls, rose above him and across the canyon. On a clear evening cliff-dwelling homes with million-dollar views shone like fireflies among the scrub oak and eucalyptus.

He hoped Janice would explain what was on her mind. "What is it you wanted to tell me?" he asked.

"It has to do with my work," Janice said. "I haven't really described to you what I do."

"No, you haven't."

He turned his head for a moment from the road to look at her briefly. She was staring at the flapping windshield wiper and was biting a fingernail. Suddenly, she shoved her hand into her lap.

"You know I'm a writer," she said.

"That's what you told me."

"But I didn't say where I worked."

"No, you didn't. That's cool. I didn't ask on purpose. I get sick and tired of meeting people who recite their entire resume within five minutes. The next thing they want to tell you is how much money they make. With us it was different. We skipped over that part."

"I *was* going to get around to it."

"You don't have to."

"Jonathan, you don't understand. I *want* to tell you. I *have* to tell you. But now I'm afraid how all this will sound. You'll think I was really conniving–"

"No, I won't. I promise."

"I was writing an article. That's why I talked to your mother. It's just that I never told her what I was doing. I wasn't up front at all."

"So what did you tell her?"

"It's not what I told her. It's what I didn't say. I pretended that I was in search of the perfect man and that I was asking the church to pray for me."

"Which is why you wrote that prayer letter."

"Yes."

Just then a horrifying thought came to Jonathan. He

hardly dared to voice it. She wrote that letter on a whim but was hitched to another guy. Maybe she was already engaged. His heart plummeted. He was steeling his nerves to hear one of those let's-just-be-friends speeches that he knew only too well. Why couldn't she have held off for a moment or two longer? Why did she have to kill the romantic mood?

"Is there someone else?" he asked.

"No, it's not that. There is no other guy."

"You're sure?" He wasn't altogether convinced.

"I swear. There really isn't another guy right now. I'm serious. The wording of that letter started out as a lark, but the desire behind it was real. You've got to believe me. I didn't make up that part. I'd been looking for a guy like the one I described." She paused.

"So what's wrong?" He stared at the road and rain, glad to have an excuse not to look at her.

"What I have to explain . . ." she went on, then hesitated.

"What is it?"

"It's like this. . . ."

Janice got no further with her sentence because at that moment a pair of blinking red lights appeared in front of them. A car with its emergency blinkers. As they approached, a figure in white stepped out and began waving frantically.

"Who's that?" Janice asked.

"I don't know," Jonathan said, slowing down. He stopped beside the stranded motorist.

"*Grazie, grazie, grazie*," the man exclaimed in a loud voice, leaning over into their window. "I am so glad you come for me." It was the chef from the restaurant.

"Can we help you?" Jonathan asked.

"*Madonna santa*, I have terrible problem. My car is dead.

Morto. It doesn't go backward; it doesn't go forward. It goes nowhere. And the rain comes down. *Piove.* It is so wet, maybe the engine is wet. Maybe it is flooded. All the time I think of my wife, my daughter. *La moglie, la ragazza.*" Here his big brown eyes flooded with tears.

"Can we give you a lift?"

"You do that?"

How can we not? Jonathan thought. It would be cruelty on a night like this to leave the man to wait for a police officer. He could be waiting all night.

"Of course," Janice said.

"Of course," Jonathan said.

"*Che gentilezza! Che bellezza!* I sit here and pray that someone come to my rescue. Someone finally come down this road and take me to my family." He ran back to his car and brought a bag of bread. "Leftovers," he explained. "*Panne.*" Then he locked his car and got in the backseat of the Toyota.

Jonathan continued driving slowly up the hill.

"You are the couple from the restaurant!" the chef observed.

"Yes, we are," Jonathan replied.

"I am Pietro," he said.

Jonathan and Janice introduced themselves.

"Now I am more sorry. You never got to eat my magnificent dessert creation. It is a *zabaglione* with pistachio nuts. You must come back."

"That's all right," Janice said. "I've eaten there before."

"You have?" Jonathan said.

"You have?" Pietro repeated. Then he leaned forward and peered from over the backseat at Janice. "I know you! You are the young girl from the newspaper."

"You are?" Jonathan asked.

"You are the young girl who writes about me. *Che bella!* What a nice story you say. You show Pietro in his genius as a cook. One of the greatest. You show a picture of me in the kitchen. I like the article so much I keep it in my wallet." He dug in his back pocket and took out a much folded clipping from his billfold.

"This is what I was trying to tell you," Janice said to Jonathan.

"You're a reporter?"

"Yes," she said. "For the *Herald News*."

"She is brilliant. Look at the things she say about Pietro." He quoted phrases from the story that he had underlined. " 'An extraordinary Italian chef bringing out-of-the-ordinary cuisine to our town.' That is wisdom. That is a very smart girl. You are a lucky man," he said to Jonathan.

"That's why we need to hurry back," Janice said, staring mournfully at the rain.

"You'd better explain," Jonathan said.

"With Pietro here?" Janice asked.

"He won't mind." And in fact, Pietro appeared engrossed in the story that she had written about him in the *Herald News*.

"It's really the whole reason we're together," she said. "The letter, the article I was writing, First Church. It all started with the newspaper."

"Please explain." Jonathan had the sinking feeling that the evening was ruined, that this woman next to him had taken him for a ride.

Lurlene woke up at 1:00 A.M. and knew that her son wasn't home. She woke up again at 2:10 and didn't even have to check his room to know he wasn't there. When she woke up for the third time, at 3:12, she got out of bed and went to the living room, picked up the unfinished crossword puzzle and sat in the Barcalounger, staring at the correct answers she had already written in. She had given up smoking before her son was born, but now she wished she could smoke.

She knew several things could have happened. Jonathan and Janice could have gone back to her apartment. They could have stayed at the restaurant, talking until all hours of the night—if there was a restaurant or bar in town that stayed open this late. Or they could have been trapped by the flooding waters somewhere.

She looked down to some cross-hatching she had made in the margin of the puzzle next to the word "tern." This was a stage of parenting that she had assumed would be easy. No diapers to change, no homework to monitor, no school dances to chaperone. In those tough days when Jonathan was five or six and had started asking all those questions about his father—*"When is he coming home? Where has he gone? Doesn't he love me?"*—Lurlene promised herself if she could just get by the early years, things would start getting easier. She wouldn't be saddled with the debts of an irresponsible man. She would be able to afford something better than tuna surprise or macaroni and cheese. Those days when she could show no anger, when she had to maintain to her son the fiction that his father was a good man who loved him, she promised herself that when her son was grown, life would be a piece of cake.

These were the days life was supposed to be easier. With

Jonathan earning his own money, Lurlene could afford a few luxuries—new pillows for the sofa, 200-point cotton sheets, a set of thick towels. She had finally bought a dishwasher after years of explaining, "I have the best dishwasher in town: my son!" She tried to pretend that her husband was someone she'd never really known. A total stranger.

She had sold his suits on consignment, put his trophies and photos in a box, shelved it on top of a chest in the garage, and put him out of her mind. Enough of him. But he still appeared in her dreams. She couldn't do anything about that. *He was my only mistake*, she had told herself again and again. *I won't make another one.*

But where was her son? Where was Jonathan?

When she had worried about Jonathan as a youngster, the worries took a tangible shape. He might break an arm at school. He might come down with a case of the measles. He might get the flu. But now, when there was some breathing room in her life, she could only fantasize about more serious scenarios. The disasters could be much worse. The stakes had gone up. The mistakes of a ten-, twelve-, or fifteen-year-old seemed tame compared to the trouble a twenty-three-year-old could get into. Trouble that could last his whole life long. A mess that could stall him forever. He could make one terrible choice and be stuck for life. The thought came to her. *As stuck as I was.*

Lurlene picked up the remote control on the TV and flipped the stations to get a weather update. Great patches of white cotton swirled in circular shapes over the bright green map of California. A mustachioed man gestured at it with a stick like a teacher in a one-room schoolhouse. White letters marched across the bottom of the screen alerting citizens in mountainous areas to watch out for mudslides and rockslides. Forest fires in the summer, landslides in the winter, it was as though California tried to make up for its wonderful temperate climate with short, dramatic, Hollywood-like disasters. Cram the turbulence of Mother Nature into one brief, spectacular appearance before resuming normalcy. The voice-over cranked up the urgency of the event with commentary, always in the conditional tense because what might be is always more compelling than that which is—in this case, a devastating rainfall. The man in the white mustache said, "They're saying this could be the worst winter storm in decades."

What might be . . . what could be. She knew people who lived their whole lives in the conditional tense, always dreaming about what was possible. *Not me*, she said to herself. Not Lurlene Scott. Maybe once she'd been that way. But now she was grounded in the present tense.

Except . . . when it came to her son. She put the rainstorm out of her mind and started imagining, as she often did. What would he become? Someday he would startle the world. Puppets? Those were only a start. He would write plays and screenplays and entertain talk-show hosts with his wit, using the puppets in bright sophisticated ways that would dazzle his audiences. TV would discover him, and movies too. Or perhaps it would be on computer . . . she didn't know. He would make millions of dollars and move out of their little brick house with the white picket fence, and when people walked by it they would comment, *"That's where Jonathan Scott grew up. He used to live there."* She had great dreams for him.

As long as he's happy in his love life, she told herself. With a secure marriage and a wife who adored him, he could take on the world. His mate would be beautiful, smart, sensitive, and caring, and she would be his partner in all his enterprises. Understanding, encouraging. Was that so much to ask? Was this begging for too much?

Lurlene could picture their relationship from a handful of couples she watched at church. The men and women who assisted each other in every social venture, the wives were independent organizers, the husbands were successful businessmen, and if they were at opposite ends of a living room during a party they seemed connected by an imaginary strand. They sprinkled references to each other in their conversation, or more likely they were so secure and happy in their spouses they didn't even need to brag. They were the world to each other. *That's what I want for Jonathan*, she thought. *It's all I'd wished for myself.*

Instead, she had been swept off her feet. No time for wishing. Her husband was not the man of any dream she'd had, because she hadn't dared to imagine that a fast-talking, hard-drinking, strong-limbed traveling salesman would woo her and win her, going against all her level-headed reasoning. If he had fallen for some other woman, she would have been the first to warn her, *"You'll pay for this."* Now she had only herself to blame. She had disregarded her own best judgment. In a momentary lapse she had ignored her inner voice. Any woman less sensible would have been less disappointed. If she were proved wrong, it would have been one thing, but being proved right was terrible. She would never forgive herself for that.

As she watched the TV and listened to the weather, she wondered what her husband looked like now. How had he aged? Was he bald, fat, stoop-shouldered, white-haired? In their courtship days she had enjoyed the attention he attracted from other women. When he walked through a restaurant, she watched the admiring gazes and appreciated the moment the looks arrived back at her. She had won the prize, reversing the logic of school gossip. The good girl, the silent one, the winner of the typing ribbon and the scholarship to business college had hooked the man about town, convincing him—so it seemed—to settle down.

In the bright glare of the TV and through the drone of the weather broadcaster, Lurlene had to admit that she had never forgiven herself for her husband's abandonment of her. She knew it was not her fault. It was his. But she found it impossible to focus her anger on him. If she had done something different, if she had handled herself differently, would things have turned out the same way? People were always praying at church for changes in their lives. *This I can't change*, she thought. It was done. Irrevocable.

With these old thoughts running through her tired mind, she fell asleep on the Barcalounger.

After several hours the phone rang, waking her. The rain was still coming down, and a hint of light could be seen in the gray sky. Lurlene opened her eyes and made her way across the room. She picked up the phone, fearing the worst. Jonathan's body had been found floating facedown in a storm drain above the arroyo. Or his car was discovered floating in the river, no sign of any passengers. His corpse had already floated out to the Pacific Ocean, and a tuna boat on a fishing expedition had picked it up.

"Hello," she answered.

"Is this the home of Jonathan Scott?" a woman asked.

"Yes, it is. This is his mother." Her stomach churned. She prepared herself to hear the worst. But first she would repeat her identity. There was great pleasure and power in those words. However Lurlene might have failed in her life, she could claim success in her son. "I'm Jonathan's mother."

There was a pause on the other line, then the speaker continued. "Mrs. Scott, this is Shelly Warner. I'm Janice Ascher's roommate. I'm worried about Janice. She went out with Jonathan last night and hasn't come back yet. Is she there?"

"No. She's not." Lurlene's heart skipped a beat.

"Do you have any idea where they went?"

"No. I'm afraid I don't. Jonathan doesn't usually tell me where he's going. I knew he was going on a date, but I didn't know where."

"Does he have a favorite place?"

"I don't know. He tells me what he wants, but I don't usually ask." Lurlene looked at her watch. It was a little after six o'clock, and no word from her son. "It's much later than I thought. Do you have any ideas of where they might be?"

"Would they have gone to see some friend of his?"

"No. I don't think so." Not without calling. Not without alerting her to where he was.

"Does he usually stay out this late?"

"I don't clock him, but if he's going to be out all night, he lets me know."

"Then I think one of us had better call the police."

"Or both of us." *The woman is right,* Lurlene thought, *Jonathan must be in some terrible trouble.* She had to let the authorities know.

"You tell them what his car looked like and when he left and where you think he might have been going," Shelly said.

"I'll do that. Give me your phone number. I'll call you after I've spoken to the police." Lurlene stepped into her efficient mode. This was how she ran the pastor's office. She was never afraid to make difficult phone calls. Where others hesitated, she got things done. It was a relief to reassume that no-nonsense personality. The one thing that silenced all worries. "Let me get a piece of paper."

Shelly started reciting the number, which Lurlene recorded in a corner of the now finished crossword puzzle.

"I'll get back to you as soon as I find out anything," Lurlene reiterated and hung up the phone.

CHAPTER 18

"SO YOU WORK FOR the *Herald News*?" Jonathan said. "My mom always does the crossword puzzle in the *News*."

He was desperately trying to make the conversation seem normal. She was a newspaper writer, she'd written a prayer letter about meeting Mr. Right, and she was very anxious about an article that was scheduled for publication soon. What was it that was so terrible? Why did he have this foreboding?

"What's your beat?" he asked, wracking his brain, trying to remember if he'd seen Janice's byline with any stories.

"I've done everything since I've been there. I started out writing wedding announcements. I enjoyed that, although the mothers of the brides could be a real pain."

"What do you do now?"

"Sometime she write about brilliant Italian cook!" Pietro muttered from the backseat.

"When I'm lucky, I write local feature stories.

Things we don't pick up on any wire service. My editor gives us a lot of room if we prove that we can come up with a good angle on something interesting.'' Janice took a deep breath. ''So I was writing a story about prayer. It wasn't going to be only about First Church, but the church ended up filling a major part of it. Several people suggested I check out the prayer letters. I wanted to do something thoughtful. Not a hatchet job. Nobody wants to hear anything nasty about a church unless it's really juicy, like a minister embezzling millions and then running off to the Bahamas with his secretary.''

''My mom is not going anywhere with Pastor Bob.'' Jonathan attempted to keep the conversation light. ''If anything, they're like a married couple forty years after the honeymoon.''

''Your mother was very helpful,'' Janice said, ignoring the joke. ''And that's what bothers me. I don't think she ever realized that I was a reporter. I'd called earlier to interview the pastor, and I spoke to her briefly, but when I called about the prayer letter, she had no idea of my hidden agenda.''

Suddenly the picture of what she had done was coming clearer, and his part in it. ''Wait a minute,'' Jonathan said. ''Wasn't I part of this hidden agenda?''

''No, not exactly.''

''You wrote your prayer letter because of the article?''

''Yes, at first. That's why I started it. That's why I put those things down and sent them off.''

He felt duped, naive. He had believed her, fallen for it, and believed that she had fallen for him. ''So what am I? Just a bit of research?''

''Not at all.''

"Is this whole date a continuation of the series? Janice Ascher exploring prayer possibilities?"

"No, no. Please don't say that. It's not true." She put her hand on his forearm.

"Does anyone want some bread?" Pietro asked from the back. He'd opened his bag of fresh bread and was ripping off a piece.

"No, thank you," Jonathan and Janice said in unison.

"*Va bene*," Pietro said.

"I didn't think I was going to like you so much when we first met," Janice stated. "I thought maybe you could tell me things . . . for the article."

"So I *was* research. . . ."

"Maybe it started out that way, but it didn't stay there. I wouldn't have come out with you tonight if it was just for the story. When I met you at Rene's, I didn't really think it would get this far. But we kept talking, and you called me back. . . ."

The rain was coming down so hard Jonathan didn't dare look away from the road, but he also wanted to see her face, to look into those eyes and know she was sincere. "I suppose I should be flattered. Being used by a beautiful girl."

"The person I've really used wasn't you. It was your mother. I was so amazed, so surprised by her response to my prayer request. I wrote the letter expecting a form letter back, you know, 'We were grateful for your letter, and now we have remembered you in prayer. Blah, blah, blah.' I didn't expect to be given the suggestion of a man to fill my dreams. I didn't expect anything practical."

"Excuse me," Pietro said from the backseat. "This is very *romantico*, no?"

"I didn't expect much either when my mother suggested

I go out with you," Jonathan said, ignoring the Italian chef.

"But there's a major difference here," Janice said. "You haven't written about it."

"Have *you?*"

"Yes," she said, "that's what's so horrible. I put all this down in a story for the paper. It's supposed to run tomorrow."

"What do you mean?"

"Your mother is right there in the opening paragraph for all to read about. The senior pastor's secretary running a dating service. 'And you thought all they did was pray at First Church.' "

"You didn't say that, did you?"

"It's pretty close. It was such a great lead, I couldn't resist it. You've got to understand. I didn't know she was your mother then."

"Would that have made any difference?" Jonathan asked.

"Of course, it would," Janice said. "I would have been more careful."

"You know she could get axed for doing something like this."

"Oh no! I feel awful."

"I'm not saying it wasn't a stupid thing for her to do. I can't really defend her. But it shouldn't be publicized. No one should have to find out about it."

"That's a mama," Pietro said. "A mama is good. A mama helps her son."

"Look, it was a lovely thing for her to do," Janice said. "It was kind and considerate. I know she meant it honestly. She's your mother. She worries about you."

"You've got to stop the story from running."

"I wish I could. But the longer it takes us to get home . . ."

"Pastor Bob will flip when he sees the story. Half the congregation will freak out. Mom will flip out."

"Jonathan, I'm sorry. I'm really sorry. If a journalist ever calls you up and says she wants to do a profile of you, say no. No good can come of it. Writers are always using their subjects in the worst possible way. I'm sorry. I'm really sorry."

"I guess the most that we can do now is get to Mom before the paper does. At least we can prepare her."

"I'd like to be the first to apologize. If I'd only known that she was your mother."

"If only she hadn't responded to your prayer letter that way."

There was a pause. "Do you really mean it?"

For a fraction of a second, Jonathan took his eyes away from the road and glanced at Janice. She was studying him so carefully, pleading with her gaze. If his mother had never written that letter, he would never have met her and the two of them wouldn't be sitting in this car together.

"No," Jonathan said. "I don't want her to get in trouble. But meeting you was the best thing that could have happened to me."

Jonathan could have said more except at that moment the headlights of the Toyota flashed on a massive mound of brown earth and white boulders. Beyond it they could see the road climbing uphill, but it halted at this mud and rock dump, the black asphalt and the white lines disappearing beneath the dirt. Nature reverting to nature. It was too steep to climb and too big to go around.

Jonathan stopped the car about fifteen feet from the landslide. "I don't think we're going any farther this way." He craned his neck around, checking behind him. "And I don't want to turn around. The road is too narrow."

"What's wrong?" Pietro asked.

"Is it worth backing down?" Janice asked.

"I can try going a little way," Jonathan said as he put the car in reverse. He backed down, looking more carefully at the hillside on his right. He wanted to find a spot where it didn't look threatening, where the slope was not so steep. But in the dark, in the rain, he could see nothing. "I can't see anything," he said.

"I never see my *famiglia*," Pietro moaned. "They worry. They don't know what happen to Pietro."

"I'm sorry."

"Any side roads where we can turn off?" Janice asked.

"Nothing that would take us out of the canyon."

"We be here all the night! *Tutta la notte*."

"What's downhill?"

"The river."

"Back by the restaurant?"

"Yes."

"So we're stuck."

"Pretty much." As if to confirm their marooned state, Jonathan stopped the car at a place where the hill wrinkled enough to hold a wild oak and two sycamores. It seemed as secure a spot as any. He turned off the engine.

"I feel terrible," Janice said. "I wanted to change the lead to the story."

"About Mom?"

"The mama is good," Pietro reiterated.

She glanced at her watch and pushed a button that made

the face illuminate, lighting up her face. "It's too late anyway."

Jonathan turned off the headlights and put on his red hazard lights so that he could be spotted by anyone coming up the road. It would be a long time before they were found. If the rain stopped or when the sun came up, it might be worth walking or he could try driving again. But for now, it was best to stay quiet in the car.

The last hour had been such a roller coaster of emotions. Discovering what Janice did and why she wrote the letter. Worrying about his mother and what would happen to her when the story came out. Determining whether he could trust the beautiful woman sitting next to him. Coping with the rain and the road.

"This isn't what I expected tonight," he said.

"I know," Janice replied.

If only she would turn the light of her watch on again so he could gaze at her face. Then he could see what she was thinking. He would know if she really meant what was in that letter.

"You've got to tell me one thing," he suddenly said.

"What's that?"

"You've got to promise me that the letter you sent to First Church wasn't all a hoax. You've got to tell me that you meant it. That it was true."

At that Janice closed her eyes and began quoting: " 'Six foot two, dark hair, a love of laughter, great sensitivity, mid-twenties to early thirties. . . . My best friend said to aim high. I'm aiming high. Pray that I don't become bitter and small-minded. Pray that I don't become desperate either, like some women I know. And pray that I'll recognize this Prince

Charming when I meet him.' "

"Your letter."

"I don't usually remember things that aren't important to me."

"It was that important?"

"Yes. Not just another work assignment."

Jonathan stared straight ahead, telling himself that he could believe her. It had to be true. The attraction between them wasn't something he was making up. She had to know it too. He opened his mouth to say something when Pietro spoke.

"Here we are stuck in a car all night long. We do something. We make the time go by. Anything."

Jonathan swung his head around and looked at the Italian chef stretched out on the backseat, his head resting against one door, his feet up on the other one.

"What did you have in mind?"

"We play games. You know any games to play?"

The mood was broken. It wasn't just the two of them in the car; there were three. They would have to do something that involved all three of them. Jonathan wracked his brain for something amusing. "Have you ever played 'They're Making a Movie of Your Life and Who's Going to Be in It'?" he asked.

"No." Pietro said.

"What is it?" Janice asked.

"It's a game I used to play with my friends. You try to cast your life story."

"How?"

"By answering this question: If someone was going to make a movie of the story of your life, who would you choose to play you?"

CHAPTER 19

THE HEADLINES IN Wednesday's *Herald News* were mostly about the Southland's devastating storm. Photos carried pictures of raging rivers, closed mountain passes, and highways blanketed with rockslides. There was a particularly vivid shot of a cantilevered house that had slid fifty yards down a hill, taking up residence in a neighbor's pool. The governor declared a state of emergency in six counties, and there was talk of the president flying in by helicopter to promise aid—it was an election year.

State officials made statements about temporary housing, low-interest loans, and guarantees to clear up roads as soon as possible. There would be bond issues for better dams in the foothills and petitions for guardrails against landslides and rockslides. Environmentalists would blame developers, and developers would point the finger at firefighters, who had been slow in responding to a brushfire in September when the Santa Ana wind had swooped down from the desert. If the soil hadn't been scorched—if it had been covered with vegetation—it wouldn't have tumbled onto the road under the onslaught of rain. "The storm was caused by global warming," stated one op-ed pundit. "Mudslides are part of our ecology," a scientist said, taking an unpopular stand. "We have to make sure a disaster like this never happens again," a bureaucrat from the Department of Water and Energy said, preferring not to call it an act of God.

For the newspaper reader who was weary of the weather, there were other stories, including a long feature piece headlining Section B called "The Amazing Power of Prayer." Beneath it was a picture of Pastor Bob and two ladies—Helen and Doris—in the room upstairs, and the caption read, "First Church marshals its forces in a room devoted to prayer."

The article opened by saying, "Some of our area churches not only make prayer a part of their service to the community, but they make sure people's prayers are answered. Not long ago a young woman wrote an anonymous letter to First Church with a prayer request to meet the right man. To her surprise she received a letter back recommending the perfect mate. . . ."

Wrapped in a plastic bag, this newspaper was dropped off at various driveways in the neighborhood of First Church. In one or two gutters it created a dam, slowing the water en route to the storm drains. At other driveways it fell on top of torn tree limbs, seedpods, acorns, and other debris. At several houses the newspaper carrier had sailed the paper over fallen trees so that it landed neatly on the porch, offering the only welcome news to residents guessing the cost of cutting up giant pines. At Pastor Bob's house the newspaper had taken a perfect flight and landed on the front path, only a foot away from the steps.

Dressed in her favorite pink terrycloth bathrobe, Mary Lou Dudley tiptoed outside in her slippers and picked up the newspaper. Normally she read the front page on her way back in—an unexamined newspaper was not worth picking up. Today she found herself doused by the water that had collected on top of the plastic bag. Holding the bag at arm's length, she shook it in the air as though it were a soggy head of lettuce, then slipped off the plastic and left it to dry like an umbrella by the doorway. Skipping the stories of mudslides and rockslides, she turned to Section B. There she saw her husband's picture.

This in itself was not unusual. Pastor Bob had made plenty of appearances in the press. Mary Lou could usually make some wry comment about his sanctimonious expression and give an argument for a better haircut. It was only when she started reading the article that she chuckled to herself and then frowned. *The woman who proved to be especially helpful was the pastor's secretary, Ms. Lurlene Scott. "This is what we do here at First Church," she explained. "Prayer is practical." And she was to show that through her action.*

"Bob," Mary Lou called from the vestibule. "I think you'd better see this." She knew he was doing his morning devotions in his home office, reading his Bible and praying. She didn't like to interrupt, but this was important.

Her slippers flapping against the hardwood floor, she made her way to the pastor's library and knocked on the open door. "You should see this," Mary Lou said. "It looks like Lurlene has overstepped the boundaries of her job."

Pastor Bob looked up from his desk. He'd just shaved and

was still wearing a glob of gel on his left ear. In a subtle gesture of ownership, Mary Lou wiped the spot off with a corner of her bathrobe as she handed her husband the paper. "I didn't read the whole thing," she said, "but it isn't a very flattering portrait of Lurlene."

Thoughtfully, deliberately, Pastor Bob spread the story out on his desk and read it very carefully, top to bottom. He would return to his prayers later. After years of experience he knew his wife wouldn't interrupt unless something was urgent. And even if it didn't seem urgent to him, he knew his wife well enough to accept her judgment of these things. She left him in silence.

The press could not always be trusted. Often they made mistakes. In his early days, Pastor Bob had courted publicity, certain that it would bring more members into the church. After a while, he became wary of it. He had never once read an article where he sounded like himself, where he was quoted accurately and in context, or where his work was given its full due. Writers either gushed or sneered. They rarely understood the struggle of faith. They were either cynical doubters or sentimentalists searching for the next Mother Teresa. It was not surprising that Christ urged his disciples to keep quiet about the miracles He performed. Publicity could not be trusted. Pastor Bob treated it as a necessary evil.

The paragraphs about Lurlene puzzled him. At first he didn't believe them. The reporter probably misunderstood. Or Lurlene was putting something over on the writer. Lurlene knew the importance of confidentiality in regard to the prayer letters. She wouldn't have broken a writer's trust.

But as he read further, he was struck by a sense of the

writer's dignity and interest. Almost despite herself, the article writer seemed won over by the idea of intercessory prayer. Her opening tone betrayed her original intent to be mildly amused, but somewhere in the body of the story, she had changed her mind. At the end she didn't gush, but she seemed to be on the lookout, as though this was the first in a series. The first step in her spiritual journey. She was searching for something. Maybe she'd found it.

Bob's pastoral instinct was to point her to the words of Doubting Thomas. *"I believe; help thou my unbelief."*

But then Pastor Bob started thinking about how this news could affect the church. That his loyal, dependable secretary had violated a cardinal rule of confidentiality. That she had actually attempted some matchmaking. This would not be helpful to First Church's mission. He had better do some damage control. Who would have read the story? What did they think? Did it make the prayer ministry look ludicrous? Why had Lurlene done it—if she did?

It was a completely atypical gesture for Lurlene, but Pastor Bob had heard enough guilt-ridden confessions in his paneled office that he'd come to accept one tenet of human behavior: The most disciplined, unswerving individuals can make the most unexpected detours. He'd listened to steadfast husbands who had found themselves in motel rooms at four o'clock in the afternoon with the wrong women. Brilliant executives could sabotage their careers with a single display of poor judgment. Lurlene had been so devoted, so hardworking, and so single-minded in her job that it was a wonder she hadn't cracked earlier. For the umpteenth time Pastor Bob decided that Lurlene needed a vacation.

Now he eyed the blinking red light on his telephone

answering machine. When he had come home from his late-night visit to the church, he had turned off the sound so he could sleep a few minutes more. And when he had awakened to say his prayers, he had noticed that a few messages had come in, but he told himself they could wait until he read his three psalms. He had a talented staff that could handle most any crisis. He had learned in his leadership role that if he occasionally made himself unavailable, others would rise to the need. With a sigh, he pressed the replay button and took out a pen to write down any essential phone numbers. The most damaging messages he would remember.

The first was from a stockbroker parishioner, an early riser who made a habit of being in his office before the New York Stock Exchange opened, anytime before six o'clock California time. "So, Pastor Bob, since when have we started a dating service?"

Mary Lou had often wondered why they couldn't have an unlisted phone number. Pastor Bob said it was like wearing a clerical collar or placing a cross outside the church. It gave the desperate a place to turn when they needed help—even if they had to speak to an answering machine.

The second call was from an older trustee. "Good morning, Bob. Sorry to call so early, but I wanted to make sure you saw today's newspaper story." The man had a profound grasp of the obvious. "The picture looks very good. I'm sure the article will bring more requests for prayer." Not an alarmist, he saw no problem. There were two calls from ladies who prayed, early morning walkers who were homebound this morning and quick to read the paper. Both of them wanted to know if Lurlene had been authorized to do what she had done and if this was a new policy for answering prayer letters. "Perhaps we should try making practical suggestions like hers," one lady said.

There was one hang-up, and one call from an obviously drunk woman, who spoke in a sultry, slurred voice. "Pastor, you don't have a prayer of a chance with me," she purred into the phone and then cackled.

In the midst of his listening, Bob heard the doorbell ring. Mary Lou would answer it since this was his prayer time. Bob could hear the sound of a female voice, the shaking of an umbrella, and the stamping of boots. "He's in the study," Mary Lou was saying as her footsteps approached. "You know I don't like to interrupt him when he's praying, but I do understand."

"It's urgent," the visitor replied, and he recognized immediately who it was. Of course she would come over right away. Naturally she would want to smooth everything out, make the best of it. And she would look for his absolution and forgiveness. But what if she tried to quit instead?

Silently daring the two women to interrupt him, Bob kept his back to the door, his fingers on his Bible. He closed his eyes. *"I will lift up mine eyes unto the hills, from whence cometh my help."*

"Bob," the familiar voice said.

The word was filled with anguish, like an animal in pain. He felt very sorry for her.

"Lurlene," he said, turning around to face the door. No "Mrs. Scott." No request for her to wait until he was done. It was clear that she was in great distress. She didn't deserve such sorrow. His pastoral instincts kicked in. He would have to comfort her, reassure her. She was clutching a sodden handkerchief in one hand. She'd bitten off all the lipstick she had put on and tears had smudged her eyeliner.

"This is terrible," she said.

"You'll have to excuse me," Mary Lou said.

Bob stood up from the chair, gestured to the sofa for Lurlene to sit down and took down a box of tissues from a shelf. "It couldn't be all that bad."

"It's terrible," she said, filled with worry for her lost son.

"I'm sure you acted in the best interest. Someone's already called me and said you should even be congratulated for suggesting a new idea."

"New idea?" Lurlene asked, looking up over the top of her glasses.

"It probably would be a good way to get more young people involved at church. You yourself have pointed out that they come because they want to meet members of the opposite sex."

"It's Jonathan," she said.

"Maybe it's not the best motive for anyone to come to church. But it can be a start. You get young people interested, and they'll come back."

"He's lost," she reiterated.

"That's exactly why they need a spiritual home. Much better than hanging out in bars. They should have a safe environment. People like your son. I'm sure he'd be glad to meet a nice woman through the church."

Lurlene's face, the mascara spreading, the lipstick gone, crumpled. She clutched the handkerchief tight in her hand and put her fist to her eyes.

"But that's how it all started," she managed to say. "I set the two of them up."

"Your Jonathan?"

"On the phone. With the young woman."

This was more than Pastor Bob had gleaned from the article. That Lurlene's only son, the tall, good-looking young man had been the suggested date? She had been a matchmaker for him? The concerned, helpful mother; the shy son. Was it possible? "You put the two of them together?" he asked.

Now it was Lurlene's turn to be surprised. "You know about that?" she asked.

"You just said it."

"I suppose I did."

"By now everybody knows, at least the matchmaking. Everybody's read about it."

"Everybody?"

"You mean you haven't seen the newspaper article?"

"No, I haven't had time to read the paper. I've been too upset."

"I'm very sorry, Mrs. Scott. This is not going to make you any happier."

"What newspaper article?"

"Here," he said, handing the paper to her.

Lurlene gasped when she saw the photo and the headline. Horrified, she took the paper out of her boss's hands. Just then the phone rang. Pastor Bob let the answering machine get it, turning down the volume so they wouldn't have to listen to the message.

From her perch on the sofa Lurlene absorbed the article, taking it in a paragraph at a time. She couldn't read something without mentally copy editing it, and so she read carefully, digesting every word, changing a few and modifying some punctuation. It was a way to postpone her anger.

Finally she looked up, bewildered. "I can't believe it! How did she know about that prayer letter and the matchmaking?"

"It must have been a setup. She probably did it herself. Reporters always refer to themselves in the third person."

"I can't believe it was the same woman. I talked to her. I helped her. She was very nice."

"She doesn't sound half-bad," Pastor Bob agreed. "These writers can go either way. Either they're cynical in a dry, tight-lipped way, or they're mushy and sentimental. But this article is thoughtful. Almost generous. She's a good writer."

"She never said she was a reporter."

"You put her right through to me when she called to interview me." Despite himself, Bob wondered why his best lines, his most quotable quotes, weren't in the story. That happened with reporters. Even when you were witty and clever, they never caught your best stuff.

"I didn't realize it was she when she called about the prayer letter."

"When did you first read her prayer letter?"

"That day."

"Which one?"

Lurlene put down the paper and began wringing her handkerchief in a nervous way that made Pastor Bob almost wish he hadn't asked for an explanation. She wound the white square of fabric from both ends, like wringing out a damp towel, then she unwound it again. "It was the day you made me go out for lunch. I decided you were being especially nice to me because something terrible was going to happen. I thought you were going to fire me."

That day, Bob thought. The day he was planning the little

celebration of Lurlene's career at First Church. He was being nice to her. He didn't want her to feel taken for granted. So much for kindness. "I was never thinking of firing you," he said.

"When I was at lunch I saw Jonathan walk by," Lurlene went on. "He stopped and waved at the girl who was my waitress, and it set me thinking about him and the women he went out with. I was feeling helpless—you have children, you know how it is—and wished I could make him happy. When I came back from lunch, I opened the letter. I don't know . . . something came over me. You're always talking about inspiration and the inner voice. I guess I was inspired."

She blew her nose and then grabbed another tissue to wipe her eyes. Jonathan lost, her career ruined—it was too much. "I'm so sorry. I didn't mean for everyone to know about it. I was going to tell you someday. It was just a little thing."

"When did you talk to her?"

"When she called back. After I talked to her, I told my son about her, and they went on a date."

"So you actually matched them up?"

"It seemed so perfect. She sounded even better on the phone than in her letter. I was sure Jonathan would like her. In fact, he's crazy about her. But I didn't know that she was the reporter. I didn't understand that the reporter and the letter writer were the same person." A muffled sob.

"That complicates things."

"It does. It's all wrong. I didn't mean for everyone to know."

"People are going to start wondering if our prayer letters are open to all."

"I didn't want that to happen."

"I know, I know," Pastor Bob replied soothingly.

Suddenly Lurlene's pink-rimmed eyes grew wide, as though something else had just dawned on her. "Oh no. This is terrible!"

"What is?"

"What she did to us."

"In the article?"

"No, not just there. On the phone. She lied to us!"

"I suppose so," the pastor said, for whom lies came in all shades. Fibs to protect feelings, white lies to get out of social obligations, evasions of the truth for expediency's sake. He never lied himself, but he understood why others did it. There was a big realm of forgiveness here. "She probably told herself that it would help her story. People do that."

Lurlene's eyes, which were now quite dry, narrowed. "It does not ingratiate her to me."

"She's probably young."

"You don't understand, Pastor Bob. My son has flipped head over heels for this woman." She checked the byline for the name, just to be sure. *Janice Ascher*. "He thinks Janice Ascher really wanted to meet a fellow like him. He thinks she's a sincere First Church young woman who had a deep, heartfelt prayer."

"Maybe she is."

"She's a phony manipulating him. She's a fake."

"How can you be so sure?"

"She faked that letter, didn't she? She manufactured it from thin air. Now we know. We can read about it in print. Anybody with half a brain can see her callousness. She could break my son's heart, all for a silly newspaper article. I wish

I had never gotten involved. I should have handled her request like all the rest of them. But when you think about it, she's the one who should be upbraided, not me. She's using the church so that she can appear clever."

Pastor Bob grew pensive. "People have always used the church. That's what it's here for."

"She wasted all those prayer ladies' time. Not to mention their prayers."

"I don't believe a prayer can ever be wasted," he said thoughtfully, as though he were quoting from one of his own sermons. "Time in prayer, for whatever purpose, is always well spent."

"The two of them are together. Somewhere. Jonathan went out with her last night, and he never came home. They're lost in the storm. Buried. Drowned."

"Maybe," Pastor Bob said gently, "they're at her place."

"No." Lurlene held up a hand. "That's not true. I've spoken to her roommate. Neither of them have come home. I'm afraid they got caught in the storm somewhere. Somewhere in the flooding or under a landslide. Jonathan is very considerate. He would have called me if he could have found a phone. He wouldn't leave me worrying."

"Do you have any idea where they went?"

"They were going out to dinner. I don't know where, but it could easily have been in the foothills or down at the beach or in one of the canyons. Anywhere. I've got to find him."

"We'll call the police."

Lurlene twisted her handkerchief into the rolled-up towel position, fighting the inclination to ask him to pray. "Do you think they're all right, Pastor Bob?" she asked.

"I sincerely hope so," he said. "I do indeed."

CHAPTER 20

JANICE AND JONATHAN played a few rounds of "They're Making a Movie of Your Life and Who's Going to Be in It" with Pietro, but he kept referring to Italian movies they'd never heard of and Italian actors they didn't know. After that they tried a version of "Name That Tune." Jonathan could stump Janice on movie themes, but she was much better on popular tunes. He could never remember which group was which or what a singer's name was, even if he could put a few words of the tune together. At the same time Pietro tried out opera arias on them, none of which were familiar.

Finally the chef said, "Pietro is very tired. I go to sleep. I say a prayer for the wife, and I say a prayer for the daughter. I pray they no worry about me, *dio buono*." And with that, he curled up on the backseat and closed his eyes.

"Maybe we should try to sleep ourselves," Jonathan whispered. In his mind he was thinking, *What a waste of time that would be. The night is spread out before us. There's no place to go. No one to interrupt us. Now is the time to explore what's happening between us.* Sheets of rain still streaked the windows, but the car was parked in the safest place possible. There was nothing else to do but get to know her better. If the hours stretched into days and the days into years, he felt as though the time would never be long enough to find out all the things he wanted to know.

"I'm not really tired," Janice said.

"Neither am I," he said.

"Should we worry about the weather? It's still raining out there."

"There's really nothing we can do about it. I think we're safe here." He leaned back in his seat and looked up to the stars–the stars that he couldn't see but were somewhere beyond the roof of the car and the thick blanket of clouds that were sending raindrops splattering onto the windshield. If he turned his body on one side and rested his head on his elbow, he could see Janice's profile as she spoke. It was beautiful to him.

"Have you ever wanted to write a novel?" he asked her.

"Sure. Everyone has, I guess. Everyone who writes. I tried several times when I was in seventh grade. I was working on a romance that had some recipes in it. Suspense and science fiction, with a bit of Betty Crocker thrown into it."

"But you don't want to be a novelist now?"

"Maybe ten years from now. Or twenty. Or never. Right now, I want to be good at writing feature stories for a newspaper. That's hard enough."

"Girls are so practical. I think girls are much more practical than guys."

"What about all the guys who go to law school or business

school or the ones becoming accountants and computer technicians? You must know guys like that."

"Yes. But a lot of them have dreams as farfetched as mine. They want to be CEO of a company or make millions developing their own software. Or they want to hang up their shingle in some ski resort and be a divorce lawyer for failing Hollywood marriages. They're not happy doing what they're doing while waiting to be what they want to be."

"So," she said, turning to him, "does this mean that you are not one hundred percent satisfied with teaching puppets to school kids?"

He sighed. "I always told myself that if I became a waiter, I wouldn't tell people that I was waiting tables because I was an out-of-work artist. I wouldn't say that this was my 'money' job while I was waiting for my big break."

"You're a good teacher."

"Yes, I am. I like kids. And I like the projects we do. But I have all these other dreams too, and if I don't put time into them, I'll feel like I'm going nowhere."

"What else are you going to do?"

"Someday I'm going to make a movie. And I'll start a company that does special effects using puppets in TV movies." He was on a roll. "And I'll do a show with puppets for a museum, inspired by the great forgotten works of literature. When I talk about my ideas to you, or to anybody else for that matter, they sound so half-baked. They sound that way to me too, but they're ideas that have stayed with me so long I know I have to do something with them. I'll feel like a failure if I don't."

"People need dreams."

"When I meet adults and say that I'm working in the

theater or that I write and make puppets, I hate it when they respond with 'I would have been an actor, but I had to earn some money first' or 'I could have been a great singer, but I had to go into my father's business.' I want to say to them, 'You didn't become an actor or singer because you didn't have it in you. You didn't want it badly enough. If you had wanted to become one, you would have.' "

Janice turned her head to the side so he couldn't see her profile anymore, and it was so dark he couldn't quite make out her face, but he thought he could feel the warmth of her breath and hear a soft swallow. No mistaking it, she was the real thing.

"What's stopping you?" she asked.

From the backseat came a snort and snore from Pietro.

"*I* am," Jonathan whispered. "I just can't figure how it all fits together. I don't know how to get there. It's not a job that I can find advertised in the *Times* or the *Herald News*." He grinned and thought he could spot the ghost of a smile on her lips. "I can make puppets in my basement workroom for an idea I've had. And I can work all night long writing a script I think would be good. I can teach all the skills I know. But I don't really know how any of those things will get me where I want to be going."

"I'm not you, so I don't exactly know how it works with you, but I've found that if I keep doing what I want to be doing, the right opportunity comes along."

Outside the rain continued to pelt the car, and from the bottom of the canyon came the rush of running water, but in the quiet of the night with no cars or trucks rolling past, it was a comforting background noise.

"I just write," Janice continued. "I go into my office and

do it. It helps having a deadline and assignments and a boss breathing down my back. What you are trying to do is much harder. You have to come up with the project ideas all on your own. But I think I know the feeling you must get, the anxiety to produce something."

"Before I start a new project I think I'm a nobody. I don't believe I have any talent. I think, 'What a lot of nerve.' Beginning something new is like jumping off a cliff."

"Then what happens?"

"I jump, if I get up the nerve."

"It has gotten easier for me. I used to hate interviewing people for stories. I would get so nervous calling people up out of the blue and saying, 'I'm Janice Ascher from the *Herald News*.' But after doing it for a while, it got easier."

"Jumping off a cliff gets easier," Jonathan mussed.

"They say the first step is the hardest."

"It's often the last step that's the killer," he concluded.

Jonathan looked out at the rain beating against the windows and wondered how long before he'd hear helicopters coming to rescue the people stranded in the canyon. Surely the news media would be arriving soon. They usually covered disasters from the air. He hoped his mother had slept through most of the storm. He didn't like to think of her worrying about him—it embarrassed him somehow. She did her best not to be overprotective, but sometimes he could sense her mother-hen instincts being held in check.

"Doris Day," he said suddenly, the name instinctively popping into his head while thinking about his mother.

"What?" Janice asked, confused at this sudden turn in the conversation.

"My mother could have been played by Doris Day. Perky, upbeat, sharp."

"What about Debbie Reynolds?" She made a quick comeback.

"She's a little too theatrical. Too campy. Too manic."

"Who would you cast for Pastor Bob?"

"Have you ever seen him?"

"I've heard him preach, and I've talked to him on the phone."

"An untwisted Robert Mitchum maybe would do."

"That sounds a little dark."

"I think he has a dark side. Mom says he can be moody at times. That's part of his charm. He's less one-dimensional than you'd think."

"How about Andy Griffith?"

"Possibly."

A silence fell between them. It made them both aware of Pietro sleeping in the backseat. Jonathan half wished for the distractions of a restaurant. A menu to study, other diners to analyze, the possibility of getting up and going to the restroom. Janice finally broke the quiet.

"Can I ask you a question?" she asked.

A dozen possibilities careened through Jonathan's mind. *She wants to tell me how much she likes me. She wants to say how irresistible I am.* Or the downside. *She has to confess that she's engaged to a bond salesman in Beverly Hills, and she's just going out with me out of pity.* "Sure. What is it?" He tried to sound casual.

"Can I have Rosalind Russell do me?"

"Rosalind Russell!" His heart skipped a beat. Saved! The

moment could go on. "I can't believe you thought of her. You mean, like in *His Girl Friday*?"

"I guess so. That's probably what I was thinking of. Classy and smart. Quick on her feet."

"I'm no Cary Grant."

"Neither was he."

What a nice thing to say. He didn't even have to fish for it. The moment was so right. He wanted to stretch his arms across the back of the Toyota, then lean across and kiss her. It would be so easy. But there was one thing that still really bothered him, and he knew if he brought it up, she could ruin everything with the wrong response. But he had to know. He had a right to know. He folded his arms across his chest and stared at the ceiling of the car.

"Janice, you didn't have to go out with me tonight," he finally said.

"I know I didn't."

"I wouldn't have minded if you had said no." This was a lie, but he would convince himself it wasn't if he had to. Preserve his dignity if necessary.

"I wanted to come."

"You've told me enough about your prayer letter for me to understand your motivation for writing it. That's cool. I think it was a gutsy thing to do. Anything for a good story and all that. But can you tell me one thing?"

"What's that?"

"Did you really mean it?" A note of earnestness entered his voice, lowering it an octave and giving it a slight tremolo.

Janice looked at him. She held his eyes in the dark of the storm. She remembered answering this same question from her roommate back in their apartment living room, but there the stakes were not nearly so high. Now she felt everything riding on her response. She closed her eyes to concentrate and said, "You know, when you write something, sometimes you have to put down the first thing that comes into your head. Some people call that the rough draft or the first draft. I call it the zero draft to take off any of the performance anxiety. It doesn't have to be good. It doesn't even have to be right. It just needs to be words on a page in some vague order."

"Like a sketch," Jonathan said.

"Yes, I think so. That's the way I wrote that letter when I first put it down and sent it to the church. Words on a page. A bunch of thoughts. Punctuated and spelled correctly, I hope, but nothing fancy. I never expected that they would come back to me. I never expected, beyond a form letter, that I'd get a response."

"You can thank Doris Day."

"Your mom?"

"Doris."

They both laughed, then Janice went on. "When I did get a response, I had to think really hard about what I had said in that letter. 'Six foot two, dark hair, a love of laughter, great sensitivity, midtwenties to early thirties, nice singing voice, stable in career, willing to travel.' Those aren't such bad qualities."

"I'm not very stable in my career."

"You're going places. You're aiming high. You're dreaming."

"Thanks," he said. "So you did mean it?"

"Sometimes after something's all finished, you look it

over and discover it was the truth. It didn't start out that way, but it became that way."

"I've had sketches that turned out like that. Where I discovered things that I didn't know were there. Good things, good ideas."

"I guess that's what happened to me. After I wrote it, I realized I believed it. Every word."

He smiled. What a relief. "Look at what you discovered!" he said. And without really planning or choreographing it, he leaned toward her and kissed her on the cheek. She turned her face to his. And then he kissed her on the lips. A real kiss that she seemed to want as much as he did, a kiss that could have lasted a long time. He didn't feel awkward about it at all.

CHAPTER 21

IN THE GRAY LIGHT of the waning storm, Lurlene walked to her office from her meeting at the manse with Pastor Bob. She trusted her boss. She was reassured. She had done all she could do for the time being. She hoped a search party would go out soon. Something had to happen. But in the end, Jonathan would be found. He was an adult, responsible and mature. He was probably managing fine. There was no need to worry.

As she walked through the rain, which seemed to be coming down in softer drops, she glanced at the oak leaves swirling in the gutter. She thought of how Jonathan had made boats from walnut shells and sent them sailing down the gutter—streams for a suburban boy. Sometimes she wondered if this town had been the best place to raise a child. Would he have been happier getting fresh air in a small country town? Should she have taken him back East to her relatives in Ohio? Would he have been better off growing up with cousins and grandparents around? They had made veiled remarks about how irresponsible she was to raise him on her own in that god-forsaken, earthquake-ridden land. Comments that only convinced her to stay where she was. Every option convinced her that she couldn't move. She would stay where she was. The schools were okay, he had friends, and she had a job convenient to home where she had reasonable responsibilities and a decent boss. Besides, how would her husband ever find her if she moved? Just in case he wanted to come home again. Just in case.

In light of her current worries about Jonathan's mere survival, her past concerns seemed ill-founded. She shuddered inside. You could never know how things would work out. You could only take one step at a time. Life couldn't be lived backwards.

It was still too early for the office to open up, but Lurlene realized she'd worry a lot more if she were at home. At work she could concentrate on other things. There was dictation to transcribe, files to sort, prayer letters to answer. She shuddered again at the thought of the latter. That was what had gotten her into trouble in the first place. If she hadn't answered the request as she had, if she hadn't spoken to Janice on the phone, if she hadn't set the woman up with her son . . . things might have been different. Like swatting at a pesky fly, she waved the thought away. Lurlene did not like to venture down the path of hypothesizing. In the daylight she struggled to put the worries away. *"Sufficient unto the day . . ."*

She put her key into the lock of the pastor's office, pushed open the door, and flicked on the lights. The office still had the damp smell of wet plaster. The small patch of bubbling paint above the window had grown larger. The building janitor said there was nothing that could be done until the bricks outside were repainted. In inclement weather, water seeped in. It was inevitable. "Not until our next capital fund-raising campaign," Pastor Bob had said. "I can't bear giving any more bricks and mortar sermons."

Lurlene cut open a new bag of coffee and emptied it into the coffee maker. She filled up the beaker with water from the bathroom down the hall, a necessary ritual in order to have her own coffeepot dripping just a few yards from her desk. At the very least, the aroma of coffee cut the mildewy smell that came from the pastor's office in the winter. There was comfort in performing this little task.

She finished pouring the water into the top of the maker, catching the coffee spilling into the glass pot, and turned to her telephone. The message light was illuminated. With the eraser end of a pencil she punched in her code. "You have five new messages," the recording stated. Maybe one of them was from her son. Maybe he'd tried to reach her here. She listened.

"I'm appalled to read that First Church is starting a dating service," began one woman. "What is the church coming to? Prayer requests should be kept absolutely confidential. . . ." Lurlene erased the message before she heard it all. She played the next message. "Lurlene? Lurlene? Is that you? Such an odd story in the newspaper this morning. I didn't think it was about you. Was it some other secretary the writer was referring to? I can't imagine you doing something like that." Lurlene erased that one also. Next message: "I'm a new member to First Church, and I'd like to meet the right sort of Christian man. Perhaps you could make a suggestion for me, and also pray for me. What I have in mind is . . ." Lurlene didn't listen to all of this one. The last two were complaints about the story, people who wished to speak to Pastor Bob. Lurlene dutifully took down their names and numbers. Bob would have to call them back. Lurlene didn't have the heart to.

While she was writing, she heard a knock at the door. *Jonathan!* she thought. Spinning around, she caught the silhouette of a man behind the frosted glass in the door. Like a shadow behind a shower curtain.

"We're not open yet," she called through the closed door. "Pastor Bob's not here yet. His first appointment's not until ten o'clock." She remembered that from her calendar. She always turned the page the previous night before leaving work. "He's got a busy day."

"I don't want to see Pastor Bob," the man said. "I want to see you."

Her heart leaped in shock. She knew that voice. Knew it as well as she knew her son's. It had been with her, even in its owner's absence, for over twenty years. No matter how much she had blocked it out, she could still hear it inside her head, and even after all these years it still had the capacity to break her heart.

"Please let me in," he said.

"I'm sorry," she replied. "I can't." *I can't. I can't. I can't open the door on closed business. Can't face the feeling of failure again. Can't dredge up emotions that I put to rest long ago. Don't ask me to do what is beyond me. Don't interrupt the peace of my life. Not now. Especially not now.*

But the door opened anyway, and there in a black plastic raincoat, a crumpled suit, a clean but wrinkled shirt, and a fraying tie stood a man she hadn't seen in twenty years. It was the man who once had been her husband. The father of her son, Jonathan. He stood very still, waiting for some response from her.

"I'm sorry to startle you, Lurlene," he finally said.

Everything about his timing was wrong. Everything about him was wrong. She had enough on her mind. *Not now. Dear Lord, please not now.*

"I didn't know how to do this," he said quietly. "I had more courage yesterday when I came by the church. I wanted to find you, to talk to you. To tell you how sorry I am for the pain I have caused you. You weren't here, so I came back again this morning. But I came back early because I was certain you wouldn't be here. Then I could leave, telling myself I had tried to find you. I purposely tried to miss you."

"As you can see, I'm here," she said coolly.

"Yes, bright and early. You were always an early riser."

"I have work to do."

He rambled, not moving, filling the threshold with talk, launching into the sort of monologue that had once charmed her but now seemed tired and stilted. "There was no reason for me to expect that you would still be at First Church. After all these years, you could have moved. But I had to try here first. Before I went any farther, I had to see if you were still here."

They stood far apart, not bearing to touch. How much he had aged. His face had the texture of wrinkled tanned leather, doleful eyes that sagged like a basset hound's. His hair was a shock of white, and his earlobes were flat and pressed like a pancake. The life he had lived had not been kind to his face, the brazen confidence that was its former expression had been replaced by yearning and sorrow. His beaten look spoke volumes. Still, Lurlene couldn't find an ounce of sympathy in her soul for him. He was a phantom she'd make disappear with the snap of her fingers.

"You were always good with talk," she said between clenched teeth. Were it not for her natural politeness, she would have pushed him back out into the rain.

"That's why they called me Doc. At the places I stayed, at homeless shelters, people called me Doc."

"Whatever they called you, you are not the person I was expecting to see."

"I don't blame you. Turn me out. You owe me nothing. But I came to apologize to you." He stood in the doorway not moving.

For many years she had wished for his return and imagined him doing what he was doing now, looking at her office, admiring her efficiency, seeing how well she had done without him. At first she had wanted him to come back so she could adequately express her anger. *"See what I have done without you. Look at how well I survived. You are worthless, unnecessary. Your absence means nothing to my life."* Then later she wanted him to admire her success. *"See this place that is mine. See how much I'm needed and admired. Notice how well I perform."*

When she didn't respond, he went on. "I used to tell myself that I didn't deserve you. That you were too good for me. That you would be better off without me."

"You never asked me my opinion."

"I couldn't. I couldn't go that far. That's him, isn't it?" he said, pointing to the picture of Jonathan.

"Yes." Lurlene stepped back and, without inviting him in, held the door open so he could enter.

"He's a nice-looking boy. I'd like to meet him."

"Why now?"

He looked hurt. "It doesn't have to be right now."

"No," she said. "You don't understand. Why have you come back now?"

"I have changed. I didn't think it was possible. I didn't really want anything more of my life. Being a drunk on skid row gave me a good excuse for failure. And my failures gave me a reason to drink. That was my cycle. I had a world of troubles that I could feel sorry about."

"Jonathan," she said to him, the name sounding so strange on her lips because it had long ago become the name of her son. It had nothing to do with her husband. "I don't want any part of your self-pity. I don't want you here. I want you to go away."

"I expected that."

"Well?"

"Before I leave, let me do one thing. Please let me apologize and explain. That's what I came for."

Her silence was all the encouragement he got.

"I was on the run when I left here, and I thought if I told you where I was, the people I owed money to would try to get it from you. I knew you were safe because the house was in your name. I was convinced that it was safer for you not to know where I'd gone."

"Nonsense. No one ever came to me for a dime."

"I didn't know that."

"You were a coward!" She gave into her anger now. "Was it some other woman? Some other family you had set up in another town?"

"There was no one else."

"I can't believe you."

"There was never anyone else. I thought once I got out of debt, I would come home. I'd make some money gambling and put it aside, but then I'd lose it." Like a sick person who has to remind himself of his illness so as not to overstep the limits of his fragile health, he repeated his confession. "I gambled. I spent my winnings. I drank the money away. I was too proud to come back until I had money. If I couldn't be your knight in shining armor, I didn't want to be anything in your life."

"Knight in shining armor? Didn't you ever think that all I really needed was for you to be here? To be a husband to me and a father to Jonathan?

"I was selfish." He flung his hands out.

"That's not enough," she said bitterly. Jonathan, her son, was her triumph. Her biggest and best achievement. How dare he turn up and take that away from her! How dare he consider horning in on her act! She had done it all alone. Her son was her starring vehicle, the only thing that had made her life worthwhile.

"I was too proud to stay and admit my failure," he went on. "Remember how you felt when I bought you that house? Remember what you thought when I took you from that small apartment to a house that would be your very own, down to the white picket fence? You were so happy. You wrapped your arms around me and held me tight. You thought maybe I was teasing you. You made me convince you it wasn't a joke. When I handed you the keys, you threw them up in the air and danced around me. I can still see you running up the brick walk and turning the key to the front door. You were radiant. And I felt so proud that I could do this for you, give you something that would make you happy. I didn't think you could love me after what I had lost."

The image of that long-ago day was too much for Lurlene to bear. Her anger would have been easier. Stoicism would have been easier. But to be reminded of a day when her world was filled with infinite hope brought something to her heart that she could hardly stand. She turned from the ruined homeless man in front of her and sank into her office chair, the wheels gliding slowly across the carpet protector. Her head in her hands, she hid the tears dripping from her eyes.

"I'm sorry," he said.

Without looking at him, the past flooded her mind. Lurlene could hear once again the persuasive voice of the handsome, charming man she had married. His playful, boyish tones would at times give way to sudden bouts of great seriousness. He once had brought lightness and laughter to her life, giving her moments of giddiness when, with blinding sincerity, he would tell her how much he loved her. It pained her to think how far away that youthful devotion now was.

"I cannot remake the past," he continued. "I will never be able to make up for my failings. But one thing I can do is tell you how deeply sorry I am for disappearing, for abandoning you and leaving you to raise Jonathan alone. I know I don't deserve your forgiveness, but—"

From her position on the chair, Lurlene held up a hand to stop him from saying anything more.

"I believe you," she said quietly. "Someday I might accept your apology. I can't now." *"Granting forgiveness is a grace all its own,"* Pastor Bob had once said. She didn't have that grace now. Someday perhaps, but not yet.

"I didn't sleep much last night," she went on, "and my

mind is not entirely my own. I'm very worried about my son. *My* son. I won't call him yours. I can't do that yet. Jonathan has been out all night, and I'm afraid he got lost in the flood. I've talked to Pastor Bob and called the police. I hope by now they are searching for him."

"Is there anything I can do?" he asked, worry clouding his voice.

She shook her head. "I don't want to talk anymore right now. Later, maybe, but I can't listen now. I'm too confused. I won't ask you where you are staying, but I presume that you have a bed to sleep in and you have clean clothes—"

"Pastor Bob found me a place," he said.

For a moment Lurlene felt betrayed. She looked up. "You saw Pastor Bob?"

"Yes. Last night. I've always liked him. He's a good man."

"Does he know who you are?"

"I didn't tell him, but he might have guessed."

"He didn't tell me," she said. She felt the bruise to her self-esteem that her boss would hide a secret like this from her. She tried to convince herself that it was an issue of confidentiality. As a pastor and counselor, his words with her husband were supposed to be taken in private. Even so, she couldn't believe that Pastor Bob recognized her husband, Jon. She could hardly recognize the man herself.

"Can I see my son sometime?" he asked.

So this was what he was driving at. This was why he had come. "He's an adult. He can make his own decision."

"But will you let me see him?"

"It's not for me to say."

"Why?"

"That's up to him. Besides, I don't know where he is. I

don't even know if he's alive. He's lost. He hasn't come back. . . ." She dreaded crying again. She hated appearing vulnerable in front of this man. She held back the tears with a great force of will.

"Well, then," he said. "I'll pray for him."

Pray for him? Coming from his mouth, the words were a shock. She shouldn't have been surprised that God was behind her husband's change of mind and his plea for forgiveness. God seemed to be behind every transformed bum and rescued wino. Nobody could give up a nightly martini at cocktail hour without thanking God for the help. She'd heard enough testimony from saved souls and recovered drunks over the years. People who said they were made new. And all they could think of doing was to pray for others. She hated it.

"You can do what you will," she said. She even resented him sharing her worries. Her worries were hers alone. She had earned them.

"I will call you," he said.

"I don't want to think about it until I know Jonathan is safe."

"I will call to find out how he is."

"Yes," she said. "Okay. You can do that."

Quietly he backed out.

CHAPTER 22

AFTER HER HUSBAND LEFT, Lurlene sat at her desk for a long time, her mind almost blank. She stared at the letters waiting to be answered. She stared at the computer screen. She gazed at the phone, daring it to ring.

When Pastor Bob came in, he found her sitting at her usual place in a daze. He hesitated a moment, apparently unsure of what to say or do, before heading into his office.

What kept going through her mind was a phrase that was often passed around at First Church: *"The Lord never gives you more than you can bear."* She decided she must have been the exception because she was on overload. If indeed there was a God, He wouldn't do this to her. He wouldn't make her suffer this much or even ask forgiveness of her in the middle of her pain. It wasn't right. It wasn't fair.

"Pastor Bob," she wanted to say, "it *is* possible for the Lord to give you more than you can bear. He must do it to people all the time. He's doing it to me right now."

Finally she was able to begin her work and turn her thoughts away from her husband and son for a few brief moments—while standing up to file an old sermon, when pouring a second cup of coffee, when answering a call from the florist who often did flowers for weddings at First Church. The man must not have read the newspaper, because he didn't say a thing about matchmaking or prayers. He only mentioned how the storms would affect a shipment he was expecting. And mention of the storm reminded Lurlene of her missing son.

"Of course, I understand," she heard Pastor Bob say on the phone from his office. "It was highly unusual, completely unorthodox. Mrs. Scott has never behaved that way before, and it certainly will never happen again. She's been my loyal, dependable secretary for years. . . . Thank you for your concern. . . . Yes, we have the situation well in hand. God bless."

Damage control. Pastor Bob was doing damage control because of her. It made her even more hesitant to pick up the phone. Who would be next and with what accusation? She hesitated a few seconds before she gave her usual greeting, "First Church, Pastor Bob's office, Lurlene Scott speaking."

"Mom," the voice said.

"Jonathan?"

"Yeah, it's me. I'm okay."

"Where are you?" she burst out.

"I'm fine," he repeated.

"Where have you been?" Lurlene's face had become flushed in the excitement, the unbelievable relief. She was hearing his voice, and he was insisting, despite her worst nightmare, that nothing was wrong.

"We got caught in the storm and had to spend the night

in the arroyo. I took Janice to a restaurant down there last night, and we had to leave when water started leaking into the kitchen and the river rose dangerously high. We picked up the Italian chef on the way—his car had stalled—and then the road washed away. There was a big mud slide ahead of us and the bridge was out behind us. So we spent the night in the car with the Italian guy. I'm sorry if you were worried, but there was no way to contact you."

"I was very concerned."

"There was nothing we could do but wait out the storm and hope for help to come."

"How did you stay dry?" She didn't want to let him go. Every moment she heard his voice was slowly undoing the fears that had built up over the past few hours. It was a release of tension.

"We were dry in the car and up high enough so the flooding didn't reach us. We fell asleep there. Pietro snored."

"Who?"

"The Italian chef. The one I told you about. Finally this morning a helicopter came and rescued us. It was quite exciting, actually. You know me, Mom. It was an adventure more than anything else. The pilot rescued a lot of poeple from the houses around there. We heard that some of the people back at the restaurant had to spend the night on the roof. I was glad we were in the car keeping dry."

His voice resonated with his enthusiasm for the dramatic rescue. But he was fine. That was all that mattered to her. All her worrying had been for nothing. She needn't have called on Pastor Bob. She needn't have shown up on his doorstep, wringing a handkerchief into a shapeless wad. All her life Lurlene had practiced worrying religiously. If she worried about something enough, she believed she might prevent the worst from happening. Or at least she could prevent herself from being disappointed when it did occur. But with one quick telephone call her worry had turned out to be worthless. Punctured like a balloon. She couldn't let it go that fast.

"Are you sure you are all right?" she asked.

"I could have used more sleep."

"Have they taken you to the hospital?"

"Mom!" came the complaint. "It wasn't as if it was freezing outside. I was plenty warm."

"Where are you now?"

"At the police station. I have to give them a report."

"I was so worried." Finally she could say it. She had earned it. "I didn't know where you were."

"That's cool, Mom. That's why I called."

"I'm glad you're okay. I'm glad you're safe." She urged herself toward happiness. All that was gone had come back, what was lost was found. The worst wasn't even a possibility. "Everyone here will be glad. Pastor Bob was particularly concerned." This was a line she must have delivered thousands of times to parishioners in distress and now she was saying it to her own son. Never had it seemed truer. Next she'd be telling him that the church had been praying for his safety.

"The article, Mom?"

"Oh, that." If she could allow her worries to diminish, maybe she could think of that again.

"Janice told me about it. She is really sorry."

"Janice?" For a moment Lurlene even forgot who this Janice was. Then she remembered.

"She didn't mean any harm by it, Mom. When she wrote the story she didn't realize you were my mom."

And that would have made a difference? "I didn't identify you as my son."

"She wouldn't have wanted to make things difficult for you if she had known."

"That's all right," Lurlene heard herself say. "It's okay. It turned out all right."

"Really?" he asked.

"There have been calls, and some people are upset. Pastor Bob has been talking to quite a few people this morning, but he said he forgave me. He won't fire me." There was something about the power of his forgiveness that took root in her now, giving a lightness to her speech. "It's turning out okay," Lurlene said again, surprising herself.

It *was* okay. She had done something that was inexcusable, unprofessional, and the world hadn't fallen apart. She was given a new chance, a clean slate. She'd had a perfect record for twenty-two years and only one gaffe. To her amazement, it hadn't sunk her.

"You're not going to lose your job?"

"I guess not."

"Janice will be glad. She was feeling guilty. She was even hoping she could stop the article from running."

What was that Bible quote that Pastor Bob used sometimes in his sermons? *"Sparingly,"* he had said. *"It should be used sparingly, otherwise Paul's message gets distorted. 'All things work together for good to them that love God.' "* Lurlene usually found it made her wince. It seemed so exclusive. What about those others who didn't love God? How would things work for them? But now she found that phrase running, uninvited, through her brain.

"Does it change your opinion of her?" Lurlene asked hesitatingly. "Now that you know she wrote that letter to the church as research for an article she was doing?"

"I don't know, Mom," he said. "I think she also meant it."

"Are you sure?"

"That's what she says."

"I hope it's true."

"She's really great, Mom. Wait till you get to know her better. You'll really like her."

"Okay." Lurlene would take that up another day. What did she know about the young woman? Far be it for her to dictate choices of the heart to her son.

"I've gotta run, Mom. I'll come by the church when I get done here. Bye."

"Good-bye, dear." She held the phone to her ear until all she could hear was the buzz of the busy signal. Wasn't this all she had wished for? Wasn't this what she had asked for when she'd stared up to heaven the night before she read *Herald News* reporter Janice Ascher's letter? Had she made a prayer that had been answered or had she made the answer for someone else's prayer?

Giddiness mixed with sleeplessness was making her light-headed. She rubbed her eyes and stared at her computer screen. Too much was happening at once. With hands folded across her lap, she let out a huge sigh. Her son was in love with a girl who seemed interested in him. And Jonathan was convinced that the girl's interest was not phony. Lurlene would have to trust that was so. Hadn't she done enough damage already? Wasn't it best to leave meddling alone? *"Sufficient unto the day . . ."*

The outer door to her office opened and in came the two prayer lady stalwarts, Helen Bradford and Doris Matthews, one tall and gangly, the other petite and birdlike. Mutt and Jeff. "We've heard," Helen said, extending her hand, the silver bracelets jangling on it.

"You must be worried sick," Doris added, slipping her arm through the loop of her handbag.

"You mean about the article," Lurlene said, uncomprehending.

"Your son," both women said.

"Pastor Bob called me this morning to alert the prayer chain," Doris said.

"And Doris called me," Helen said.

"Jonathan just called. He's fine. He was fine all night. Stuck on a road, but fine." Lurlene couldn't bring herself to tell them that he wasn't alone.

"The good Lord be praised," Doris said.

"I'm so glad," said Helen. "You must be relieved."

"I am."

"We'd just alerted the prayer chain."

"Already?"

"With a few calls on the phone tree, we can get dozens of people praying for a specific need," Doris explained.

"A bunch of strangers praying for us?" Lurlene said.

"You're hardly a stranger around First Church."

Once again tears came to Lurlene's eyes, but these were tears of a different sort. She couldn't believe the emotion that passed through her. The sentimentality. Even after all that she'd done, people were praying for her. "I'm touched," she said. "I'm truly touched."

"Doris, we should get on the line and tell people the good news," Helen said.

"You're right."

"Do you mind if we make some calls right here?" she asked Lurlene.

"Please do."

Pastor Bob was thrilled when he heard the news of Jonathan's safety. He came out of his lair and greeted Lurlene with one of his patented bear hugs. Helen and Doris had just finished working the phones, alerting the phone tree.

"Mrs. Scott, perhaps you should take the rest of the day off," he said.

"I couldn't do that," she exclaimed. "I've got piles of work to catch up on."

"Go out to lunch and celebrate."

"Lunch is what got me into trouble in the first place."

"The Cobb salad?"

"The glass of Chardonnay." She laughed.

"We'll take you to lunch," Helen said.

"We'll just drink iced tea," chimed in Doris.

"I can't leave," Lurlene said. "Jonathan's coming."

"He can join us. It's not even ten-thirty. We won't leave till noon. We have some sorting out to do upstairs."

"I don't know," Lurlene said, running out of excuses.

"I hope you can," Helen said.

"We'll call you," Doris added.

The rest of the morning took on the painful ordinariness of life after a wedding or a wake. One is grateful for the little chores that are left to do: responding to the condolence notes, cleaning rice out of the carpet and lawn, returning rented glassware to the caterer, taking the dead flowers out of the arrangements, and consolidating the hardier blooms left. Lurlene was glad for every telephone call. She appreciated the requests for Pastor Bob's sermon and the inquiries about parking availability on Sundays and the calls from parishioners scheduling meetings with their senior minister. She was glad of the memos she had to type up and the correspondence she had to answer for her boss. Every interruption was a delight because it reminded her of the lovely normalcy of her life. The only thing that troubled her was the return of her husband. He wanted to see his son. She couldn't deny him that. But could he ever become a father?

"Mom," Jonathan stood in the doorway of his mother's office. Unshaven, hair tousled, he was exhilarated by his experience. It was as though he had spent the evening at a tropical beach on a starry night instead of trapped in a tiny Toyota in the midst of Southern California's worst downpour in decades—according to the newscasters' most recent account.

"You really are okay," she said after hugging him close.

"Mom, you've got to come outside and look. It's beautiful out there."

She looked down at her desk. "I've got so much work to catch up on."

"Come on," he said. "Just for a minute."

"Just for a sec." She headed outside, where the water was drying up on the sidewalks, leaving behind cloudlike patterns of light and dark. The trunks of the palms were still black from the dampness, but in the sunlight the grass was the green of an Irish spring and the ivy climbing the bell tower as lush as a tropical jungle.

"Look at the mountains," Jonathan said. "Come with me. On the other side of San Anselmo, there's a better view."

The storm had pushed itself against the tallest peaks, lingering there, then rising in lacelike mists from the crumpled valleys. The last bands of gray still hovered above the far slopes, but the sunlight gilded the snow-covered granite, dazzling the powder that blanketed the mountains. The trees and eaves and gutters in the foreground were still dripping from the rain, but above was the sort of pristine view that real-estate marketers had used to sell California to Easterners since the arrival of the railroads. Oranges to be plucked in the shadow of snowy peaks. Palm trees framing a distant ski slope. A climate with something for everyone.

"It is beautiful," Lurlene conceded.

"It doesn't get any better," said her son.

"Are you glad you live here?"

"On a day like today."

The sky was cleaner and clearer that it would ever be on a temperate day. It wasn't simply the contrast. The rain had washed every speck of grime away. The clarity of it made Lurlene want to ask one question of Jonathan. The murk in her own vision had to be addressed.

"Do you ever wish you had a father?" she asked.

"Sure, I do. But I don't dwell on it."

"Would you have been happier if your father had been around to raise you?"

"Mom," he said, looking at her quizzically, "why are you asking me this now?"

She hesitated to explain, then backed away from the reason. She couldn't go into it just now. "I wasn't perfect," she settled on. "I couldn't do everything."

He put his arm on her shoulder. "You did a lot."

"Thank you." Someday she would explain to him more about his father. Sometime she would talk about her anger, which was still a shock to her. Someday she might even forgive the man. But not now. She needed to get back to her office. Kissing her son farewell on the cheek, she returned to her desk and her computer.

It was odd about prayer, odd that so much had worked out. She wanted to say that was just the way things were. But so much that happened was also exactly what people had prayed for.

After lunch Doris Matthews brought Lurlene a framed plaque that said, "A friend is a gift you give yourself." And Helen Bradford gave her a potted African violet with white flowers the color of wedding silk. Several more people called about the article in the *Herald News*, and she thanked them for their interest.

In the late afternoon when her energy was flagging and the lack of sleep was catching up with her, Pastor Bob called her into his paneled office to take dictation, but he only had one letter to dictate and the rest of the time he wanted to talk.

"Mrs. Scott, I don't think what you did was a terrible thing. But I would like to make sure it doesn't start a pattern. You are not to add your comments to the prayer letters that are sent out from this address."

"Of course," she said. "I understand."

"When someone calls with a practical request you are not to indulge in your matchmaking instincts. We provide enough services here at First Church. There would be no end of trouble if we added to them the ability to match up the lovelorn with the perfect mate."

"I won't do it again." She listened to his little speech, feeling less chagrined than she would have thought. Maybe she was simply worn out from the ups and downs of her day. At any rate, from years of experience, she recognized that Pastor Bob wasn't all that angry. He had a point to make, but his remonstrances were not grave.

"We take intercessory prayer very seriously at this church," he continued, "and we don't want people out there to think their needs are being compromised by meddling. You were meddling."

"Pastor," she said, "do you believe in prayer?"

"What an odd question to ask," he said.

"Do you believe it works?"

"What do you mean by that?"

"Do you believe—do you really believe—that if I pray for something I will get it?"

"Depends on what you're praying for." He allowed the conversation to turn more serious.

"For twenty-two years I've typed up your sermons and listened to you preach. By now I think I've heard all your supporting arguments. You know, that where two or three are gathered in Jesus' name, He is there. Or that when they ask, truly believing, for a mountain to be moved, it can be moved. Or how God hears the prayers of our heart. I have heard all that and have never truly believed."

"I know."

"I hope you're not disappointed with me."

"No. You have been honest with yourself. I've appreciated that. Have you recently changed your mind about believing?"

"I don't know," she said, just comprehending it for the first time. "It's the oddest thing. Maybe I'm doubting my doubts."

"Mrs. Scott, do you mean to tell me you are a skeptic?"

"I have always been that. Now I'm something else. I'm a skeptic full of doubts about skepticism."

"What caused this change?" He leaned forward in his chair and looked across his messy desk at her. She put down the pencil and pad of paper that she was purportedly using to take dictation.

"Everything that has just happened. I made a wish—maybe it was a prayer—that Jonathan would find the right woman in his life. But then I didn't really trust it to happen, so I made it happen, and it did. Did it happen because I wished it, or will it work out because I meddled?"

The thought was so complicated she had to linger over it for a moment. Did good things happen because she prayed for them or because she worked on them? "I also think about the flood and my fears for Jonathan," she said. "None of what I worried about came true. I would have put that down to his cool-headed thinking—"

"His God-given gift," Pastor Bob interrupted.

"Or I would have said it was our good fortune. And now I discover that half of First Church was praying for him. Or at least that's what Helen Bradford told me. So now I'm wondering if his rescue and safety could have been due maybe in part to prayer."

"Either way, aren't you glad?"

"Pastor," she said. "I've always tried to be very fair. And I'd like to be fair now. That's what scares me. If all the good things that have happened to me—or the bad things—have come down from Providence, then I owe God a few words. In fact, I can't begin to say the many things I would have to say."

It was all Pastor Bob could do to prevent a huge smile filling his expressive face. "All you have to do is to say, 'I believe.' "

"I want to try that."

"Pray with me for a moment."

"You mean, say something?"

"No, just listen and close your eyes," he said. "I will pray for you. The only thing you have to do is remember the phrase, 'Help my unbelief.' That's it. 'Help my unbelief.' "

"Okay," she said as she bowed her head in the stillness of her boss's office.

CHAPTER 23

DOC—OR JON OR MR. SCOTT as he really was—was given a bed at another church to sleep in the next night. The basement shelter at First Church was full. It had provided him an emergency bed for one night, but he was the twentieth man, and normally the facility took only nineteen homeless guests. The extra cot was for just such emergencies. Besides, after his conversation with Lurlene, Doc realized it would be easier to stay in a place where he didn't run into her day to day. He wasn't ready for that kind of regular contact, and neither was she. He had come here to beg forgiveness. He'd come a step in that direction, but for now he'd leave things as they were. He had another mission in mind.

After leaving First Church he walked to a park in town. With the food coupon he'd been given at the church, he bought a tuna sandwich and a Coke at a little convenience store. Sitting on a bench in the park, he ate it and watched a group of school kids playing their games—volleyball and soccer—the children kicking the ball across a turf of dark green. At the low end of the field, water from the storm had gathered, and a few of the youngsters tested fate by kicking the ball around the pond, proving they could keep it and themselves out of harm's way.

"Here, over here. Kick it to me," one boy yelled.

"I'm free," shouted another.

They could have been in third or fourth grade, much younger of course than Jonathan, but for Doc, these kids reminded him of all he'd missed of his son's boyhood. The birthday parties, back-to-school nights, soccer matches, Little League games. The bedtime stories, camping trips, fishing expeditions. Did Jonathan ever play Little League, and if so, what position? Who was his coach? How good was he at hitting a ball? And when he got older, did he play any sports in high school? Or was he one of those kids who shone in other areas—Glee Club, band, Student Council, the senior class play? Did he ever miss his father? Did he wish he had stories to trade about his dad?

As Doc watched the kids, one boy chased the ball around the edge of the pond, and as he was leaning into a turn, he lost his footing, skidding and tumbling into the water with a terrific splash. For a moment all the other kids stopped, horrified at what had happened. They waited, watching, as the boy lifted his head like a crocodile out of a swamp, and then arose, fully covered with mud. At once, one of the crueler teammates burst into malicious laughter, and the others followed. Soon the whole class was laughing, and the kid covered with mud tried to make light of it.

It made Doc think of all the disasters that might have befallen his son over the years: strikeouts in the ball field, a lost election for class officer, speeches where everyone laughed at the wrong moment. Wanting to be a part of a group and finding himself alone on the outskirts. It was all very well to say that such events were simply part of growing up or that they helped developed character, but Jonathan would have had no refuge, no sanctuary except for his mother when life's disappointments hit.

"Fine time for thinking of all this," Doc said to himself. "There's not a thing I can do about it now." When he was a younger man, he had run away from the responsibility of raising a family. He had anesthetized himself from the remorse and regrets that plagued him. He had drowned himself in booze and a wayward life. But now that he'd turned away from that—now that he'd said yes to something else—the remorse returned, more powerful and potent than ever.

Closing his eyes, he said a prayer of apology. "Sorry, Lord. I really botched up fatherhood." But it was an empty prayer that sounded hollow in his head without any action behind it—when action could be taken. *That's why I'm here,* he thought. *That's why I came back.*

He blew up his empty bag and popped it—an old habit. Tossing the bag into a trash can, he set off on the second part of his mission. The air smelled clean and fresh, as though it had been filtered through the night's turmoil. The wind still blew, sending clouds racing through the sky and leaves flurrying across the sidewalk, but it wasn't a breeze that promised more storm clouds. It was one to bring clearer, cleaner air—a day perfect for a new beginning. It was something that could match the new convictions Jon had brought to his life. "God, give me courage," he said aloud.

How well he knew the route. How little had changed. Houses had been added on to, painted, reroofed, relandscaped, but he recognized each one of them. Sometimes names of former residents popped into his mind. The Lacys had lived in that split-level, the Howlands lived in the Spanish-style bungalow, an older couple used to live in the clapboard home. He half-expected windows to open, distant friends to hail him, or waves to come from front doors as though he were the paper boy and had just lobbed the evening news onto the front porch.

Had he ever really been happy here? No, it was only an imitation of happiness, a sham. Pushing his son around the block in his stroller, nodding to neighbors, he had always expected that he would be found out. That these good, upstanding folk would discover he was barely holding the job he said he had and that he could barely provide for the son in the stroller. He had feared they would soon find out about the many times he left their leafy neighborhood and checked into a bar, where friends could be had for the price of a drink and friendship lasted no longer than the foam on a glass of beer.

A terrier yipped at him from behind a hedge and a chain link fence. A large dog picked up the refrain from across the street. Doc moved off the sidewalk and took a few ragged steps along the gutter, as though he'd somehow be safer there.

There was only half a block more to go. He knew Lurlene still lived there—he'd seen an envelope on her desk at First Church. It bore the same address, the one he'd repeated night after night, promising someday he'd return to the place and make the owner of it proud. Before he left First Church that morning he'd heard from Rocco—who'd heard from the bookkeeper who'd heard from one of the prayer ladies who'd heard from Pastor Bob—that Jonathan had been found. They'd all been praying for him, and their prayers were answered. He was safe. Now it was Doc's assumption that his son would be back home after his overnight ordeal. Lurlene would still be at the office, and Jonathan would be at home.

There the place stood, secure and solid behind its white picket fence. Maybe the door and window frames needed a new coat of paint, perhaps the grass could use some weeding, but the house was exactly as he remembered it. The oak in front that had once been a sapling held up by wooden stakes was now a self-supporting, strapping tree. With or without him to water it and trim it, the tree had grown. Like his son.

Doc walked up the brick walk. He paused at the front door, then finally rang the doorbell. Even its chimes played the same tune, the same notes of a chord.

"Coming," a voice called from within.

Doc waited, hearing footsteps coming from the back, from the kitchen to the front hall. Finally the door opened. No one peeked out from behind a hidden spyglass, no chain held the door latched. No one here seemed timid about a stranger ringing a doorbell at one-thirty in the afternoon. The person who answered was tall, as tall as he himself had once been. Thin but not gaunt, with a friendly expression on his face and blue eyes that showed trust.

"Yes?" the young man said. "Can I help you?"

How many times had Doc rehearsed the speech he would give? How many times had he rewritten it over the years? In shelters, on the street, sitting on park benches. He had wanted to justify himself in one long sweeping monologue—the sort he had been able to pull off in his sales days. Blow smokescreen over himself and his product with a lot of hot air. Sometimes he thought he was able to get people to buy things because they wanted to get rid of him and his talk. But where had the words gone now? His gift for gab escaped him. For too long his stories had seemed like a pack of lies.

"I came here to find you," he finally said.

"I'm sorry," Jonathan said. "I wasn't aware that I needed to be found."

"No. I needed to come see you. I was in the neighborhood."

"Who is it you're looking for? Sometimes these houses can all look alike. It's easy to get turned around," Jonathan said, assuming the man before him was confused or lost. "If you give me a name, I might be able to find the person you're looking for. Or I can look up the address in a phone book."

"Jonathan Walter Scott Jr."

This should have been enough to tip off Jonathan. No one ever thought of Jonathan as a Junior, and no one ever used his middle name. With Jonathan Sr. out of the picture for such a long time, Jonathan had dropped the Jr. from his name.

"That's me," he said.

"I am your father," the old man said.

Now at this point, Doc had always imagined opening his arms and reaching out to embrace his son, but somehow he'd never expected his son to be as tall as he was, even though he knew that Jonathan was a full-grown adult. This young man was standing a step up at the front door, almost towering over him. Doc kept his hands stiffly in his jacket pockets and watched the changing expression on his son's face. Irritation, wonder, bewilderment, curiosity, horror.

"I didn't mean to do it this way," Doc said. "I didn't intend to shock you like this. I wanted to write you a letter first. Give you time to take it in. . . ."

Jonathan, still rooted to his place, said, "No. I did know about you. Mom had told me. She didn't know where you were, but she said that you were still alive."

"Any letter I ever started didn't have room for all the things I would have put in it. That's the only excuse I have to make, and I know it's a bad one."

A car drove past the house, and the cool breeze sent a small branch that had come down from the tree tumbling across the lawn. Doc raised his shoulders against the cool air.

"You better come in," Jonathan said. "Please come in."

"Thank you."

What is it about a house that it can smell the same after decades? he wondered. The residents might have changed, the cooks might have transformed their menus, but the house can still give off an odor of oak, pine, plaster, and wool that is its own. Doc could have closed his eyes, could have gone blind in the years since he'd stepped foot in the house, but he would have known it in an instant. It smelled sweet like an apple tart and reassuring like nutmeg. On the table in a dish were Lurlene's car keys.

"She always liked to walk to work, didn't she?"

"Mom?" Jonathan said. "Yes. She walks every other day."

"It's good exercise."

Jonathan stood staring at the man who claimed to be his father, and he still didn't know what to do. He wanted to ask a thousand questions, starting with, "Why did you leave us?" "Why didn't you get in touch with us?" and "Why did you come back?" But something else was going on. Even with the fatigue of an exhausting night weighing him down, Jonathan wanted to love this man. He wanted to show him that in spite of the past he was ready to love a man who said he was his father—however hard that might be. The presence of this tall, stooped, worn-looking figure in his house made him realize more than ever what a terrible absence his father had been in his life.

"Have you seen Mom?" Jonathan asked.

"Yes, this morning. She was still very worried about you. Everyone was."

Jonathan laughed. "It was quite a night."

"Thank God it turned out all right."

"Yes. Thank God." Jonathan wished he could call his mother right away and ask for her advice, her thoughts on what to do with this intruder in their lives. Why hadn't she said anything this morning? Or was that why she asked him if he missed growing up without a father? Now he had a fear that this man would move right into their house, and Jonathan wasn't ready for that. He wasn't even ready to offer his father a place to sit down.

"She's still angry with me," his father said in measured tones. "And she has every right to be. I expected that."

"But did she know you were going to talk to me?"

"She said that I could. She said you were an adult and you could make your own decision about me."

What decision? What was he supposed to do? Besides pepper the man with questions. Besides try to figure out what he had missed out on for these twenty-odd years. Jonathan glanced at his watch. "Oh," he said. "I've got to go. I've got to take Mom's car and pick up some stuff for a class I'm teaching this afternoon. I can't stay here and talk."

"My timing has never been great."

No, Jonathan thought, but he still couldn't leave his father standing inside or out. "Come with me," he said. "Come with me on the errand. I need some more Styrofoam and glue. I teach puppetry in an after-school program. It's my money job. The pay is okay, and I enjoy the work. Where are you headed?"

"I'm staying in a shelter at a church."

So the man was homeless. Just what he looked like. A neatly dressed, well-spoken homeless bum. His father.

"Last night I stayed at First Church," his father continued. "I was very comfortable there, but they don't have room to keep me for long. And I didn't think I wanted to be so close to your mother just yet." He let out a sigh. "This is going to take a long time . . . so I'm being put up at another church."

"That's cool." Jonathan picked up his keys from the dish and headed toward the kitchen and then the basement for a bag of things for his afternoon class.

When Jonathan returned, the two of them got into Lurlene's car, Jonathan behind the wheel and his father sitting awkwardly in the front seat beside him. If Jonathan had been a little younger, they might have looked like a father teaching his son to drive, but Jonathan was anything but hesitant behind the wheel. His father was the unsure, tentative one.

"The Hobby Shop has most of the stuff I need," Jonathan said. "They know me pretty well by now."

"How long have you been doing this?"

"The teaching?"

"Yes."

"I started while I was still in college. It was a way to make money, and I discovered I liked it. I enjoyed working with kids. We seem to get along okay. I get them to put on plays with the puppets they build, and the parents come and see what they've done. It makes them proud–'' Jonathan stopped. *They come to shows. Unlike you. They show up for their children's lives.* The vehemence of his thoughts surprised him.

''I'm surprised how little things have changed,'' his father said. ''The streets seem the same. The directions for how to get to places are still in my head. We turn here, don't we?'' he asked, as indeed Jonathan turned.

''Yeah. The Hobby Shop has been around for ages, I guess.''

''I saw other kids when I was away. In parks I liked to watch the kids play. When I was in church shelters, I looked forward to the times when families visited us. Sometimes I went upstairs and stood in the back of church and watched the kids there. I saw girls and boys receive their Bibles or show off the passages they had memorized. I listened while they sang songs with their Sunday school classes.''

''I suppose that was entertaining.''

''I never once heard a child or saw one without thinking of you.''

Jonathan nodded his head. He dared not turn to look at this man who was his father. He couldn't listen to that voice and also see what expressions his face wore. It was all that Jonathan could do to take in the talk.

''Have you ever made a puppet that you weren't happy with?'' his father asked him.

''Sure. All the time. I come up with things that don't work all the time.''

''Do you let people see them?''

"Not a chance. I throw them away. If a head doesn't work right or the costume is wrong or the eyes or nose or mouth, I don't want anyone to see it. I get rid of the stuff and start over. I only want to show the very best puppets."

"You're a perfectionist?"

"Just practical. This is what I do. I want what other people see to be my best work."

"There's the post office," his father said, gesturing to an old stucco building that still wore enough decorations on the outside to be nicknamed the Wedding Cake Building. "It's still here."

"There was a big effort to save it when the postal department wanted to build a new, more modern place. Everybody complained. Nobody would let them give up the Wedding Cake."

"Well, I was thinking of your puppets," his father said, reverting back to the former subject. "It was sort of like me. I didn't want to come back here until I was perfect. I didn't want you to see me until you could be proud of me. I didn't feel I was worthy of you or your mother. It won't explain everything to you, but it might help you understand. So much time went by that I couldn't come back. I was too scared."

"You were a perfectionist?"

"No, I was a failure. And I pretended to be a perfectionist. I pretended to think I was doing you a favor. I was wrong."

Jonathan was pulling into the Hobby Shop parking lot. He aimed for a slot nearest to the back door and steered the car into it with one try. Still, the two of them sat without moving. His father was staring down at his hands and biting his lower lip. Jonathan took the keys out of the ignition, then held them in his hand without opening the door.

"I want to tell you that I'm sorry," his father finally said. "I'm sorry for all those years that I missed out on. I'm sorry I wasn't there for you and your mother."

"That's cool," Jonathan said, unsure of how to respond. His father's outburst both warmed him and embarrassed him.

"I would like to make it up to you somehow. It will take a long time, I know . . . I've been gone so many years. That's why I want to stay here–not right here, but near enough to see you sometimes, if that's all right."

"Sure."

"It's what I need to do."

Jonathan wished somehow he could hug his father or shake hands, but he couldn't see doing it in the car, and it would be all wrong to hug standing outside the car in broad daylight in the parking lot of the Hobby Shop. He reached over, car keys still in hand, and patted his father on the back.

"You know what you can do with me?" he said.

"What's that?"

"You can come with me into the store while I buy the Styrofoam."

"I would love to."

CHAPTER 24

DURING THE WEEK Jonathan had briefly spoken to his father about the party that was happening for Lurlene. They both decided it was best for him to stay away. Mr. Scott was getting used to his new shelter across town, and he felt he needed to stay put there in the evenings. He was volunteering for several duties, and he wanted to make a good impression. Besides, it had been an emotionally exhausting week. He didn't want to add much more to the burden he was already carrying. That said, he hoped to visit Jonathan again.

The prayer ladies had festooned balloons from the acoustical tiles in the fellowship hall. Half a dozen loops of crepe paper drooped beneath the heater ducts in the ceiling, the blasts of warm air fanning them like waves in a field of wheat. One of the assistants in the business office had printed a sign on her computer that said, "Thank You, Lurlene. You're Number One at First Church!" It hung in front of a row of casement windows, the light coming through the purple and fuchsia ink that filled the black printing like colored shards in a stained-glass window. Round tables were set up on the green linoleum with pink paper tablecloths left over from Valentine's Day. The centerpieces were small bouquets of carnations with hearts floating over them—more leftovers—with notes that said "We Love You, Lurlene."

Sixty people milled around one end of the room where a punch bowl had been set up at a long folding table. They were drinking out of clear plastic cups, part of the vast supply in stock for Sunday morning fellowship for those who did not drink coffee. These were the stalwarts of First Church: the fundraisers, trustees, Sunday school teachers, and prayer leaders. If there was a shortage of younger members, it wasn't because they weren't also pillars of the church. It was mostly because the guests were chosen from a list of people who had known Lurlene the longest.

This was Lurlene's community, her extended family. They knew they could call on her from nine to five, Monday through Friday, and she would tell them whether Pastor Bob was preaching, what his topic was, and which Bible passages he would read. She could give them the phone number of a new member, let them know when the next stewardship meeting was, or fax an extra copy of the minutes. They depended on her ability to guess their unarticulated demands, and they could count on her recognizing their voices before they even identified themselves on the phone. Most important, they knew that if there was a crisis at hand—a beloved member in the hospital or a death in the church body—Lurlene would have all the latest details, like the hospital room number or the address of the funeral home. Although none of them would have wished Lurlene ill, they found it a bit of a relief that the latest little crisis that circulated in church gossip had revolved around her.

When she walked into this room, she would spot couples whose weddings she had scheduled and parents of children who'd had their Bibles inscribed by Pastor Bob when they joined the church—the names spelled correctly on the *ex libris* plaque inside, thanks to Lurlene's diligence in checking and double-checking through the church directory. She would greet others who had eulogized their best friends at church memorial services for which she had typed up the church bulletin, knowing just which quote from Ralph Waldo Emerson or psalm would be appropriate to print on the cover. She would see her colleagues, her boss, her son, and his new girlfriend.

"I can't believe that this time we're going to surprise her," Doris Matthews said to her dear friend Helen Bradford.

"I never thought the day would come when we could pull something over on her," Helen responded.

"We haven't had a surprise party here since Dr. Sandifur's days," Doris said.

"Was it when he and his wife were going on a cruise to Hong Kong and we had little British flags at all the tables? We sang 'God Save the Queen' and 'Jesus Loves Me.' "

"Yes, I believe we did."

The plan was that Pastor Bob would bring Lurlene to Fellowship Hall after the long, dull conference at which she'd been taking notes all day. Jonathan had been concerned that she'd be dressed in slacks and a blouse—the perennial sweater draped over her shoulders—and he knew she'd be embarrassed to discover herself at a party, especially as the center attraction, in her Saturday lounging clothes. "Mom," he had said, "you'd better dress up." Her first hint.

Other hints had come her way. On Friday when the florist delivered two buckets full of tulips, Gerbera daisies, mums, and forced sprays of dogwood, he signed off saying, "See you tomorrow," which Lurlene thought odd. Surely the florist was not attending the long-range planning session.

Lurlene hated surprises. She loathed not knowing things. In her position, she knew almost everything that went on at First Church. She was very good at keeping secrets. But Saturday morning she had a sense that the big secret going around was about her.

Finally her son, out of kindness, confessed. "They're giving you a surprise party."

"What on earth for?" Lurlene said, horrified.

"As a thank-you for all the work you've done over the years. It's a special recognition day."

"But," she said, "I'm dressed all wrong." She looked down at the utilitarian gray skirt she was wearing and the blue blouse.

"Then change."

"How can I dress in party clothes if I'm supposed to be working all day?"

"Mom, it's something nice they're doing."

"I suppose if I put on a dress it would give it away."

"Just do me one favor. Act surprised."

At 5:25 that evening when she walked into Fellowship Hall dressed in a sunny, springlike green print, she didn't even have to act. She was completely overwhelmed to see all those faces staring at her. To hear them say, "Surprise!" To read the sign that had been taped to the back wall. To look at the album where cards and notes and letters of appreciation from hundreds of First Church members, past and present, had been compiled. She was speechless for a few moments.

"I had no idea!" she finally burst out. "How did you do all this? You never let me know!" All she could think was *Why me?* What difference could she possibly have made in their lives? Hers wasn't the primary signature adorning the birthday cards that she put in the mail every week for parishioners. She wasn't the one giving the sermons, teaching the Sunday school classes, or raising funds for church improvements. She, Lurlene Scott, had worked hard to remain steadfastly in the background. How had they noticed? Why were they putting her in the limelight?

Out of her mouth she heard herself utter the most amazing clichés: "How could you?" "You shouldn't have." "This just isn't fair." She looked at one familiar face after another and exclaimed, "You knew all about this and didn't say a thing!" "I can't believe it." "I can't believe you've all been keeping this secret from me."

Thanks to the warning from her son, she managed to have a good time at her surprise recognition party. She shook hands, received kisses, and graciously thanked all for their words of appreciation. It was only when someone presented her with a framed copy of her infamous newspaper interview that something dawned on her. These people liked her just as she was. Lurlene Scott, faults and all, counted for them.

After the lasagna, after the Jell-O salad, after the lemon meringue pie, she listened, entranced, to Pastor Bob's short speech. How many times had she heard that voice wax eloquent for the causes of justice, salvation, charity, and love?

How startling to hear it raised only for her. His conclusion brought tears to her eyes.

"Without Lurlene Scott's hard work for twenty-two years, I would not have been able to do the job you've asked me to do. She has been my right arm, my left arm, and quite often my brain. I want to thank her for all that she's done to make me successful in being your pastor."

To a standing ovation she walked forward to receive the envelope he held out for her. With nervous fingers she opened it. Inside was a certificate for an all-expenses-paid vacation of two weeks in Hawaii. "But . . . but . . . but," she stammered. "I can't be gone from the office that long." Everyone laughed. "Someone has to hold down the fort," she said.

Jonathan was at the party, of course, with his new girlfriend. People frequently came up to Janice and introduced themselves. A few of them made the connection. "Were you the one who wrote that story about our prayer ministry?"

"Yes," she admitted to that inquiry, blushing.

"So who was it who wrote a letter asking to be matched up with the right man?" another questioned.

"The letters are all confidential."

"But how did you find out about that one?"

"Well, to tell you the truth . . ." she began, holding Jonathan's hand as he squeezed it, giving her a dose of confidence.

At one point during the party Lurlene was standing near her son and Janice when someone exclaimed, "What a charming couple. How did they meet?"

"I introduced them," Lurlene said.

"You did?" the woman replied. "I've never been able to

introduce my son to any girl he's ever liked.''

''Well,'' Lurlene hesitated. ''It wasn't exactly all my doing.'' She was still surprised that this lady didn't already know the whole story. Or maybe she hadn't put the newspaper story and Jonathan's girlfriend together.

''Someone helped?''

Lurlene took a deep breath. ''Yes, you could put it that way.'' That was the truth of the matter. Someone helped. Was it possible that a higher Someone—God?—had planned and designed the whole thing? She was going to try to see it that way. The truth of the matter was, the end result was far greater and better than she could have arranged herself, even with her years of experience arranging things and running things for Pastor Bob. *''All things work together for good to them that love God''* . . . even those things that are beyond imagining. The words she'd heard Pastor Bob quote rang in her ears.

Life would certainly be different looking for God in the picture. Not just in Pastor Bob's sermons as she typed them, not only in the hymns and anthem listed in the program, not solely in the Bible passages quoted by the senior minister of First Church. Lurlene would be on the lookout for God in all those busy events of the day, from answering the first call at the office to turning off the copy machine. She would look for Him in the walk home from work and in the crossword puzzle she did in ink and in the TV shows she watched. After all, hadn't this business with Jonathan started when she made a wish on a clear winter's evening not long ago? Who would have thought that a wish could lead to answered prayer?

At nine o'clock, Pastor Bob started yawning. ''You'd better

get started home,'' Lurlene said. ''You've got your sermon to prepare.''

''You know me well enough, Mrs. Scott,'' he said, ''to know that it's already written.''

''Well,'' she smiled, ''perhaps it needs a little more practice.''

Others were leaving Fellowship Hall and came up to Lurlene, wishing her the best as they said good-bye. Pastor Bob wandered off to say good-night to some old friends and remind them of the worship committee meeting on Thursday. As the party organizers began cleaning off the tables and putting away folding chairs, Lurlene approached her boss.

''Words can't express . . .'' she began. That was as far as she got. Pastor Bob wrapped her in one of his patented hugs and held her tight for a moment.

''You're the very best, Mrs. Scott,'' he said. ''I would be nothing without all your help.''

A bit out of breath, she backed away and smiled. He was absolutely right. She was indispensable. Behind every great man is a great secretary.

''We'd better be going,'' she declared. Picking up their cue, her son and his new girlfriend gathered up her presents, put them in large shopping bags, and followed her out to the car.

As the moon shone over the bell tower behind the palm trees and the stars twinkled in a velvet sky, she felt like the most fortunate woman in the world. For the moment she decided if that was what it meant to believe, she would believe. She'd do her best. For now thanks would be enough.

''Thanks,'' she said to her son.

"Sure, Mom," he replied.

Then on her own, before she stepped into her Pontiac, she looked up to the heavens and said inwardly, *Thank you, God, thank you. Thank you very much.*